Pride Publishing books by Nikki McCoy

Everything That You Are
My Forever
Shattered Heart

Keepers of the Gods
Son of Death
Master of Wrath
Keepers of the Night
Slave to Chaos

Of Blood and Spirit
Crimson Mate
Darkness Entwined

I0663069

Of Blood and Spirit

LOVE ETERNAL

NIKKI MCCOY

Love Eternal
ISBN # 978-1-78686-376-8
©Copyright Nikki McCoy 2018
Cover Art by Emmy@studioenp ©Copyright October 2018
Interior text design by Claire Siemaszkiewicz
Pride Publishing

LOVE ETERNAL

Dedication

To my husband for his undying support and to all
my fans who share in the joys and tribulations of
my characters.

Chapter One

Tailor checked the blades of his shuriken, running his thumb over their razor-sharp edges before tucking them back into the straps across his chest. From his car, he looked out into the dead of night lit only by sparse lamp posts. The rural neighborhood was silent, except for the lulling song of crickets in the background. The street he waited on was cloaked in shadow and hedged on one side by a row of concealing evergreens.

Here, nature had been sculpted into a tamed display of wealth and prominence. The large houses spaced for privacy boasted only greens that could be cultivated into perfect, eye-pleasing designs. Trees were trimmed and flowers were planted instead of let loose to flourish.

Tailor curled his lip in disgust. He expected as much of the humans. Theirs was a way of life that promoted superiority in all things, including nature, but the owners of the house he'd been watching for the past three weeks were *Ba'Kal*, children of the Goddess *Miel Se Luuda,* and bound to nature by the spirits tied to their souls. Like him, they'd each been given the gift of an animal soul that had bonded with theirs upon maturity, allowing them to shift into the form of their animal at will.

When the full moon rose twice each month, their spirits took dominance, making the change inevitable. It was a beautiful communion that gave worship to their Mother and allowed them to reunite with the power of creation.

Yet, the ones he watched had forsaken their bond with the Mother. They had chosen affluence over the wilds of the forests and destruction over creation. Their allegiance was to *Roh Se Kahn*, the brother and exact opposite of *Miel Se Luuda*. The two Gods were as day and night, good and evil. For all that *Miel Se Luuda* had done to create her children and bless them with the natural gifts of the world she had provided, *Roh Se Kahn* wanted to destroy them all and reign over what remained as the one true God.

Despite all that Tailor had heard and witnessed over the past year, it still amazed him that *Roh Se Kahn's* followers could continue to believe the mad God would keep his promise to them. That he would give them a place at his side when he ruled over this realm as king. Then again, it wasn't that much of a surprise. In this, they and the humans were alike. Since the dawn of man, there had always been sheep willing to follow blindly in the path of those who offered riches, and there always would be.

True power was often hidden behind the strength of pretty words.

Tailor gripped the gun at his belt as a shadow flitted across his rearview mirror. When a large form appeared outside the passenger window, he cocked the gun and aimed, only to lower it with a growl of frustration.

Cyrus' familiar face came into view as the man entered the car and peered over at him. His long black hair was pulled back into a leather ponytail wrap and his hard features, made pronounced by pale skin, were softened in the dim light. While his physical characteristics were typical for a *Vam'kir*, there was a very noticeable difference about him. Piercings of every size decorated his face and parts of his body Tailor didn't want to contemplate. They gave him a sinister look that was somewhat appealing in an unnerving kind of way.

Tailor holstered his gun and returned his gaze to the street in front of him. "What are you doing here?"

"What the hell do you think?" Cy retorted. "I'm here in case you do something stupid like get yourself killed."

Tailor grunted. "That hasn't stopped you from standing back and letting me do all the hard work before."

"Hey, this is your crusade. Far be it from me to interfere with you murdering every son of a bitch that worships *Roh Se Kahn* for information you know they don't have. I had a life once, you know. One that didn't involve me babysitting a man hell-bent on revenge."

The anger that always dwelled beneath Tailor's cold visage rose to the surface. "I didn't ask you to join me, and I sure as *fuck* don't want you here. If you have better things to do, then get the hell —"

"Stand down, warrior," Cy said with just as much vehemence. He pursed his lips then looked away. "You know I agree with what you're trying to do, but the ends aren't justifying the means. You've lost sight of your goal. In the past six months since I've been with you, not a single follower of *Roh Se Kahn* has had any knowledge of how to get your mate back. You're chasing the sheep when you should be hunting the wolf."

"Don't you think I know that?" Tailor seethed, then took a deep breath to calm his nerves. Cy wasn't his enemy, and while he resented the man's very presence, he had to admit he liked the guy.

When Rowan's *Meraan*, a personal bodyguard in the language of the *Vam'kir*, died a year previously, Rowan had chosen two others. Half a year ago, he'd sent one of them, Cy, to accompany Tailor on his quest to find Dhani. If not for the strong friendship between Tailor and Rowan, Tailor would've refused the help. At times, he still did, but he knew Rowan wouldn't have sent anyone he didn't trust with his own life.

After a stretch of silence, he sighed then said, "The sheep are all I have. At least until I can find the wolf."

When Cy didn't argue further, Tailor's mind drifted back to the reason for his current circumstance. The beginning of it all.

It was almost hard to believe that at one point in time, his life had made sense. After nearly a century of brutality in the art of war, he had finally found happiness in the form of a mate. The other half of his soul gifted to him by the Mother. The only one who could give his life meaning and erase his loneliness and suffering.

Then, in two short weeks, his happiness had been ripped away. Dominic had been murdered before they could link their life forces together. The bond would've enabled Tailor to follow his mate into death with the blessing of *Miel Se Luuda,* but without it, his only choices had been to either forfeit his soul through suicide or go on living an empty life.

After months of pain and despair, he'd chosen life only for his friendship with Manning, heir to the king of the *Ba'Kal*. At the time, Manning had been close to taking over leadership from his father and had needed Tailor to help him guide their people in the war against the *Vam'kir*, their twin race. Though also born through the creation of *Miel Se Luuda*, the *Vam'kir* weren't gifted with animal spirits. Instead, they sustained themselves on the life-giving blood of humans, which granted them exceptional night vision, strength and speed.

Two millennia ago, their races had originated as one, the *Bassen'kir*, who possessed all the traits of both kinds. However, through a violent fallout between the *Bassen'kir's* princes at the time, brought about by *Roh Se Kahn*, they'd been divided into separate races and pitted against one another. Their war had raged on until only three years ago, when a chosen one had reunited them and given rebirth to the *Bassen'kir*. Only the high-borns of each race had been made *Bassen'kir* and given the ability to shift, as well as take blood for sustenance, with the responsibility to pass on this gift to their descendants.

For two years afterwards, Rowan, the *Magnique* and king of the *Vam'kir*, had worked alongside Manning to solidify the alliance between their races. All had gone considerably well until a new threat had made its presence known. *Roh Se Kahn,* banished at the start of the war to an alternate realm, had reemerged to once again complete his plans to destroy *Miel Se Luuda's* children and reign over the human realm.

For three decades, he'd kept his presence hidden and sired four sons to aid in his plans. The first son had been born of his union with a highborn *Ba'Kal* and his next three from a simple human. The *Ba'Kal* hybrid, Keenan, had turned out to be more powerful than *Roh Se Kahn* could've imagined. The dark God knew that one day, the power of darkness mixed with light in Keenan might eventually lead to his demise if Keenan were ever to turn against him.

In his fear, *Roh Se Kahn* had made Keenan his slave, a puppet in his strategy to destroy *Miel Se Luuda's* children. Keenan had escaped when he was sixteen, however, and had befriended another *Ba'Kal* named Dhani. Their friendship had grown strong for years, even surviving their capture by rogue *Vam'kir* who'd held them and many others prisoner during the war between the *Vam'kir* and *Ba'Kal*.

One year ago, Tailor had helped Manning and Rowan rescue the prisoners of war. Tailor had known instantly that Dhani was his mate. Defying logic and all the laws of nature, the draw of their souls to one another was unmistakable. Throughout the history of *Miel Se Luuda's* children, there was one truth that had never changed. Each child was granted only one mate. One person to complete the others' soul. In the span of their long lifetimes, it was rare for them to meet. Many things stood in their way, such as distance, fate or death.

Tailor had denied it at first and treated Dhani as if nothing existed between them. He couldn't believe it was possible that he could have a second mate even when all the signs were there — his unrelenting desire for Dhani and the younger man's unquestionable faith in him, despite the fact that they'd hardly known each other. He hadn't wanted to open his heart to the possibility of what another mate could mean for him.

Regardless of his brusque demeanor, though, Dhani hadn't given up. He'd waited patiently for Tailor get his head out of his ass and admit to their connection as mates. Tailor had been so close. He'd been tired of fighting logic and had been ready to follow his heart.

Then, for a second time, it had all been ripped away from him.

Roh Se Kahn had formed an army of minions to defeat the warriors of the *Vam'kir* and *Ba'Kal*. He would've succeeded in killing all who opposed him if it hadn't been for Keenan. In the final battle, father and son had warred against each other and, quite literally, killed each other in the process. While only the dark God's physical form was killed, Keenan had managed to banish his father's soul from the human realm before he himself had died.

Dhani had been right there witnessing it all, though instead of standing by meekly, he'd delivered a spell that had brought Keenan back to life. In doing so, he'd left himself vulnerable to *Roh Se Kahn's* attack and had been pulled into the alternate realm by the dark God. He had sacrificed himself so that Keenan could live, giving all that he had for the love of a friend.

In the wake of this, Tailor had fallen into a depth of self-loathing he'd never known his soul could harbor. Doubts and contempt plagued his every thought. He thrived on the revenge he wanted to take on *Roh Se Kahn,* but it was his hatred for himself that kept him going.

It was he who had spurned Dhani's willingness to accept him. He who had turned away from the second chance at love Dhani had offered in the moments of secrecy they'd shared. Maybe if he had admitted his fears to Dhani... Maybe if he hadn't cast aside what had been so obvious between them...Dhani would still be here.

In his arms.

In his life.

Tailor squeezed his eyes shut and raked a hand through his blond locks. "Is there any word from Keenan?"

Cy shook his head. "Last I heard from Rowan, the kid is exhausting himself looking through the library of texts *Roh Se Kahn* kept on the dark arts. He doesn't trust anyone else to go through the material with him. Says it's too dangerous."

Despite his frustration, Tailor nearly smiled at the ongoing joke between Keenan and Cy. While Keenan was only twenty-seven years old to Cy's three hundred years plus, Keenan was a demigod and likely immortal. A 'kid' who would outlive them all, except for Rowan, his mate. The bond between them would probably keep Rowan alive with him. No one knew for sure. Unlike *Miel Se Luuda*, who had created her children, *Roh Se Kahn* had devised a spell that had allowed him to physically sire Keenan, making him the first demigod in history.

The texts Cy was referring to were those the dark God had had in his possession the day Keenan had banished him from the human realm. Tailor knew Keenan was doing his best in searching through them to find a way to bring Dhani back, but the wait was growing unbearable. They had no idea what kind of realm Dhani had been dragged into, or even whether it could sustain life. The thought that Dhani might be dead, however, was one Tailor refused to contemplate.

"We'll find him," Cy said in a low voice. "Just have a little more patience."

Tailor bit back a sharp response then straightened in his seat when he saw a black limo pull into the driveway of the house he was surveying. He checked his watch, heart rate quickening with grim satisfaction. It was exactly midnight. The same time the limo arrived every Friday night with the handful of *Vam'kir* who'd been meeting with the group of *Ba'Kal* in the house. The driver was human, although from what Tailor had observed, the man seemed to have just as much invested in the meetings as the others.

"Tell you what," Tailor said as he pulled on a pair of leather gloves, "I'll go in and get some information while you enjoy your patience in the safety of my car." He stepped out before Cy could reply and shifted to the majestic form of his golden eagle. Once in the air, he flew towards the back of the large house and perched on the branch of a tree. There was no security alarm or watch dogs, though neither was typical for *Ba'Kal*. Normally, they lived in secluded communities in the woods where the security of valuables was not an issue.

Through the blinds covering the windows, he saw the lights come on in the downstairs study where they usually congregated. There were nine in all. Five *Ba'Kal*, three *Vam'kir* and the human. Since the start of his search, this was the most activity he'd seen among those who still served *Roh Se Kahn*. In the beginning, he'd only been able to find them individually or in pairs. Over the past few months, however, they'd begun meeting frequently in groups.

Something was going on, Tailor could feel it, although he hadn't been able to glean any more information from the groups than he had the individuals. They were all privately funded to maintain their secrecy, having as little to do with outsiders as possible.

He waited just long enough for the group to get comfortable then flew to the back door and shifted to his human form. After picking the lock, he crept inside and made his way to the study. He put his ear to the closed door and listened to the muffled voices within.

Only pieces of their conversation came through, but one word came out loud and clear.

Vane.

Tailor tensed at the mention of the name. Vane was Keenan's half-brother, another demigod who had escaped during the battle waged to rid *Roh Se Kahn* from their realm. Where Keenan had the power of *Miel Se Luuda's* light in him inherited from his *Ba'Kal* mother, Vane had been birthed from a human woman. The darkness in him eclipsed whatever good might have come from his mother, making him pure evil.

Tailor knew with *Roh Se Kahn* gone, it would only be a matter of time before Vane gathered his father's followers to his side and made another attempt to take control over the races. Vane had nearly succeeded once in overthrowing Rowan's crown and reigning over the *Vam'kir* in his place. Whatever his plans were now, death and chaos were sure to come with them.

He screwed a silencer onto his revolver, palmed a knife then kicked in the door. The looks of alarm on the faces of the men as they jumped up were priceless, and lasted for only a second. Tailor focused himself in that moment then sprang into action.

There was no fear, no guilt or hesitation. The rage that always burned inside him was masked behind a layer of detachment. Not even the lust for blood fueled him as it did so many warriors who faced battle. All the emotions that came with the deliverance of death had been beaten out of him years ago. With a weapon in his hands, he was no more than a machine trained to kill.

He sank his knife into the gut of the nearest man and yanked upwards, splitting the man from belly to sternum. With a vicious kick, he shattered the kneecap of a second man then put a bullet between the eyes of a third. Three more men charged him at once and he took the form of his eagle, hooking his talons into the eyes of one of them. The man went down with a howling screech that rose above the angry shouts.

Instinct alerted Tailor to the immediate threat at the other end of the room. The *Ba'Kal* in charge was standing behind his desk with a gun pointed at him. Tailor shifted back and let loose one of his shuriken before his boots touched the ground. Blood spurted from around the blades in the *Ba'Kal's* throat as he dropped to the ground in a lifeless heap.

Tailor ducked the left hook of a *Vam'kir* coming at him, then twisted the man's arm behind him. He used the man as a shield to block the attack of a second *Vam'kir* who lunged forward with a small dagger. When the attacker paused in shock at his mistake, his dagger buried hilt deep in the man Tailor held, Tailor shoved them both out of the way.

A strong punch caught him in the ribs from the side and he turned to face his newest opponent. He slammed his knuckles into the man's nose three times, then brought up his gun and fired two rounds into the man's skull. He spun around to aim his gun at the man still writhing on the floor from his gouged eyes and put an end to his screams.

Movement at the door made him pivot and put a hole in the back of the head of the human who was trying to flee. Behind him, the loud shot of a pistol rang out, but the bullet ricocheted off a cast-iron end table three feet away. Not even close. He turned around and sneered at the *Ba'Kal* who had inadvertently killed his own associate, more out of annoyance than any kind of emotion. The first lesson he'd learned in his warrior training was to never draw a weapon unless you were sure of the kill.

He holstered his own gun then kicked the one from the trembling hands of the *Ba'Kal*. The man flinched away as Tailor yanked him up by his shirt and brought their faces to within inches of each other. "Where is Vane?" he growled.

The man only shook his head vigorously.

"Where is he?" Tailor yelled. "Does he have Dhani?"

"H-h-he'll kill me if I tell you," the man stuttered.

"I'll cut off parts of you that'll make you wish for death before I kill you if you don't."

With a pathetic whimper, the man shook his head again. "I d-don't know where Vane is. He's only contacted us by phone and told us to gather our forces. I've never heard of a Dhani."

Tailor bared his teeth in a feral snarl and paused for a moment, feeling out the man's energy to sense if he was lying, but there was only truth. He took another knife from his belt and slit the man's throat. Eight down. One left.

He stalked the last *Ba'Kal* still lying on the floor from his shattered knee. The man's eyes widened with fear then narrowed to slits in false bravery. Tailor could smell the nauseating stench of panic on him. He knelt down, fisted the man's hair in one hand then brought the edge of his blade to the man's throat with his other. "Same question. Where are Vane and Dhani?"

The man thinned his lips in a look of mockery. "He will come, and he will surpass his father and take his rightful place as ruler. Nothing you do will stop that."

The madness in the man's eyes was enough to make Tailor recoil within. He knew most of *Roh Se Kahn's* followers had been bought with promises of riches and grandeur, but this was one of the few who offered his devotion freely. Despite the fact that he was obviously no warrior, it made him twice as dangerous.

In one last effort, Tailor pressed the tip of the blade into the man's jugular, piercing the skin. "Tell me how to get Dhani out of *Roh Se Kahn's* realm and I'll let you live."

Before the man could respond, another knife was thrown from somewhere on Tailor's left and embedded itself deep into the side of the man's neck. A gurgling sound passed the *Ba'Kal's* lips as he slumped to the ground in death. For the first time since entering the study, emotion flooded into Tailor. Fury filled him, swift and fierce. He jumped to his feet and aimed his gun at the person who'd thrown the knife.

It had come from a woman who met his rage with a calm expression. Tailor instantly felt the presence of a spirit in her, letting him know she was a shifter as well. She was petite, yet held the build and carriage of an experienced warrior. Her pants and vest overlaying a black top were brown, supple leather that fit snugly on her pronounced curves. Tailor was momentarily caught off-guard by the striking angles of her face. They were stunning and vaguely familiar. Creamy skin lent the perfect contrast to her shaded, hazel eyes and dark red hair pulled back into a ponytail.

She was exactly the kind of woman Tailor would've have gone for if he hadn't met Dhani. Beautiful and independent. His tastes had leaned toward men when he was younger. And when he'd found his first mate, it had come as no surprise that his mate was male. Then, after his world had shattered with Dominic's death, he hadn't been able to bring himself to touch another man. They had all reminded him of the one he'd lost.

Since then, there had been only women. Endless scores of women who could never affect him the way his first mate had. They had been a safe escape from the desolation of his soul.

With Dhani's appearance, though, his need to fill that empty space inside him with the warmth of women had fled. Dhani had consumed him, in spite of his efforts to push the younger man away out of his own insecurities.

Yet, there was something compelling about this woman — who had just killed his target.

He shook off the odd sense of familiarity and cocked his gun. "Who are you?"

She raised her hands in a gesture of submission and tilted her head to the side. "I've never seen anyone fight like you do. I didn't think it was possible, but the rumors were true. You hold no equal."

Cy seemed to materialize from the shadows on her right and put the muzzle of his gun to her temple. "He asked you a question."

The woman stiffened, then flexed her jaw with a piqued expression. "We don't have time for this. The gunshot from that *Ba'Kal* was loud enough to alert his neighbors. The police will be here soon. We need to go."

Tailor approached her menacingly and touched the muzzle of his silencer to her forehead. Familiar or not, she was an unknown, and therefore a threat. "Why did you kill the guy I was interrogating? Who. Are. You?" he asked, punctuating each word with his anger. If there was even the slightest chance he'd lost out on information from the *Ba'Kal* regarding Dhani, this would be the first time he'd felt the urge to kill an unarmed woman.

Precious seconds ticked by as she bit her lip in deliberation. Finally, she lowered her hands and took a deep breath. "My name is Layzani. You can call me Laya. I've been tracking *Roh Se Kahn's* followers for years. I was at the battle when he was cast out of this realm. Since then, I haven't been able to find any information on their whereabouts until I heard of a man who was seeking them out and killing them. A blond warrior who looked like he should be holding a surf board instead of a gun."

Cy lowered his gun and let out a bark of laughter, then sobered when Tailor shot him an ominous glare. He shrugged, not at all intimidated. "You do look like a surfer."

"I heard of a man searching for a *Ba'Kal* named Dhani," she continued, "who had been pulled into an alternate realm by *Roh Se Kahn*. I also have a vested interest in finding Dhani. I've been tracking you for the past four months, or rather, the trail of blood you've left behind. I had to find out if you were trying to find Dhani for the right reasons. I had to know…" Her voice faltered, then she cleared her throat. "I had to know whether I could trust you."

"Trust me for what? What is Dhani to you?"

More seconds ticked by before she exhaled, as if in resolve. "He's my son.

Chapter Two

The gun became a lead weight in Tailor's hand and he let it fall to his side.

Her son. It couldn't be.

Dhani had been adopted at the age of six following the deaths of his parents. His foster mother had died five years ago after being beaten to death by his foster father. From what Tailor had discovered, the couple hadn't been mates and had abused Dhani from the start of his time with them. Dhani had no known living family and the woman standing in front of Tailor was definitely not his foster mother.

Which could only mean…

"You're his birth mother."

Laya gave a reserved nod.

A slew of questions crowded into his mind, but the woman was right. This wasn't the time or place for that particular conversation. He turned and began rifling through the clothes of the *Ba'Kal* in charge.

"What are you doing?" Laya asked.

"One of the men said Vane had contacted them by phone. There's a chance I can trace the number back to him." He found the *Ba'Kal's* cell phone, slipped it into his pocket then took Laya by the arm. "You're coming with us."

She tried to wrest her arm from his grip as he hurried out of the house, but he refused to let go. "You don't have to use force," she hissed. "I was the one who sought you out, remember? Besides, I have my own car."

"Which I'm sure you were smart enough to park where the cops won't find it. I'm not letting you out of my sight until I get more answers." All three loaded into his car and he took off. After the distant lights of the police cars faded from his rearview mirror, he released the vice-like grip on his emotions and glanced over at Laya threateningly. "Tell me everything. If I detect even the slightest lie, I won't hesitate to use any means necessary to get the truth out of you."

It was harsh, but he couldn't take any chances. If she was working with Vane and meant to sabotage Tailor's search for Dhani, he had to know immediately.

She turned to face him squarely. "You first. I've told you who I am. Now tell me why you're so desperate to find my son."

He ground his jaw in impatience. Dhani's relationship with him was still a sore subject. Then again, he no longer held the desire to keep it secret. He'd come to terms with the fact that somehow, against the natural laws of his kind, he'd been given a second mate. All that mattered now was what he did to fix the mistake of driving Dhani away. "He's my mate," he said tensely.

Laya merely nodded. "I thought as much. No one would go to the lengths you have unless it was for love. Having said that, if your intentions toward my son are anything less than honest, I'll kill you myself."

Her words rang with truth and made Tailor wonder just what kind of mother she could be to abandon her son into the care of an abusive foster family then worry about his safety years later.

Before he could get off a sarcastic reply, she asked, "This must mean he's still alive, right? Or else you would've sought out your own death by now."

He shifted uncomfortably in his seat. "Dhani and I never bonded. When we met, it...wasn't the right time."

She was quiet for a moment, then shifted her gaze to the dark scenery outside. "My mate and I bonded the night we met, about three decades ago. I loved him madly. He was a fierce warrior like you, proud and strong. He fought with passion in our war against the *Vam'kir*. Later, when I became pregnant with Dhani, he started to grow distant. He hid parts of his life from me and would leave for weeks at a time. Whenever I confronted him about his secrecy, he would always say he was doing what was best for our family. That, one day, he would reveal what he was hiding and I would join him when the time was right."

Her voice took on an edge of animosity. "Eventually, I grew tired of his disappearances and decided to follow him all the way to England. He met with a large group of others in a remote location. Some of them I recognized as *Ba'Kal*. The others were a mix of *Vam'kir* and humans. I couldn't believe he was conversing with our enemy. Then I saw five men being taken in as prisoners. These were *Ba'Kal*. They were being handled as if they were the traitors and not the ones my mate was meeting with."

"They were trying to release *Roh Se Kahn*," Cy said grimly from the back seat. When Tailor looked at him sharply, he said, "Keenan was born nearly thirty years ago, and all of *Roh Se Kahn's* followers you've found in the past year have been *Ba'Kal, Vam'kir* and humans all working together. That's never happened before under any circumstances."

Laya nodded. "He's right, only my mate and the others didn't try. They succeeded. I heard awful screams coming from inside the building and had to know what was going on. The others wanted to kill me as soon as they saw me, but my mate convinced them I wouldn't interfere. He explained to me that they'd been in contact with *Roh Se Kahn* and that the dark God had revealed to them his plans for peace.

"He claimed *Roh Se Kahn* knew the Mother's children would annihilate each other in their hatred and that the only way to stop it was for all the races, including humans, to acknowledge one true God. My mate said *Roh Se Kahn* would lead them into an age of peace under his rule and they would be saved."

Her tone grew hushed and she brushed briskly at her eyes, as if wiping away tears. "I loved my mate, but what I saw in his eyes that night took everything away from me. He was insane. While most of the other followers boasted about *Roh Se Kahn* making them wealthy, I knew my mate was following out of blind servitude."

Tailor thought back on the zealous look he'd seen in the eyes of the *Ba'Kal* he'd been interrogating before Laya had killed him. It raised chills across his flesh that Dhani's father had given in to that same madness. It must've taken extraordinary strength for Laya to resist the lure of darkness that had consumed her mate, yet it didn't explain why she hadn't followed him. Mates were alike in almost all areas. Why had she kept her faith in *Miel Se Luuda* when her mate had forsaken it?

When he asked her this, she looked at him and didn't bother to hide the moisture brimming on her lashes. "The bond of a mate is strong, but the bond between a mother and her child is even stronger. I knew if my mate was caught for his treason, my child and I would be put in danger as well."

Though Tailor didn't doubt that, he couldn't help but notice her choice of words. She hadn't said that worshiping *Roh Se Kahn* was wrong. Rather, that she'd been afraid of the consequences.

"The spell they performed to free *Roh Se Kahn* from his realm failed the first four times they tried it," she continued. "They succeeded on the fifth *Ba'Kal*. His spirit was torn from him, and the separation of his animal's soul from his own caused a rift in our realm that allowed the dark God to pass through. The creation of the rift broke the spell that kept him from taking any form in our realm and his essence entered the body of a willing human.

"I wasn't a warrior then. The fear I had caused me to go into labor and I gave birth to Dhani that night. For the next six years, my mate held me and our child captive. He couldn't kill me even though I defied him since it would mean his own death, so he tried everything to convince me that his allegiance to *Roh Se Kahn* was right. Finally, I managed to escape with Dhani. I knew my mate would never stop looking for us, so I took Dhani to a faraway community and told them to give him to a good family. I never gave them my name or the name of Dhani's father. I couldn't risk my mate finding him."

She took a shaky breath, then said, "I disappeared after that. I was too afraid to keep in contact with Dhani, in case my mate ever found me. I did what I had to do to keep my son alive."

And delivered him into the hands of monsters, Tailor thought. The cynicism and hatred that rose up made him look away in disgust, although he had to admit, only a portion of his hatred was for the woman next to him. What had he done to keep Dhani safe? He'd been so wrapped up in his own pain and confusion after meeting Dhani that he was responsible for delivering his mate into the hands of a much worse monster.

He cleared the ache in his throat and asked, "If you let him go, how did you find out he'd been taken by *Roh Se Kahn*?"

"When the *Jaes'din* had his men search for the families of the *Ba'Kal* who had been kidnapped by the old *Vam'kir* king, I heard that Dhani was one of them. I tracked his location to the *Jaes'din's* mansion, then to the *Magnique's* palace. I went to Ireland to fight in the war against *Roh Se Kahn,* hoping to hear more about my son. That was where I learned he'd been taken by the dark God. Since then, you've been the only link I have to my son."

Tailor swallowed heavily. In spite of his suspicions, he wanted to believe that she had Dhani's best interests at heart. That her presence was an asset and not an omen. However, he couldn't let his guard down yet. There was still too much at stake.

"We'll go to my place for now," he said. "In a few days, after the heat dies down from the police, Cy will take you back to get your car."

"The hell I will," Cy spoke up. "It's bad enough I gotta watch over you. I have better things to do in my off time than play chauffeur to a woman who's not going to give me anything in return. No offense," he said to Laya.

Laya smirked. "None taken. When I kiss a man, I like to feel skin, not steel piercings."

Tailor gave a low chuckle, feeling his mood lighten with her quick barb. "If I recall, weren't those the exact words of the last woman you tried to get with?"

"Like you're one to talk," Cy replied with a snort. "I heard you slept with so many women, you lost count. And how many of them wanted to kick your ass for not calling them afterwards?"

Tailor grinned, recalling the days when he would've done anything to get into a woman's bed. When all he'd needed was a drink and a warm body. He shrugged. "A whiskey glass or a woman's ass will turn any man into a horse's ass." At the bald glare he received from Laya, he quickly wiped the grin from his face. "So I've heard."

When the ring of his cell phone saved him from the blistering comment he knew Laya was about to make, he pulled it from his jacket and answered.

Manning's voice came on the other line. "Where are you?"

"On the way to my place. What's up?"

"You need to drive to the community near Salt Lake City in Utah."

Tailor restrained his irritation. "I know I've been gone for a while, but I can't start working yet. I think I'm getting close to something." As Manning's *Ketai,* his personal guard, it was his duty to assist Manning in all the affairs of Manning's role as *Jaes'din.* For the past year, however, he'd been in dereliction of his duties. While Manning was aware of how important it was for Tailor to find his mate, Manning had also repeatedly expressed his concern over Tailor's welfare.

"This isn't about me," Manning said. "I just received a call from the Alpha of that community saying a *Ba'Kal* had come to him asking for a man named Tailor. A young *Ba'Kal* with long red hair and no family. Ring any bells?"

Tailor clenched the phone in a tight fist, his chest seizing with hope he didn't want to give in to just yet. "Dhani," he said in a choked voice.

"I don't know for sure. The Alpha said the man wouldn't give him his name. Only that he wanted to speak with Tailor, my *Ketai*. Tailor, be careful. If this is Dhani—"

Tailor ended the call and spun his car around in a 180. He gripped the steering wheel as he headed for Salt Lake City, trying to gain control over the storm of his emotions.

"What is it?" Laya asked.

"Boss?" Cy said at the same time.

Tailor ground his teeth, refusing to let hope weaken him. After so long, could it be true? Could Dhani be waiting for him at a community…safe…alive?

"That was Manning. He says he knows where Dhani is."

A heavy silence filled the confined space, then Laya glanced at him with a small smile on her lips. "If it is Dhani, thank you for taking me with you."

Tailor kept his expression cold. "Don't thank me. Like I said, I'm not letting you out of my sight until I know I can trust you."

* * * *

Dhani stared through the window of the guest bedroom he'd been given in the small mansion. It was spacious and well-furnished, befitting an Alpha's wealth. Central heating kept winter's bite at bay and outside, the dawning sun shone on a thin layer of frost. The surrounding greenery was welcoming with the promise of a fresh, new day.

It was all so beautiful and comforting. Everything he'd prayed to enjoy again over the past year and all that he'd feared was forever lost to him. At any moment, he expected the light to dissolve, plunging him back into an abyss of darkness. The scenery would melt away and the heat would fade, leaving him once more naked and so cold, his bones would ache.

What surrounded him now seemed like a dream. An illusion conjured by his insanity and overwhelming need to feel something. Anything other than the pain and emptiness he'd lived with for too long.

He reached within for the soothing presence of his spirit and felt the leopard purr in assurance. For so long, he'd been without that presence, trapped alone in his mind and shell of a body. In the alternate realm, where he'd lived with *Roh Se Kahn,* there had been no light. Even the blessed light of *Miel Se Luuda* that resided in his soul, marking him as one of her children, had been suppressed. The darkness had taken away his ability to communicate with his leopard and held him in agonizing suspension.

Dhani shivered at the memories that still consumed him. He tugged at the jeans and T-shirt he'd been given, uneasy in their confinement, yet grateful for their cover. In the alternate realm, he'd been stripped of his clothes, along with any other form of privacy. There, only the essence of a being could exist. Material things were lost or destroyed. He wasn't quite sure. It had been *Roh Se Kahn's* power that had kept Dhani's physical body from fading along with his clothes.

Although *Roh Se Kahn* had preserved his human form, it hadn't been without consequences. In that realm, time only existed in the soul. While Dhani's body had lain dormant, his mind had still felt the effects of time passing. Hunger, thirst, cold. All the things he would've experienced physically without warmth, food or water over a year's time on earth. In many ways, the realm had been his coffin and he a prisoner that had been buried alive with no chance to escape in death.

He clawed his hands through his long hair, trying to dispel the memories.

I'm not there anymore, he told himself. *I'm not trapped in the darkness. I'm on earth, alive.*

But not free.

In his faint reflection in the window, he caught sight of the single lock of white hair falling from his left temple like a bright wing shining out from the rest of his red hair. His hand shook as he touched it. To anyone else, the white lock might seem harmless, but he knew what it was. A shackle on his soul. The mark of a brand tying him irrevocably to the being that had tortured him mercilessly for an entire year.

At the sounds of raised voices, he turned to face the door to his room. A familiar voice shouted, "Where is he?" seconds before the door was flung open. Adrenaline spiked in Dhani's blood as the man he never thought he'd see again ran in then came to an abrupt halt. Dhani's heart seized and his hands began to tremble.

His spirit surged forth with aching need to go to the man and touch him to make sure he was real. At the same time, Dhani's body reacted in a way it had only once before—the first time he'd met the man. His skin tingled and blood rushed to his groin, filling him with nearly uncontrollable desire. It took all that he had not to fall to the floor in relief, yet his fear still clung to him like an iron weight.

Tailor was even more handsome than he remembered. In place of his normally casual attire, he wore black leather pants, a skin-tight shirt and a black jacket that enhanced his large frame. A dusting of blond whiskers covered his jaw and his multi-faceted blond hair fell in wild waves past his shoulders, as if he'd been up for days.

The small arsenal of weapons strapped to his chest and waist gave him a feral look that matched the fierceness of his posture. Every line of his body was rigid and the energy rolling from him exuded intimidation, yet it was his eyes that held Dhani.

They were clear blue and so intense with emotion that Dhani couldn't look away. He saw disbelief, shock and a depth of hunger in them so great, it made Dhani quiver with anticipation. For endless days, months, he had envisioned the warrior before him. Dreamt of what it would be like to see him again. Now that the moment was here, Dhani found he couldn't trust it. What if this Tailor was just another illusion his mind had conjured to stave off insanity?

Then the moment was broken when several others entered the room. Alarm spread through him and he drew back until the window behind him cut off his escape.

A man with long black hair and several piercings on his face moved to stand next to Tailor, and beside him entered a petite woman. There was something familiar about her, though Dhani couldn't remember ever meeting her. By the energy of her spirit, he knew she was *Ba'Kal*. The other man lacked that same energy, however, which meant he had to be *Vam'kir*.

The Alpha, Grayson, who had taken him in hours ago, came in with a slightly irritated expression. "Like I was trying to tell you earlier," the Alpha began, "the boy is safe and appears unharmed. One of my Betas found him last night coming into my community in his leopard form. It took my man some time to convince him to meet with me. He was scared and badly shaken. When I finally got the boy to take back his human form to tell me who he was, he was completely naked. Wouldn't give me his name or birth community. All he said was that he had to talk to you."

Dhani winced inwardly at the description of his sudden appearance in the Alpha's community. Upon reentering their realm, he hadn't thought of clothes or decorum. His mind had only been on one thing — finding Tailor. He'd run as far and fast as he could from the darkness of the alternate realm and it had been only by sheer luck that he'd found this community.

"How long has he been here?" the woman asked.

"About six hours. He won't eat or sleep. Hasn't spoken a word, except for demanding to speak with you," he said, nodding to Tailor.

Tailor approached slowly, his gaze locked on Dhani. "I came as soon as I could, *daishen*. I'm sorry it took so long."

Dhani watched him, caught up in the calming timbre of his voice and the confidence in his attractive features, his mind barely registering the *Ba'Kal* moniker roughly translated to 'sweet love'. As Tailor drew near, his natural scent wafted over Dhani. He smelled of the forest after a heavy rain. Of the intoxicating aroma of fresh earth and musk. Beneath those scents was a hint of old blood that gave him a dangerous appeal, but Dhani wasn't fazed by this.

What did hit him, however, was the energy in Tailor that grew stronger with every step he took. Dhani could feel the man's life force, his essence. It was raw and commanding, like the essences of the damned souls that dwelled in the alternate realm. Theirs had been powerful as well, and they had used their power to violate him every chance they got. They had torn through his soul like a vicious storm, inflicting waves of pain he could still feel.

When Tailor stopped a few feet away and reached out, Dhani flinched and squeezed his eyes shut. He tensed in expectation of the suffering he knew would come. Then, after several pounding heartbeats, he finally opened his eyes and met Tailor's gaze. Instead of the promise of hatred in them, he saw only hesitancy and…guilt?

Tailor lowered his hand. "I won't hurt you, Dhani. I swear, no one will ever hurt you again. You're safe from *Roh Se Kahn* now."

"Wait," Grayson broke in. "Is this the Dhani who helped end the war against *Roh Se Kahn*? The boy who was pulled into the same dimension the dark God was banished to?"

"This is my mate," Tailor said without breaking eye contact with Dhani, "and I'm taking him home."

34

"Your *mate*?" Grayson exclaimed, before his expression hardened. "I'm sorry, but that doesn't change the fact that this boy has been with *Roh Se Kahn* for a year now. I was at the battle and heard about what happened. I can't just let you take him. For all we know, he's been corrupted. He could be a spy sent here to betray us all. He could be serving *Roh Se Kahn* — "

Before anyone could blink, Tailor drew a knife from his belt and threw it at the Alpha. It hit the wall beside the Alpha mere inches from his face. In the next instant, Tailor backed Grayson to the wall with a hand around the man's throat and another knife pressed to his jugular.

In a deadly tone, Tailor said, "Call him boy one more time and it'll be the last thing you do."

Grayson's eyes widened and he sputtered past the choke hold around his neck. "You are *Ketai* to the *Jaes'din*. You can't just take this boy — *Dhani* — to your home without first contacting the *Jaes'din* of your intentions. He's too much of a risk. Think about it. Dhani appeared out of nowhere. How do we know he wasn't released from *Roh Se Kahn's* realm on purpose, or that *Roh Se Kahn* doesn't have a plan for him?"

Dhani tensed, afraid that Tailor might believe the Alpha. That he would be held prisoner again until he could prove his loyalty to his kind, which would be impossible. Most of all, though, he feared Tailor might distrust him as much as the Alpha did.

Before Dhani had been pulled in by *Roh Se Kahn,* he'd known he and Tailor were mates — had been overjoyed to find the one person who was destined to love him completely. But Tailor had rejected him repeatedly, giving no other reason than the fact that Tailor was sure their link as mates was a mistake.

As crushing as that had been, however, Dhani hadn't stopped longing for Tailor in the bleakness of his imprisonment. He hadn't given up hope that maybe, by some miracle, Tailor might learn to accept him.

Now, that hope could be torn away by the very real accusations of a well-respected Alpha.

Then, to Dhani's incredulity, Tailor reached into his pocket for his cell phone, dialed a number then put the phone to the Grayson's ear. "Talk to the *Jaes'din* yourself," he said in a daring tone. "Tell him you want to keep me from my mate."

When Grayson took the phone and began talking, Tailor turned and strode back to Dhani. Concern lined his face and Dhani could see the restraint in his posture as he was about to touch Dhani's cheek, but instead, reached for his hand. "Are you okay?"

Dhani nodded, dumbfounded by the faith Tailor was displaying in him.

"Will you come with me?"

Again, Dhani tipped his head and took his mate's hand. As they headed for the door, he heard a deep voice yelling through the other end of the cell phone pressed to Grayson's ear and watched the man's tan skin turn pale.

Grayson mumbled a quick apology before Tailor yanked the phone from him and returned it to his pocket.

"You ever doubt me again," Tailor said as he pulled his knife from the wall, "and you'll be bowing down to the Alpha that takes your place."

Dhani let his mate lead him from the small mansion, trying and failing to tamp down the desire that was flooding his system. In all the time of his captivity, he'd never once envisioned a scenario where Tailor would not only want him, but threaten another's life just to keep him. It had always been him dreaming of a way keep Tailor. An impossible dream that had given him the only warmth he'd known over the past year.

As soon as they exited the front door, Tailor surprised him again by pulling him into a tight embrace and capturing his mouth in a kiss. The move was so abrupt, Dhani didn't have a chance to prepare. He was swamped by the ferocity of Tailor's energy, so strong that his first instinct was to retreat. His heart pulsed frantically in terror and he struggled in the man's hold.

But Tailor wouldn't let him go. The band of his arms only tightened around Dhani and crushed him closer.

Dhani's mind froze in panic at first, then his body seemed to take over. Need, stark and demanding, took control and seemed to beat back the fear that had been his constant companion. His spirit leapt up from within, denying him the caution he still harbored.

Dhani released a breath in shock that was swallowed by his mate. The firmness of Tailor's hand delving into his hair and bringing him closer drew a moan from deep within his chest. Tailor's rumbling approval vibrated along his lips, causing his dick to swell painfully. When Tailor's other arm circled his waist and brought their groins together, sparks danced beneath Dhani's skin. The steel rod of Tailor's cock rubbing along the length of his own through the rough material separating them sent his senses into overdrive.

He surrendered to the claim of his mate's tongue dominating his and forcing him to feel what he'd only fantasized about in the other realm. The world fell away, time stopped and instead of darkness, all that existed was the heat of Tailor's body against his.

Then, slowly, Tailor drew back, leaving Dhani gasping for air he couldn't quite pull into his lungs. Dhani felt a sliver of trepidation enter his mate's energy as Tailor brought their foreheads together.

"I'm sorry," Tailor panted. "I know I had no right to do that, but I couldn't stop myself. I thought I'd lost you again."

The words fell on Dhani in a blissful haze, until the last one registered.

'Again'.

He stiffened as realization set in. Tailor wasn't talking about losing him to *Roh Se Kahn*. He was referring to his first mate, the man he'd lost before Dhani had come into his life. Dhani pushed away and looked up at the man with a challenging stare. "Who did you think you'd lost — me, or your first mate?"

Guilt crept over Tailor's handsome countenance and he shook his head in denial. "Dhani, I didn't mean — "

"I know what you meant," Dhani said through the constriction of his throat. His thoughts were thrown back to the one and only time Tailor had deigned to touch him in the past. It had been with a kiss as searing as the one they'd just shared.

The memory was as clear as if it had happened yesterday. They had been standing in the kitchen of Rowan's palace. Tailor had just admitted the reason for his reluctance to accept Dhani as his mate. He'd said it was impossible because he'd already met his mate, and that his mate had died before they could bond. He'd told Dhani there was no way he could love again, then he'd kissed Dhani as if his life had depended on it.

At that moment, Dhani had been determined to help his mate love again despite the cynicism in Tailor's heart. He'd been willing to look past the multitude of women Tailor had bedded in his attempt to forget the pain of losing the one man who had been his destiny. All that had mattered was that Tailor was his, and he'd wanted to do anything to heal the man's heart.

Then, when Rowan had entered the kitchen and caught them unawares, Tailor had pulled away as if appalled by what he'd done. In the wake of the embarrassment and rejection, Dhani had run.

Later, when he'd recited the spell to bring his best friend Keenan back to life, a part of him had still clung to the hope that he could help Tailor love again, even in the face of his own death.

Now, however, that hope seemed like a fool's dream. Tailor would never get past his devastation over the death of his first mate, and Dhani would never be the man Tailor truly wanted.

The man with the piercings came out then, followed by the red-headed woman. "I gotta say, your balls are a hell of a lot bigger than I gave them credit for," he said to Tailor. "I've never seen an Alpha ready to piss his pants like that, and I've killed more than my share during the war between our kind. You ready to take your mate home now?"

Unbridled rage stole the last of Dhani's patience. He met Tailor's tempered gaze with fierce resolve. "He's not taking his *mate* anywhere. That man died years ago, didn't he?"

A flicker of wounded resignation entered Tailor's eyes, but Dhani ignored it. During his months on end of torture, the dream that his mate might still be out there searching for him had been all that'd kept him going. Then, when Tailor had been ready to kill to protect him, his fantasies had become a reality.

For a very brief moment.

The guilt that remained thick in Tailor's energy gave Dhani pause. Tailor *had* stood up for him, defended him. Only Dhani couldn't bring himself to settle for being second best, despite how damaged he was.

"Dhani," Tailor began stiffly, "don't do this. Neither one of us was given a choice in being mated."

Given a choice? *Given a choice?*

Fury surged through Dhani's veins and the anger he'd suppressed over all the injustices in his life boiled to the surface. He pointed at Tailor, then at the other man, saying, "Fuck you, fuck him and fuck this whole Gods-damned realm! I won't go with you just because you think you're obligated to protect me. I survived a whole year in a pit of hell I wouldn't wish on my worst enemy. If you think I'm going to let you tell me what to do, you can go screw yourself. I'm not your mate. I'm not the one you want."

He swallowed the tears burning his throat and tried to still the tremors shaking his entire body. A small part of his brain told him he was being irrational. That Tailor didn't deserve his hatred. But a larger part of him screamed at the audacity of *Miel Se Luuda* tying them together as mates. What right did she have to link him to a man who'd already given his heart to another? Hadn't he suffered enough for one lifetime?

The man with the piercings threw up his hands. "Whoa, little guy. I know Tailor's ugly puss is enough to make a runway model sign up to be a nun for the rest of her life, but don't go blaming me for that. I'm just the man sworn to keep his ass alive so he can piss you off."

"Cy, not helping," Tailor ground out.

"Oh, you want me to *help*. In that case, run Dhani. Somewhere out there's a man who can love you with the brain in his head, not the one in his —"

Tailor pulled the gun from his side holster and aimed it at the man's head. "Finish that sentence and you won't have a brain."

Almost simultaneously, Cy drew his own gun and faced off with Tailor. "I guess we're gonna find out who has the bigger balls."

Alarm diverted the anger in Dhani to the new threat and he jumped in front of Tailor, barricading his mate with his own body. "Stop! Don't kill him."

Tension clogged the air, mingling with Dhani's primal instincts and something else. Something alien that reared up within him. It was dark, chaotic and thrashing against his soul to be let loose. It thirsted for death, building inside him until his blood raced and skin burned with the need to release it. His palms blazed with energy that didn't belong to him. It was an infection, growing more powerful with his anger until he didn't think he could control it any longer.

Then Cy flipped his gun and holstered it. "Seems Tailor isn't the only one who wants to protect his mate out of obligation."

His own words being thrown back at him shook Dhani into awareness. He had been ready to protect Tailor, whether his mate wanted it or not. The irony of that knowledge dispelled his anger, but the darkness was still there, hammering at his resolve. It intensified with his effort to force it under his control, beating at his temples with nauseating impact. He looked down at his palms and saw blue sparks dancing over his skin, then fisted them tightly.

As he turned to meet Tailor's gaze, the earth tilted and blood rushed to his head with dizzying speed. Just before his knees gave out and the world went dark, he felt Tailor's arms catch him and the deep tenor of his mate's worried voice calling out his name.

Chapter Three

"You've been pacing for thirty minutes now," Manning said. "You're starting to make me nervous. Get a beer, or better yet, get a bottle of whiskey."

Tailor suppressed a snide remark and continued to pace the length of the hallway on the second floor of his cabin. Manning was more than his *Jaes'din*. They were best friends and had seen each other through bad times and worse. The man deserved better than the short end of his temper, though at this point, Tailor was finding it next to impossible to rein in.

"I don't need whiskey. I need to know whether my mate is alive or not."

"He's alive. If anything's changed, the doc would've let us know by now."

Tailor glanced down at Manning where he sat in the hall with his back to the wall. They were similar yet different in so many ways. Both shared the characteristic tan skin and toned physiques of the warriors of their kind. Manning, however, had trimmed black hair and black eyes to Tailor's blond waves and blue eyes.

They also differed in their personalities. As leader of the *Ba'Kal,* Manning had earned the respect of his people through the stable and responsible traits of his nature, whereas Tailor had almost always been carefree, even reckless at times. He didn't care what anyone thought of him and didn't give a damn about authority. All that had ever mattered to him was his loyalty to those he cared about.

And right now, one of those few was lying in a bed, unconscious and beyond his ability to care for.

Tailor raked his hands through his hair. "Four days, Manning. My mate has been in a coma for four days. What if this is an aftereffect of being trapped in that realm with *Roh Se Kahn*? What if he never wakes up?"

"Then we'll find out just how charming you are and see if true love's kiss will break the spell."

Tailor sneered at Manning on his next pass, not at all impressed by his sense of humor.

Manning shrugged with a half-grin. "Worth a shot."

Tailor stopped when he saw Laya enter the hallway from the staircase at the far end. She looked good in snug clothes with her hair pulled back in a braid, though the bags under her eyes told him she hadn't gotten any more rest than he had since Dhani had passed out at the Alpha's mansion.

To her credit, her story that she was only there out of concern for her son had held true over the past several days. Which was fortunate for her, considering Tailor would've kicked her out of his house at the first sign of betrayal. The only times she'd left had been to get food and supplies in the community Tailor resided in with Manning. She hadn't even wanted to pick up her car from the location where they'd met for fear of being absent when Dhani woke up.

She nodded in greeting to Manning, then looked to Tailor. "How is he?"

"Not sure," Tailor replied grimly. "Doc hasn't come out yet."

As if on cue, the door to the bedroom Tailor had given Dhani opened and the community doctor came out. Quinn, Manning's mate, came out as well and shut the door behind him. Quinn was a good-looking man around Dhani's age with the same slim build and long hair, although his was as black as a clear, midnight sky.

The doctor closed his medical bag and met Tailor's gaze with a sigh. "There's been very little change. His heart rate and blood pressure are still extremely low, but his reflexes are fine. There's no sign of brain trauma and his temperature is normal."

Tailor shifted nervously. "When do you think he'll come out of the coma?"

"I'm not sure this is a coma anymore. His body is…not reacting like that of a coma patient. While his oxygen levels are fine, there's been no need for a catheter and if what you're telling me is true, he hasn't defecated either. His body is also rejecting the IVs I've tried giving him for fluid and dietary supplements. He should be suffering from severe dehydration by now, but he seems to be fine. I've never seen anything like it."

"Then why isn't he waking up?" Tailor asked through clenched teeth, unable to stifle his irritation at the helplessness of the situation.

Before the doctor could answer, Quinn intervened, "Thanks, Doc. We'll see you in a few days for another checkup."

The doctor nodded gravely then headed for the stairs. When he was gone, Quinn looked to Tailor. "I need to speak with you alone." He glanced with meaning at Laya, who shook her head adamantly.

"He is my *son*. I deserve to know everything you do."

Quinn looked back to Tailor and only continued when Tailor nodded. "I've been talking with Cher, our historian. She thinks Dhani's condition may be due to the realm he was in. The spell that was used on *Roh Se Kahn* didn't necessarily banish him to a different realm. It merely revoked his ability to take any physical form in this world. Since his essence can't be destroyed, the only alternative was for it to be forced out of this realm and into another.

"The realm *Roh Se Kahn* went to would have to have been one that could contain essences with no physical forms. In Dhani's case, that would mean his body would've been held in stasis while his mind and soul were still active."

"I don't understand," Tailor said, shaking his head.

Quinn bit his lower lip. "It means that his body was held in suspension. It didn't age, didn't eat, didn't sleep, but Dhani's brain still registered all the effects of his hibernation. For example, when you get hungry, your nerves relay the message to your brain which then gives you the impulse to eat and if you don't, you feel the pain of starvation. Dhani's brain has been receiving all those messages, but his body hasn't been able to respond."

Tailor's blood ran cold at the significance of what Quinn was telling him. "Do you mean Dhani has been starving and unable to sleep for the past year?"

"Essentially...yeah. I think when you found him at the Alpha's house, he was running on pure fumes."

"What does that have to do with his condition now?" Laya asked.

"His body is trying to get used to functioning again. It's slowly coming out of hibernation and catching up on the sleep it needed. I have a feeling he'll be able to start eating again once his metabolism speeds up and returns to normal."

"Dear Mother," Laya breathed. "Having full awareness and going for that long without food or sleep is enough to drive a person insane."

Quinn kept his gaze on Tailor. "It is. We won't know more until he wakes up. Tailor, you should know, he's not going to be the same man you once knew."

Tailor swallowed past the dryness in his throat, his mind still trying to grasp the enormity of his mate's situation. The words, *I can't lose him. I can't lose him again,* circled endlessly through his mind. Although Dhani had misinterpreted those words when he'd said them outside the Alpha's mansion, he had no doubts as to who he was thinking of. The death of his first mate had devastated him, but that was in the past. Dhani was all that mattered to him now.

Dhani was his mate—his life—and having a mate before him only made Tailor more aware of how precious a gift Dhani was to him.

He nodded absently. "I understand."

"I don't think you do," Quinn said with a tortured note in his tone. He glanced at Laya again, as if unsure he should keep talking in her presence, then back to Tailor. "Dhani was in a realm filled with the essences of beings that were probably almost as vicious as *Roh Se Kahn.* While his body was in stasis, his own essence would've been unprotected from them."

When Quinn's voice became tight and his eyes shimmered with moisture, he glanced at his mate. Manning stood and went to Quinn, wrapping his arms around the smaller man. They shared a very private look, then Quinn met Tailor's gaze again. "You know that I was held prisoner and raped repeatedly for four years."

Tailor dipped his head in acknowledgement. He recalled Quinn's history and his importance to their race. Quinn had been the chosen one meant to unite the *Vam'kir* and *Ba'Kal* and bring about the race both had originated as, the *Bassen'kir.* His father, the former *Magnique,* had sought to use Quinn's power to annihilate the *Ba'Kal* by bonding Quinn to a *Vam'kir* of his choosing. Since the ritual of bonding required sex, Quinn had been the victim of rape for the length of time his father had kept him prisoner.

The memory of Quinn's story brought chills to Tailor's flesh. There could only be one reason why Quinn was referring to his imprisonment while discussing Dhani's past.

Quinn took a deep breath. "Being raped is like feeling a thousand demons rip through your soul, trying to tear you apart. There is no shelter, no escape. Dhani wouldn't have been able to protect himself from the other essences, let alone *Roh Se Kahn.* That may have damaged him irreparably."

Tailor walked to Dhani's door and put his hand against it, feeling Dhani's faint energy on the other side. He closed his eyes and bowed his head as guilt, hard and swift, speared him. He knew of Dhani's past, of the suffering he'd gone through as a child. The knowledge of what Dhani had suffered while with *Roh Se Kahn* made bile churn in his stomach.

Yet, he couldn't stop thinking about the kiss he'd shared with his mate outside the Alpha's mansion. It had been full of passion and desire. And when Cy had pulled his gun on Tailor, Dhani's first response had been to protect him.

There was still good in his mate. No matter the circumstances of Dhani's imprisonment, he wasn't insane.

Tailor was sure of it.

He met Quinn's gaze, and said in a ragged voice, "He's my mate. I won't give up on him...ever."

His answer seemed to satisfy Quinn who gave him a bittersweet smile. "I know you won't. I'll call you if I learn anything else."

"Let us know if his condition changes," Manning said quietly, then left with his mate.

In the ensuing silence, Laya stared at the door to Dhani's room. "This is my fault," she said softly. "Maybe if I had taken him on the run with me, I could've kept him safe."

"That depends," Tailor replied in an acerbic tone. "Was your mate a child-beating pedophile like the foster father you abandoned your son to?" He instantly regretted his harsh words, but he couldn't get the image of Dhani being violated out of his mind, physically or spiritually. The hatred he felt wasn't even aimed at Laya. He was cursing himself for his own stupidity. It was he who had rejected his mate instead of being there to support him.

If he had only gotten past his own selfish pain, he might have —

A small sob pulled him from his thoughts and he saw streaks of tears staining Laya's cheeks. She shook her head and let out another wrenching sob. Her shoulders were slumped and forehead creased in disbelief, so at odds with her usual unyielding countenance.

It was then that Tailor accepted the truth she'd been trying to give him all along.

She hadn't known the hell she'd delivered her son into years ago. She wasn't a spy or a traitor. She was simply a mother who had tried to give her son the best future she could.

No one could fake the hurt and shame emanating from the woman in rolling tides. Tailor would know. He'd learned from the best.

He cursed inwardly then walked to Laya and enfolded her in a tight embrace, rocking gently to soothe her. In this vulnerable state, she seemed nothing like the hard-as-nails woman he'd grudgingly accepted as part of Dhani's life. "I'm sorry. I wasn't sure if you knew."

She jerked out of his arms and punched him in the chest. "What do you mean, you weren't sure? You think I would willingly put my son through that?"

And...there she is, he thought with a small grin. "Come on. I think we could both use a drink right about now."

He led the way to the kitchen on the first floor and filled two tumblers with whiskey.

Laya downed hers then gestured impatiently for a refill. Tailor chuckled and filled her glass again, then sat down with her at the breakfast table in a corner of the kitchen. Several minutes passed as they nursed their liquor, then Laya gulped back her third glass and served herself a fourth.

"So, my son was abused" — she said matter-of-factly — "by the man I gave him to."

Tailor peered over, taking note of the way her skin had turned ashen and her eyes had become red and swollen. For a brief second, he thought about telling a white lie to ease the brutality of the truth, but they were too alike. He knew she wouldn't appreciate a lie any more than he would.

"After Dhani was taken by *Roh Se Kahn*," Tailor began, "I investigated further into his past on the off-chance it would lead me to any clues on how to find him. I discovered that his foster father had beaten his foster mother to death five years ago. After that, an investigation had begun and the man had stood trial for the alleged rape and assault of several minors prior to his wife's death.

"None of the accusations dated back before the year 2006, however, which was the same year Dhani ran away from home at the age of seventeen. His foster father was found guilty and put to death shortly after his trial, so I didn't have a chance to interrogate him about Dhani, but I didn't have to." Tailor took a long draw from his glass then set it down to stare at the golden liquid.

"A monster like that doesn't just wake up one day and decide to start abusing strangers' kids. He chooses a child who's close to him. One he knows is too weak and afraid to defy him. A child he can control within his own home." Memories crowded into Tailor's mind of his own childhood. Of the monster he'd lived with until he'd grown strong enough to barely escape with his life.

He shook his head then grabbed the bottle to pour more whiskey. "As much as it pains me to say this, I like you. And I don't think you should blame yourself for what happened to Dhani. When I first met him, he'd just been rescued from being held prisoner for two and a half years by a band of rogue *Vam'kir*. Before that, he'd lived on the streets until he met a good friend of mine, Keenan. For years afterwards, they lived together in a shitty apartment in Detroit.

"He had every right to be a jaded, self-centered, stuck-up little brat, but he wasn't. He was happy." Tailor laughed and shook his head. "He's like no one I've ever met. Hell, he was even willing to accept me after I pretty much threw him away."

Laya reached across the table and punched him in the arm. "You threw my baby away?"

"Ow!" He rubbed his arm then leaned back out of her reach. "Okay, so I'm an asshole. You knew that about me already."

Surprisingly, she merely smiled. "That I did." She raised her glass in salute and waited for Tailor to tap his glass against hers. "Here's to the man we love. May he forgive us our many faults."

As soon as they'd downed their whiskey, Laya pierced him with a penetrating glare. "Especially yours. I know about your reputation with women. If you hurt my son, I'll cut off your manhood and choke you with it, assuming it's long enough to get the job done."

Tailor grinned. Oh yeah, he definitely liked this woman.

They passed away another hour drinking and talking until Laya admitted defeat. When she tried to stumble to her guest bedroom, Tailor picked her up and carried her there, laying her down in the bed and tucking her under the blankets.

He went upstairs to his own bedroom next to Dhani's, but couldn't bring himself to go inside. Instead, he found himself entering his mate's room and taking the seat he'd been sleeping in for the past three nights beside Dhani's bed.

He leaned forward to take Dhani's limp hand into both of his then rested his forehead on his mate's knuckles. Dhani's clean scent permeated the blanket covering him, filling Tailor's senses with the lure of dark spices.

Since he'd arrived at his home with Dhani, he had refused for anyone other than Quinn and the community doctor to touch his mate. He'd been the one to bathe Dhani and change the sheets on his bed. Every inch of his mate's thin body was etched into his mind from the hours he'd taken to ensure Dhani was comfortable.

He had no right to such intimacy, he knew this, but neither could he bring himself to allow anyone else to get so close to his mate. At times, his possessiveness over Dhani scared him. In truth, they hardly knew each other. During the few weeks after they'd met, Tailor had been too consumed over the memories of his first mate that Dhani's presence had induced. He'd been unable to appreciate the gift that was right there in front of him.

I was a fool, Tailor berated himself. For as much as Dhani was still a stranger to him, he felt as though he'd learned all he needed to about his mate during the handful of times they'd interacted.

Dhani was loyal to a fault. He'd been willing to accept a mate who didn't deserve him and sacrifice himself for a friend, knowing what it might cost him. If Tailor had been in his shoes, he didn't know if he could've been so altruistic.

He leaned back to scrub his face then stilled when his mate jerked suddenly. Dhani's brow furrowed and his head began to shake from side to side. His eyes remained closed as his back arched and mouth opened to let loose a scream that echoed throughout the room.

When Dhani started to thrash his arms as though warding off an invisible threat, Tailor grabbed hold of his wrists and pressed them into the mattress next to Dhani's head. "You're okay," Tailor said softly. "Everything's fine. I'm with you."

But whatever nightmare held Dhani in its grip only worsened. Dhani cried out again as tears fell down his temples. He fought wildly against Tailor's hold, bucking his frail body until Tailor had no choice except to straddle him.

Tailor pressed down with the full weight of his body and willed the panic from his energy, knowing it would only provoke Dhani's fear. He brought his mouth to Dhani's ear and said, "Enough. I won't let him have you anymore. You're mine, you understand that? You belong to me."

Dhani bucked again, though his strength seemed to be fading.

Tailor continued to whisper in his mate's ear, commanding him to calm down. For several minutes, he spoke quiet nonsense, saying anything and everything he could think of to draw Dhani out of his nightmare.

After what seemed an eternity, Dhani's resistance eventually faded and his body sank slowly back onto the bed.

Tailor buried his face into the pillow under Dhani's head and loosened his grip on his mate's wrists, taking deep breaths to calm his nerves. Exhaustion crept in, reminding him that he hadn't slept in days, and the haze of the whiskey he'd consumed blurred his thoughts.

He slumped to Dhani's side and wrapped a protective arm around him, telling himself he would only steal five minutes of his mate's comfort.

Just five minutes to take away his own nightmares.

Chapter Four

Dhani's mind stirred at the feel of luxurious heat surrounding him. It was everywhere all at once, enveloping him in a cocoon that was all too real to be an illusion. He reached within himself for the source and felt his spirit respond with joy. His leopard purred in happiness, telling him he had missed the communion of their souls as much as Dhani had.

Dhani felt his cat stretch within, urging him to do the same. He tried to extend his arms only to pause when a heavy weight restricted his movement. Tight bands were tethered around his arms and legs, caging him in.

A rush of terror seized him and he sought out the security of his spirit. Bones reknit themselves and skin transformed to a thick white pelt with reddish-brown spots. A sliver of hesitancy sparked from his leopard, but he ignored it in favor of the strength his animal form gave him.

He twisted out of the bands holding him down and flipped over to take on the unknown threat. Bloodlust sang in his veins as he pinned the alien body beneath his substantial weight and clamped his jaws around vulnerable flesh.

Flashbacks of the pain and violation he'd been subjected to in the vast realm of his prison crowded into his thoughts, taking over.

Never again, he told himself. *Never again will I be that weak.*

He had the power of his leopard now, and he would kill anyone who dared take it away from him again.

He bit down harder and growled his dominance when the sweet tang of blood spilled onto his tongue. Triumph reeled through him, urging him to take more—to demand his vengeance.

Then his spirit yowled ferociously within, clawing at his soul to force him to back off.

Dhani's thoughts glazed over in confusion. Why was his leopard challenging him now?

He unclamped his jaws with effort then drew back. Tailor's handsome face came into view, his blue eyes staring up at Dhani with an unfathomable expression. There was no fear or even the slightest trace of apprehension in the man's gaze. Only utter patience and a disturbing amount of acceptance.

Small bite wounds marked both sides of his neck where Dhani's canines had punctured his skin. They wept twin trails of blood over bruises that were already starting to form. If Dhani had applied any more pressure, his canines would've broken his mate's jugular and possibly ended his life. Yet, Tailor hadn't made a single move to defend himself.

That was when Dhani recognized what lay beneath the patience in his mate's gaze. It was trust, blind and terrifying.

Tailor had been willing to give his life just to prove that trust.

The realization made Dhani rear back in bewilderment. At the same time, Tailor bolted upright with a sharp gasp, yelling, "Wait!"

Too late, Dhani felt his hind claws dig into his mate's groin as he scrambled backwards. Tailor sprang forward in a failed attempt to protect himself and rolled with Dhani off the foot of the bed. More accidentally than out of intention, Dhani reverted back to his human form just as his back hit the floor. Tailor landed on top of him with a grunt, his head bent and face screwed up in a rictus of pain.

"I'm sorry!" Dhani exclaimed. "I didn't know it was you. Are you okay?"

After several shallow breaths, Tailor raised his head and gave him a sardonic half-grin. "I guess I deserved that. Just don't expect me to function properly for the next week."

Despite Tailor's obvious pain, or perhaps because of it, Dhani lips curved up in a smile. He temporarily forgot about the reasons for his fear and cocked his head to the side. "Have you ever functioned properly?"

Tailor's grin widened and his chest rumbled with deep laughter. "Keep it up and I'll show you just how well I can function."

The teasing humor in Tailor's eyes slowly changed then, becoming something else. Something more. His irises lightened and took on the golden hue of his eagle spirit, signifying his arousal. The enticing smells of fresh earth and musk enveloped Dhani in a seductive embrace.

Dhani felt a sudden urge to pull his mate close. To sink back into the heat of Tailor's body and lose himself there. It would be so easy, and in that moment, he had no doubt Tailor would let him.

The temptation to crawl into his mate's arms and stay there until nothing else existed was nearly overwhelming. The way Tailor looked at him now, like he was the only person on earth that mattered, was an aphrodisiac. Tailor's energy was so strong and confident.

In the back of Dhani's mind, an alarm went off, telling him he should be afraid. Yet, he couldn't bring himself to take heed. There was a gentle edge to Tailor's stark arousal that let Dhani know the man wouldn't hurt him.

Then Dhani's stomach growled loudly, breaking the tension.

Tailor dropped his head to Dhani's neck and chuckled softly. When he looked back up, his irises had returned to their original sky blue. "I'll get you some food. There's a bathroom through that door," he said, tilting his head to a corner of the room. "Take a shower and relax. And whatever you do, don't shift again until I'm prepared for it."

Dhani smiled in embarrassment as he watched his mate leave. It was only then that he became aware of his nakedness under the blanket tangled around him. Tailor had been fully clothed, which meant he hadn't tried anything while Dhani had been asleep.

While Dhani was grateful for that, he recalled the stories he'd heard of Tailor's promiscuity among women. How the man had bedded any willing female he could find. At the time, that hadn't bothered Dhani. He'd been positive he could show his mate how to truly love again.

Now, he wasn't so sure about anything anymore. Tailor was dangerous, attractive and larger than life. He'd also had an entire year to forget about the complications of another mate and return to his single life. In that year, all Dhani had become was damaged goods. Did he really have any right to hope Tailor would accept him now when he hadn't before?

Dhani shook his head and pushed aside the blanket to stand. A wave of dizziness hit him and he immediately leaned on the bed for support. His body felt sluggish and hollow and his stomach cramped painfully.

He walked carefully to the bathroom then grimaced when he saw his reflection in the wide mirror above the sink. His lips matched the color of his pale skin and his hair was unkempt. He peered closer and touched the wing of white hair at his left temple among his red locks. Dread coursed through him when he noticed there was more white than there had been before.

The shackle was tightening.

As if in response, the darkness that infected his soul rose up like a putrid current, reminding him of the reason *Roh Se Kahn* had released him from the alternate realm. As bad as it had been in his prison, he hadn't wanted freedom at the price *Roh Se Kahn* had demanded of him. He would've stayed and suffered for an eternity rather than give in to the dark God, but *Roh Se Kahn* hadn't given him a choice.

The dark God had forced a sliver of his soul into Dhani to ensure Dhani carried out his plans in the human realm. To make room for his soul, he had taken a part of Dhani in exchange. Dhani felt the absence of what *Roh Se Kahn* had taken from him keenly, but he closed those thoughts from his mind. Although *Roh Se*

Kahn's power was growing stronger within him, he was still in control. He still had some time before the darkness took over completely.

When that happened, he swore to himself he would be as far from his mate as possible.

For a second, he was tempted to try suicide again. He'd already tried it as soon as he'd been thrust back into the human realm by the dark God. *Roh Se Kahn* had just given him the orders he was to carry out and the thought of completing them had filled every ounce of him with the desire to die rather than follow through.

The darkness in him hadn't allowed it, however. It had blazed him, inside and out, with a burning so intense, his very will had been taken from him. In the countless minutes of agony he'd endured, the darkness hadn't relented until he'd given up his thoughts of suicide. Dhani had known right then it was only a matter of time before the sliver of *Roh Se Kahn's* soul would dominate his every move.

For now, though, he still had time.

He found a new toothbrush, brush and everything else he needed stored neatly in the drawers by the sink. After taking a shower, he deliberately combed his hair to one side to hide the streak of white then went in search of clothing. It came as no surprise to find the closet in the room filled with clothes his size.

He smiled, rifling through the expensive collection he could never have afforded in several lifetimes. It reminded him of the day his best friend had been treated to such luxuries by his own mate. Dhani and Keenan had lived together for years, scraping by on just enough money to keep them off the streets. Then when Keenan's mate, Rowan, had found them, Rowan had showered Keenan with gifts most would take for granted. Like food, a car and clothes that didn't come from a second-hand store.

A pang entered Dhani's chest at the thought of his friend. He wanted to see Keenan badly, but knew he couldn't. Not while he still had some control over the darkness within.

He chose casual jeans and a shirt and was dressed just as his mate came in with a tray of food.

Tailor paused in setting the tray on the dresser to stare at Dhani. "You look good. Really good."

Dhani felt heat rise in his cheeks and looked away. "Thanks." When Tailor didn't stop staring for several more seconds, he tugged at his clothes self-consciously then pointed at the tray. "Is that for me?"

"Yeah," Tailor said abruptly. "Yeah, I, uh…may have gotten a little too much. Doc said you probably wouldn't be able to eat a whole lot at first. I want you to eat as much as you can, though. And I brought some vitamins you need to take. Drink all of your milk and call me when you're done." He pulled a cell phone from his pocket and placed it next to the tray. "I don't want you walking around too much. You need to rebuild your energy."

Dhani smirked in slight irritation. "Anything else, Dad?"

Tailor smiled uneasily. "Guess I am going a little overboard. I'm just worried about you."

"You didn't worry about me a year ago when you were sleeping with all those women." The words were out before he could stop them, and instantly, he wanted to take them back. *What the hell am I doing?* he castigated himself inwardly. *I didn't care about that before. Why the hell is it bothering me now?*

Guilt speared him when Tailor's face became a stone mask. Even the calming feel of Tailor's energy seemed to disappear, which should've been impossible. The energy of any *Ba'Kal* or *Vam'kir* was akin to the heat generated by any living being.

In a tone lacking all inflection, Tailor replied, "Since the first time I saw you, there's been no one else. Even when I thought I'd lost you forever, you were still all that mattered."

Dhani bowed his head, unable to meet his mate's emotionless gaze.

A loud stretch of silence passed, then Tailor walked to the door. He paused to turn back to Dhani. "By the way, I spoke with Keenan. He's anxious to see you. I've arranged to pick him up from the airport tomorrow. He's going to take the first flight he can find out of France."

"No!" Dhani exclaimed, then tamped down the fear spiking through him. "I mean, not yet. It's too soon." He couldn't risk contact with Keenan. If their meeting accelerated the control *Roh Se Kahn's* power had over him, it would be game over.

Tailor frowned. "Whatever happened to you in the past year, whatever *Roh Se Kahn* might've done, none of us think you've been corrupted by him. Keenan loves you. That'll never change."

Despair gripped Dhani as his mate's words hit too close to home. If only they knew the truth… "I just can't do it right now. Please don't make me."

Concern flickered in Tailor's gaze before he nodded solemnly and left.

Dhani took a deep breath then turned to glare at the food on the tray, his appetite gone. He covered his face with one hand and snarled angrily. The darkness in him was like a cancerous growth that would win in the end. It was inevitable. Why, then, couldn't he forget about his resentment and make the best out of the time he had left?

Tailor would probably always consider him as a replacement for his first mate, but it was getting harder and harder to think of that as a bad thing. When you only had weeks to live, it wasn't so easy to live on pride alone.

He forced himself to eat as much as he could, put the cell phone in his pocket, then left the room with the tray in hand. The thought of calling Tailor as he'd asked him to came and went just as quickly. Dhani knew he was in his mate's house. Tailor's masculine scent clung to everything, faint yet undeniable. He wanted to explore the place his mate called home without being looked after like a child.

He found a staircase leading to the ground floor and, despite the lethargy that still dragged him, couldn't help but become mesmerized by the beauty of the expansive house. Or rather, cabin. There was not a single sheet of drywall or plastic panels in sight. Every wall and floor in each room he passed consisted of hard-wood logs polished to perfection. Most of the furniture was also made of wood and appeared to be antique.

All of it, from the intricate rugs on the floors to the old-fashioned fireplaces and tapestries hanging on the walls, was like a picturesque scene from a wealthy person's villa constructed two centuries ago.

Everything seemed so incongruous with the playboy attitude he knew his mate was known for. It made Dhani wonder whether Tailor had inherited the cabin from his parents.

When he eventually found the kitchen, he almost changed his mind about washing his own dishes. The sink was gold-inlaid porcelain mounted by granite countertops. A wood-fueled stove restored to mint condition sat opposite it and cast-iron lanterns were affixed to the walls, filled with oil and wicks. It was all so old-fashioned, he was afraid he might break something.

Carefully, he washed his dishes then set them to dry. Through one of the windows, movement drew his attention. Three men stood at a distance from the cabin. They were all bare-chested with long swords in their hands glinting in the bright sunlight. Dhani recognized Tailor instantly from his waves of golden hair. Then the men lifted their swords and began attacking each other.

Alarm gripped Dhani and he ran back through several rooms to a back door he'd seen previously in an indoor patio. He paused at the glass door, ready to protect his mate, until the movements of the three men took on a distinctive pattern. They weren't fighting. They were sparring, he realized.

One of the men was covered in what appeared to be Celtic tattoos. Dhani made out the multitude of piercings on his face and recognized him as Cy, the man who had threatened Tailor at the Alpha's house. Apparently, the two had worked through their differences. The third man with short, black hair was vaguely familiar, but Dhani couldn't focus on him. Instead, he was held mesmerized by his mate.

Tailor moved unlike any warrior Dhani had ever seen. The sword in his hands seemed to weigh nothing as he wielded it with amazing power and speed. His motions were graceful and lithe, as though he was moving in a calculated dance rather than fending off his opponents. Even from where Dhani stood, he could see the clear definition of Tailor's muscles rippling beneath tan skin. The man's body was a work of art, sinuous and far too tempting.

Dhani felt arousal spark in his blood as he watched his mate. Tailor was magnificent in every aspect. It was no wonder women had flocked to him at even the slightest hint of his attention.

A flicker of insecurity passed through Dhani. There was no way he could compete with his mate's natural beauty. Tailor was the stuff fantasies were made of, and he was, well…him. Skinny and small with no traits or value that set him apart.

"I know that feeling," a voice said from behind him.

He turned and smiled widely at the familiar face staring back at him. It was Quinn. For the first time since being forced back into the human realm, he felt the burden of his secret lift and simple joy spread through him. He reached out and hugged his friend tightly. "It's good to see you again."

"And you," Quinn said with laughter in his voice. "Tailor called a little while ago to let me know you were awake."

A year ago, when Dhani had arrived with Keenan at the *Jaes'din's* community, he'd been sick with pneumonia. Quinn had kept him company during the long days of his recovery. Although they'd only known each other for a few weeks, they'd become good friends. Quinn was so much like Keenan, non-judgmental and fierce in his loyalty.

When they drew apart, Quinn tilted his head in the direction of the three men outside. "You were thinking you don't deserve your mate, weren't you?"

Dhani frowned. "Sort of. How did you know?"

"Because I thought the same thing when I first saw my mate half-naked with more muscles than the man had a right to," he said, pointing to the man with short, black hair.

Dhani's brows lifted as the identity of the man dawned on him. It was Manning, Quinn's mate and *Jaes'din* of the *Ba'Kal.* The leader Tailor was sworn to protect as Manning's personal guard.

He thinned his lips in cynicism. While it was apparent Quinn was trying to give him confidence, their mates weren't entirely the same. "Did your mate also have a reputation for sleeping around?"

Quinn grinned wryly. "Point taken, but when Manning found me, he *was* looking for a female mate. That didn't exactly give us the best start. He'd never been with a guy before. Hell, he didn't even know how to date me. At least you can be sure Tailor won't have a problem with you being male. You've heard about his first mate, right?"

Dhani nodded as he continued to watch Tailor. "He told me his mate died years ago before they could bond, and that's why he's never wanted to be with another man again."

"Then you know how hard it must be for him to have found you."

"I know," he said in a hard tone. "I was there every time he rejected me because I'm not the man he loved."

"That's not what I'm talking about."

Dhani tore his gaze away from Tailor. "What do you mean?"

Quinn sighed and sat down on one of the patio chairs, gesturing for Dhani to sit next to him. "I'd always thought Tailor didn't care about anything except his position as *Ketai.* He always had a smart-ass comment about everything. To tell the truth, it kinda got on my nerves. The only time he wasn't making a joke was when he was in battle. During those times, I noticed he had no emotions at all. Like he was a killing machine with no thought or feeling."

Dhani remembered his discussion with Tailor earlier. How Tailor's energy had seemed to disappear when Dhani had upset him.

"I asked Manning one day why Tailor was like that," Quinn went on. "He told me Tailor hadn't always been carefree. Tailor's father had been a psychopath. A man who'd lived and breathed his hatred for the *Vam'kir*. One day, Tailor's mother had shown up on his doorstep when Tailor was only two weeks old and told him she didn't want to care for a bastard child from a one night stand with him. Instead of giving Tailor up for adoption, which would've been merciful, the guy kept him.

"He saw Tailor as the perfect opportunity to create a soldier in his image. The art of killing was drilled into Tailor before he could walk. Manning said when they were growing up, there wasn't a single time he saw Tailor without bruises or broken bones. When he'd ask about them, Tailor would only shrug, saying he'd made the mistake of showing emotion. Happiness, anger, it didn't matter. Tailor's father tried to beat it all out of him to fashion him into a living weapon."

Dhani swallowed heavily. He thought back on his own past, of the abuse he'd suffered from his foster parents. His life had been a nightmare until he'd run away, but there had also been times of joy and kindness among the friends he'd had. Surely Tailor had some good childhood memories with Manning.

When he asked, Quinn merely shook his head. "Tailor's version of a friend at the time was someone he didn't want to kill. Manning had never seen him smile. He wasn't even sure if Tailor knew how to. Then Tailor found his mate and for the first time in his life, took a break from fighting the *Vam'kir*. His father was furious, but he didn't care. He fell in love with his mate immediately. Two weeks later, their community had been raided by a band of *Vam'kir*."

"Is that how Tailor's mate died?" He tried unsuccessfully to keep the sadness from his tone. He would never have guessed the violence of Tailor's past. It seemed so unreal, that the man had been denied even the right to feel emotions. What must it have been like?

Quinn shook his head. "No. Tailor left afterward in search of the group of *Vam'kir*, determined to kill every last one of them, despite the fact that his mate begged him to stay. After a week with no luck, Tailor went back and inadvertently led a different group of *Vam'kir* to his community. They attacked and killed nearly everyone. Tailor had told his mate to run, but at the end of it, there was no sign of his mate anywhere. Tailor had to accept the fact that his mate had been murdered.

"Tailor's father had also been killed during the second attack. Since then, Tailor hasn't cared about anything. All he had left in the world was Manning, so he agreed to become Manning's *Ketai* and swore never to love again. On the outside, he was the most laid-back, happy-go-lucky guy you could ever meet, but inside, there was nothing. Until he met you."

Dhani frowned. "He doesn't want to love me. He told me that a year ago."

"He was afraid to feel emotions again," Quinn replied gently. "He still is. All those women he slept with were just a distraction to keep him from reverting back to the unfeeling soldier his father had molded him into. When you were gone, he became that soldier again. He left to hunt down what remained of *Roh Se Kahn's* followers in search of you. He refused to keep in touch with any of us. That's why Rowan asked Cy to watch over him six months ago. We were all afraid he'd get himself killed trying to find you."

Chills raced over Dhani's flesh. Tailor had tried to find him? It didn't make sense. The man had been so forceful in rejecting him before. Could what Quinn was suggesting be true, that Tailor really did want him?

As if in answer, Quinn said, "He needs you. He needs to learn how to love again."

Dhani wanted to believe that more than anything, yet he couldn't bring himself to trust in something he'd given up on a long time ago. More than that, he knew he had no future with Tailor. Not with the sliver of *Roh Se Kahn's* soul growing stronger inside him with each passing day.

He stood up to look out on his mate, heart aching with the injustice of the situation. The memory of Tailor had been all that had kept him sane during his imprisonment. Now that Tailor was finally right there in front of him, it was he who would have to reject the man in the end. It was the only way he could keep Tailor safe. But maybe it didn't have to be as painful as before. If he could find a way to show Tailor how to love again, maybe his mate would learn to find happiness after Dhani was gone.

Maybe…

Chapter Five

The sun was starting to set when fatigue finally wore at Tailor's muscles. He lowered his sword when Manning held up a hand to catch his breath. He knew his friend would continue to spar with him for as long as it took for Tailor to work through his issues. It wasn't the first time they'd spent hours on end in combat.

Growing up, Manning had been the only one to understand the cathartic release Tailor got from sparring. It helped him to focus and clear his mind of emotions he didn't know how to handle. When Manning had arrived that morning after Tailor had called to say Dhani was awake, he'd sensed something was wrong. Without a word, he'd gone to the weapons room in Tailor's cabin, chosen a sword, then walked with him to the backyard to begin sparring.

Tailor was grateful for his friend's silence and Cy's willingness to join them. Although he hadn't confided in Cy the reasons for his difficulty with emotions, the man had never questioned him. Another thing he was grateful for.

Tailor still couldn't erase from his thoughts the edge of anger that had been in his mate's voice earlier. Dhani had every right to despise him for his reputation, and for pushing him away after they'd met. The alienation of his mate was a mistake he'd replayed in his mind over and over again since Dhani's capture. He would do anything to take back his actions and restore the faith Dhani had once given him blindly. Only, he had no idea where to start.

He shook his head when Manning prepared for another round. Cy stood from where he'd been resting on the ground near them, ready to switch off with Manning again.

"I'm done," Tailor said. "Go home, both of you. I'm sure your mate's missing you," he told Manning, then said to Cy, "I've already informed Rowan of Dhani's return. You should go back to your king. I'm sure he's missed you by now."

Manning met his gaze with concern. "Will you be all right?"

Tailor mustered a small smile and nodded. "Yeah. Thanks for coming. I'll, uh… I'll call you in a few days."

Manning continued to stare at him as if trying to gauge the truth of his promise, then picked up his shirt and left.

Cy grabbed his shirt as well, then clapped Tailor on the arm as he walked by. "I'll make myself scarce for the night while you talk to your mate. See you in the morning."

"I said go home," Tailor called out after him.

"This is my home until I know you're going to pull through," Cy yelled without turning around. "You got a problem with that, take it up with Rowan."

Tailor growled as he snatched up his own shirt. He knew exactly what Rowan would say and the pointlessness of having that conversation. It was at times like this he regretted making friends at all.

He went inside to his room and took a shower in the adjoining bathroom. After getting dressed, he steeled himself to knock on Dhani's bedroom door. He still had no clue how to handle his mate, but he'd gone for hours without seeing Dhani and the urge to reassure himself his mate was safe was more than he could suppress.

When no answer came at his knock, he went inside only to find the room and Dhani's own bathroom empty. By the time he'd searched the kitchen and living room with still no sign of Dhani, panic began to take hold. He rushed through the other rooms of the cabin, simultaneously reaching out with his senses for Dhani's unmistakable energy.

Finally, in a section of the cabin that was still being constructed, he found his mate in what would eventually be a library. Bookcases lined the walls, empty of shelves Tailor hadn't gotten around to installing yet. Dhani was standing on a ladder in front of one of the bookcases holding a cherry oak shelf with a leveler on top of it. He was so absorbed in what he was doing that he didn't notice Tailor enter. A pencil was held between his teeth and when he grabbed it to mark where the supports would go, his tongue stuck out in concentration.

The comical sight made Tailor grin. "What are you doing?"

Dhani jerked in surprise and dropped the shelf. At the same time, he lost his footing and stumbled backwards. Tailor raced across the room and caught him before he could hit the floor. Dhani stared up at him as Tailor gently lowered him. Their proximity caused heat to wash over Tailor. The smell of dark spices on his mate's skin filled his lungs and the dark rim of Dhani's lashes around hazel eyes was innocently erotic.

He couldn't believe he'd almost forgotten how handsome his mate was. When he'd found out Dhani had prostituted himself for a year to survive on the streets after he'd run away, Tailor had been furious. Apparently, when Dhani had met Keenan later and stopped selling himself, a few of his regular johns had stalked him, refusing to let him go. Tailor still had a hard time coming to grips with that part of Dhani's past, yet it hadn't been hard to believe. Dhani was gorgeous without even trying.

When Dhani gained his feet, he took a few steps back and smiled shyly. "I saw this room and thought…maybe I could help you finish it. I want to apologize for what I said earlier."

Tailor cocked his head, wondering whether Quinn had anything to do with his mate's change of attitude. He'd known Quinn had come with Manning that morning to check on Dhani. "Don't worry about it," he said casually. "Do you know anything about putting up shelves?"

Dhani shrugged. "A little. I worked construction for a while when I lived in Detroit. Your house is beautiful. Did you inherit it?"

He glanced around the room with pride. "I built it after my father died."

"You built all of this?" Dhani exclaimed in disbelief. "For your father?"

"No," he said with a snort. He went to the boxes on the other side of the room and knelt down to dig out some materials. "More like because of him. My father never let me do anything that took time away from my training. He wanted me to become a warrior, just like he was. The man was obsessed with our war against the *Vam'kir*."

"Sounds like he was a little psychotic."

Tailor paused at that description, the same one Manning had always given his father. "Quinn told you about him, didn't he?"

Dhani looked away as if in guilt. "I'm sorry. Don't be mad at Quinn. He just wanted to help me understand you."

Tailor waved a dismissive hand. "Quinn has a tendency to butt into other people's business, but he does it with a good heart. It's actually a relief that you know. I tend to forget that trust goes both ways." He gathered nails, a second hammer and two supports for the shelf then went back to Dhani. "I know I was an idiot when we first met, but I want you to trust me now. Ask me anything you want and I'll give you the truth."

Dhani creased his brow in deliberation. "What was your favorite thing growing up?"

He laughed out loud. "*That's* what you want to know?"

"You said anything."

With a shake of his head, he handed his mate the supports and began hammering nails into the bookcase where Dhani had marked it. "A car. 1929 Bugatti Type 46 Semi-profile Coupe. It had a midnight blue and ivory exterior, black leather seats, sweep panels, sleek fenders and a brass steering wheel. I'd chrome plated the engine and chopped the top to make it a convertible. She was the sweetest thing on four wheels. Riding her was better than sex."

He winced at his choice of words. "In her...the car. Not that she — it — was like a woman. She was just a thing. The car — "

Dhani rolled his eyes and cut him off, "Stop before you hurt yourself."

Tailor grinned as he reached down to grab a couple of anchors from an open container on the floor. "Anyway, Manning's parents let me store it in their garage so my father wouldn't find out. I didn't get to drive her often, but when I did, it was like freedom."

Dhani nodded then went on to ask him several more questions. Some were more difficult than others, though Tailor didn't mind. As the time passed, the tension between them abated and he felt a tiny spark of joy each time he made his mate smile.

Talking with Dhani was a lot easier than he'd thought it would be. Even easier than it had been to talk to his first mate. Dhani held no expectations or doubts. His genuine honesty in all things was refreshing and put Tailor at ease, even while discussing areas of his life he'd only told Manning about. Like how he'd accidentally run into his mother once at a community he and his father had defended against an attack. How his father had purposefully introduced them, knowing the woman would reject him just as she had when she'd abandoned him as a baby.

Instead of commenting on the fact that Tailor had rejected him several times as well, Dhani simply nodded as though he understood. Which, of course, he would. Only, Dhani had been old enough to remember his mother abandoning him. Tailor was thankful Layzani had decided to stay at a hotel in the community for a few days to give him some alone time with his mate.

When Dhani yawned, Tailor glanced at his watch to find more than two hours had passed. "It's getting late," he said, packing up the materials. "I should get you to bed."

"Not yet," Dhani said hastily. "I'm not tired, really." When Tailor merely peered at him, he shrugged a shoulder. "Besides, if either of us should be tired, it's you. What are you…twenty times my age?"

Tailor dropped his jaw in false indignation and narrowed his eyes. "Come here. I'll show you just how old I am."

Dhani squealed and tried to dodge Tailor's advance, but he wasn't quick enough. Tailor picked him up with one arm around his waist and began tickling him. Dhani laughed hysterically as he twisted in Tailor's grasp. Finally, Tailor relented and pinned his mate by the wrists against the nearest wall. They were both out of breath and Dhani's eyes danced with humor when he looked up.

Without thought, Tailor leaned down and took possession of his mate's mouth. Dhani's lips were warm and pliant, then they became rigid as his body stiffened. A current of fear filled the air around them and Tailor drew back. Dhani's expression was veiled, hesitant.

It pained Tailor to see the resistance in his mate, though it wasn't anything he didn't deserve. In his stupidity, he'd only added to the suffering his mate had known all his life. It was a miracle the younger man wasn't the jaded, sarcastic asshole Tailor had become.

Just as Tailor was about to pull away, however, Dhani lifted himself on his bare feet and pressed their mouths together. Pleasure hit Tailor hard as he delved into the kiss, breathing in Dhani's heat. The shroud of fear was replaced with arousal and it was all Tailor could do not to strip his mate right there and devour every inch of his body.

When Dhani moaned into him, the vibration sent a shiver down his spine. His cock strained in the confines of his jeans and his head swam in relief at his mate's willingness. No woman had ever made him feel this way, and thinking back on the momentary comfort he'd taken in their bodies made him realize just how much of a fool he'd been. There was no comparison. With Dhani, he felt alive again.

Reluctantly, he drew back and rested his forehead on Dhani's. As much as he wanted to take things further, he didn't want to scare his mate away. Dhani was safe now, and Tailor didn't want to screw things up between them like he had the last time.

"Let's get something to eat. The Doc will kill me if he finds out I haven't been feeding you."

Dhani's low chuckle sang along his nerves. He led his mate to the kitchen where he took two beers from the fridge and offered one to Dhani. He downed half of his in an attempt to flag his aching erection, then began taking out food for sandwiches.

He frowned when someone knocked on the front door and told Dhani he'd be right back. As he opened the door, apprehension speared him when he saw who it was. *Great, just great,* he thought with an inward groan. *This is all I need.*

Tula smiled at him with all the seductive grace of a wolf on the prowl. She was one of the women he'd slept with occasionally whenever he was in the community. Her bobbed hair framed a face painted with too much makeup and the slinky shirt she wore over a miniskirt rode low on her ample breasts. Perfume wafted over Tailor as she stepped forward and rubbed her slender body along his.

"Hello, handsome," she purred. "I heard you were finally back and wanted to welcome you personally. It's been so long." Her bottom lip pushed out in a pout. "What's kept you?"

"Tula, uh…" He stepped to the side to put distance between them, but she only followed until he was trapped against the foyer wall. Gently, he removed her wandering hands from his chest. "Look, now's not a good time. I think you should go."

"Why? Do you already have another female here?" Her eyes perked up. "I know! We can all play together. I don't mind. Besides, it looks like she's already gotten you hot and ready."

When her hand squeezed his cock, still hard from Dhani, he jerked and pushed it away. "Whoa!"

Cy entered the foyer then with a hand shielding his eyes. "Don't mind me. I'm not here. Just wanted to grab a—"

"Oh!" Tula exclaimed, clapping her hands in delight. "Your visitor's a man. Even more fun."

Cy practically skidded to a halt and looked over in surprise.

"And he's just as attractive as you are," she commented, licking her red lips.

"Thank you," Cy said as he moved to a nearby wall and leaned against it. "I was just *not* leaving."

Tailor growled at the amusement shining in Cy's eyes. "My foot and your ass are about to become real good friends."

Cy raised his hands in an innocent gesture.

"What's going on?" Dhani came in at that moment and froze when he saw Tula still crowding Tailor.

Tailor gave him a weak smile, dying a little inside.

Tula frowned. "Two men? I'm getting confused."

"Tula," Tailor started, "This is Cy and Dhani. Dhani is my..." he hesitated over the word mate, unsure of whether Dhani wanted him to broadcast their relationship yet. Once Tula knew, so would the entire community by the next day.

But Dhani made that choice for him.

"His mate," Dhani ground out.

"His...mate," Tula repeated, then looked sharply at Tailor. "Your *mate?* But he's a guy."

"Caught that, did you?" Dhani said bitingly. He strode to the door and proceeded to push Tula through it. "I'm his mate, he's taken, and you're no longer necessary. Have a good life and don't come back again." He slammed the door then turned on Tailor, fuming.

Tailor's stomach plummeted. "Dhani, I—"

Dhani reared back and punched him hard across the jaw. In the next instant, he was marching toward the staircase.

"Dhani, wait!"

"I'm not talking to you right now!" Dhani yelled back.

Tailor rubbed his jaw, cursing under his breath. He caught Cy's wide grin and glared at him. "Thanks for the help."

"Hey, I'm on your side, stud. I think what happened is a good thing. At least now you know how your mate feels about you."

With a grunt, Tailor headed back to the kitchen. "Pissed off? Betrayed?"

"Possessive," Cy corrected. He took a whiskey bottle down from a cabinet and poured two glasses, handing one to Tailor. "There's a fine line between love and hate, my friend, and I think your mate just crossed it. I've lived over three centuries and have never seen emotion like that unless love was involved."

Tailor mulled over Cy's words as he sipped from his glass. Was it possible Dhani loved him, even if it came from just a small part of his heart? Dhani certainly had no problem telling Tula they were mates, and before that disaster, things had been going so well. The tension that had always existed between them had disappeared.

He scrubbed his face. "I just don't know what I'm doing. With my first mate, Dominic, it was so easy. We fell in love instantly and would've bonded if I hadn't been required to investigate a few skirmishes during the war. Then I got him killed and I…lost myself."

After he upended his glass, he took a deep breath. "With Dhani, there were so many complications in the way. I got scared," he admitted, not caring if he sounded like a vulnerable coward. Dhani was all that mattered. "I pushed him away, right into the hands of *Roh Se Kahn*. For the past year, all I've been able to think about was that I'd killed another mate. A *second* one. No one gets a second chance, so why is Dhani here? Goddess knows I don't deserve him."

Cy refilled their glasses and shook his head. "I don't know, but my parents were mated and if there's one thing I've learned from them, it's that love is a scary bitch. There's no hiding from it and there damn sure ain't no running from it. You need to keep trying, for his sake and yours."

"It's not that easy."

After a stretch of silence, Cy said, "When Dhani was taken by *Roh Se Kahn,* you spent a year searching for him. You put aside your obligations as *Ketai* to your best friend and *Jaes'din,* you left all your friends behind and I've seen you kill dozens of *Roh Se Kahn's* followers with no fear for your own life. That's not the kind of thing you do out of guilt alone. Then when Dhani came back, you were the first person he asked for – the only one. He's here, right now, with you, because he chose you. He trusts you. If that's not love, what is?"

Cy clapped him on the shoulder then turned to leave. "Good luck, buddy."

A smile lifted a corner of Tailor's mouth. Surprisingly, Cy's words made sense. It wasn't guilt that had driven him. Dhani had wanted him from the start, and even after he'd been a fool, Dhani hadn't given up. That kind of love was unconditional, and that was what he'd been chasing for the past year. Dhani could've gone anywhere, sought out any one of the people who cared for him, yet it had been Tailor he'd asked for.

With newfound determination, Tailor poured his liquor into the sink, finished the sandwich he'd been making Dhani, then cleaned up. He put the food on a tray and headed for his mate's room.

"Dhani," he called out, knocking on the door. "I'm sorry about what happened. I wasn't sure about telling Tula we were mates because…" *I didn't know if you wanted to claim me,* "she loves to gossip. Telling her something is like announcing it to the world. I didn't know if you were ready for that. Dhani?"

Dhani stood on the other side of the door with his back to it. His body was trembling and hands shook violently. Within, the darkness was rising like black tendrils through his veins. The sliver of *Roh Se Kahn's* soul beat at him, trying to tear down his will and replace it with its own.

It became active from its near dormant state by his anger, he was sure of it now. Just as it had been triggered outside the Alpha's house when Cy had drawn a gun on Tailor. Before that, it had almost taken over when Dhani had tried to kill himself out of fear and rage. It was feeding off his aggression, getting stronger each time he lost control.

"Dhani?" Tailor called again, knocking harder.

He tried to calm himself, but it was no use. Terror made him gasp when he looked down and saw bright, blue sparks spitting in his palms. Dread made him look up at his reflection in the dresser mirror across the room. Right there in front of his very eyes, another lock of his hair turned white. His pupils flashed to silver then back again.

"Dhani, she means nothing to me. She never has. Please talk to me," Tailor called out.

Dhani clamped his eyes shut and balled his fists. He wasn't even mad at his mate anymore. When that woman had been rubbing her breasts all over him, Dhani hadn't felt a single thread of arousal in his mate's energy. It had just been a knee-jerk reaction to someone trying to seduce Tailor that had fired up his anger. He'd been unable to control it.

"*Daishen*, you have every right to be mad," Tailor said in a stern tone, "but I need to know you're okay. I'm coming in, all right?"

He glanced around frantically, searching for anything that might calm him. Tailor couldn't see him like this. Dhani wanted more time with him. Just a little more time.

When the doorknob turned, Dhani spun around, yanked the door open and leapt into Tailor's arms. What sounded like dishes clattered to the floor, but he didn't care. He circled his arms around Tailor's neck and kissed him hard. At first, Tailor didn't move, then he wrapped him in a tight embrace and opened his mouth to deepen the kiss.

Dhani strengthened his hold and concentrated on moving his tongue around Tailor's. Part of him was desperate and the other part afraid Tailor would let him go. This was the only time he'd felt any kind of peace, in Tailor's arms, and he was hoping this time wouldn't be any different.

Sometime between his panic and the rush of Tailor's alluring scent filling the air, the kiss changed. It became pleasure instead of work. The potency of the darkness inside him began to wane and his thoughts stopped spiraling. He loosened his grip and sank into the wonderful heat of his mate's firm body enveloping his.

Gradually, Tailor eased back to look at him in concern. "What's wrong? You're shaking."

For a brief moment, Dhani considered telling him, but he couldn't bring himself to do it. The darkness was still volatile within and he wasn't sure what it would do if he made it known. He bit his lip in turmoil. "I need you."

"You have me," Tailor said, hugging him close. "I'll stay with you all night if you want me to."

"No." Dhani pulled back just enough to meet his mate's gaze. "I mean I need you. Right now." He poured all of the desire he felt for Tailor into his voice. It was the truth. He needed the light of Tailor's spirit, his affection and warmth to chase away the darkness still competing for dominance inside him.

Seconds ticked by, and just when he thought Tailor might question him further, Tailor grabbed his waist and lifted him. Dhani circled his legs around his mate and gave in to the crush of Tailor's mouth on his. This time, Tailor took charge and fisted a hand in Dhani's hair at the back of his head to keep him there. His embrace was strong and his tongue demanding as he plunged into the cavern of Dhani's mouth.

Dhani was barely aware of Tailor walking into his own room and kicking the door shut. He flipped the switch to turn on two lanterns hanging from either side of the bed which bathed the room in soft light. When Tailor laid him on the bed, he looked around in amazement. Everything was so rustic and obviously hand-chosen with care. A tribute to all the comforts nature had to offer and so far from the playboy persona Tailor had once cultivated. It was exactly the style Dhani would've chosen for his own house.

Tailor took off his shirt then blanketed Dhani's body to resume their kiss. His hard muscles stretched beneath Dhani's hands as he gathered him close and threaded his fingers through Dhani's hair. The strength of his passion was almost overwhelming, as if he'd been starving for this.

Dhani let himself go. He forgot about his worries and surrendered to the intensity of his mate's hold on him.

Tailor's energy was everywhere, enticing and rousing him even as it calmed the frenetic violence his anger had unleashed earlier. He could feel the darkness shrinking back into dormancy.

Just a little more. He was almost in control again.

Then Tailor rubbed his solid erection into Dhani's groin and a jolt of electricity raced up Dhani's spine. He gasped as his cock thickened, begging for the pressure of Tailor's steel column sliding along it through the rough material of their jeans. Dhani dug his nails into his mate's back and arched up, nearly whimpering when Tailor paused to stare down at him.

"Are you sure, baby? We don't have to do this if you're not ready." Although his words were couched in patience, his voice was strained and his blue eyes couldn't hide the lust in them.

In the horror of the alternate realm where he'd been held prisoner, Dhani had imagined this moment a thousand times. He'd dreamt of it and held it close where none of the other essences could steal it away. Now, with his mate willing to accept him, his dream was a reality. Maybe it wasn't all he'd hoped for. He didn't expect Tailor to love him, but it was a start.

If this was all he could have before the darkness took over, he would gladly take it.

"This is where I want to be."

Tailor smiled widely then fused their mouths together again. He moved his lips down the curve of Dhani's neck and grazed the sharp tips of his canines along Dhani's collar bone. The sting made Dhani's breath catch in his throat. He raised himself to let Tailor pull off his shirt, but when he reached for his pants, Tailor held him down.

"Don't move." Tailor's voice was deep and commanding, and sent a shiver through Dhani's chest.

He lay there and watched his mate strip his pants from him then slowly brush his mouth across every inch of his chest. Tailor teased Dhani's nipples between his teeth then moved lower, grasping at Dhani's narrow waist and licking the trail of fine hairs that led from his flat belly to his groin.

As Tailor's mouth traveled closer to his weeping cock, he strained with the urge to switch their positions. No one had ever gone down on him. It had always been his role to please first, whether for money or fear of pain, even during the few times he'd had sex for pleasure. It came naturally to him. Yet, at the same time, he didn't want Tailor to stop. His skin quivered in anticipation of his mate's mouth surrounding him.

Tailor flicked his tongue over Dhani's slit then lowered his lips down the throbbing shaft. Dhani threw his head back in shock. Incredible heat engulfed him all the way down to his base and his hips bucked of their own accord. Tailor restrained him with strong hands as he brought his mouth up then lowered it again, creating a tight suction that scattered Dhani's thoughts.

He'd never known it could feel like this. The hot rasp of Tailor's tongue on his sensitive flesh and the press of his lips were almost more than he could bear. He curled his fists to keep from moving as Tailor quickened his pace. The friction blazed along Dhani's nerves and his balls drew up tight, preparing for his imminent climax.

Then Tailor gently cupped his balls and pulled them down, stemming Dhani's release. He groaned loudly in frustration.

Tailor chuckled softly. "I'm not letting you off so easily. I owe you for that mean left hook." He stood up and began stripping out of his clothes.

Dhani laughed. "You deserved that." He watched as Tailor grabbed a bottle of lube from his nightstand then climbed back onto the bed, placing Dhani's legs over his thighs.

Tailor poured the lube onto his fingers then started to massage Dhani's hole. He leaned forward and stared into Dhani's eyes unerringly. "I deserve a lot of things, but I've never deserved you." He inserted one finger and rotated it, then a second and third.

Dhani let himself relax, caught in the force of Tailor's gaze. The impact of his mate's statement humbled him and made his eyes fill with moisture. It should be the other way around. He was the one who didn't deserve Tailor. His mate was a man of action, and all Dhani had done was run from the pain in his life. He couldn't look away, though, and couldn't deny how much Tailor wanted his trust.

Another sensation hit him when Tailor twisted his fingers and hooked them forward, grazing his prostate. They rubbed it mercilessly, causing blood to engorge his member to the point of pain. He reached down to alleviate the pressure, but Tailor pushed his hand away.

"That's mine," Tailor said, full authority in his voice, which only made Dhani squirm with need. Tailor poured more lube onto his considerable length then placed the tip of his cock at Dhani's entrance. When Dhani closed his eyes, Tailor brought their bodies together and whispered above him, "Open your eyes, *daishen*. I want you to see me."

As soon as Dhani obeyed, Tailor pushed into him slowly, filling him completely. The burn of entry was quickly replaced by a sense of thrilling contentment so deep, he could only cling to Tailor's large torso. This was nothing like his dreams. It was so much better and frightening at the same time. He felt like he was where he should've been all his life. Like he had finally found where he belonged. And he was suddenly scared to death of losing it.

"Stop," Tailor told him. "I can feel your fear coming back. Don't think of anything except me. I'm here, right now, and I'm never going to let you go again."

A single tear escaped before Dhani could blink it away. Tailor caught it with his tongue then captured Dhani's mouth with his. He pulled out and thrust back in over and over again, burying himself deeper each time.

Dhani clutched his mate's broad shoulders to anchor himself as the penetrating force of his mate's unyielding length drove the fears from his mind. He moaned into Tailor's mouth, needing more, craving all of him.

Tailor lifted Dhani's legs higher and began to pump furiously. The new angle placed the head of his cock in a direct line with Dhani's prostate, making Dhani cry out with need. He was so close. Then Tailor gripped his cock and began stroking in time with his thrusts.

Dhani's body seemed to shatter into a million pieces as his orgasm bowled through him. He shouted into his mate's mouth, every muscle in his body tensing with the depth of his release. The strength of his orgasm was prolonged as Tailor slammed into him harder until he found his own climax. Tailor buried his face in Dhani's neck and moaned, his body shaking with aftershocks.

They lay tangled in each other for some time. Tailor's heavy weight made it impossible for Dhani to take a full breath, but he didn't mind. He didn't want to move at all. Everything was so perfect.

This was the memory he wanted to cling to, no matter what happened.

Eventually, Tailor slid off to resituate the comforter on top of them. He pulled Dhani's head onto his chest and pressed his cheek to Dhani's brow. "Thank you," he murmured, "for giving me back my life."

Dhani's eyes pricked with more tears. *So this is what it feels like,* he thought, *to be cherished and wanted.* He moved closer to wrap himself around Tailor's large breadth and gave in to the lure of sleep, wishing, in the back of his mind, that he might never wake up.

Chapter Six

The next morning, Dhani awoke to the smell of coffee and the distant sound of a buzz saw. He was alone in Tailor's bed with no sign of his mate anywhere. On the nightstand was a tray of food and a note.

Good morning, daishen.
I'm in the library. Join me after you eat.
T

Dhani smiled at the pet name. He ate the food then barely remembered to shower and dress in his hurry to get to the library. After he washed his dishes in the kitchen, he made his way to the other end of the cabin.

Just as he approached, apprehension gripped him. He wasn't sure how Tailor would react to him after last night. While it had been amazing, the circumstances surrounding it hadn't exactly been normal, and their relationship was still new. What if Tailor was under the impression that Dhani's eagerness had been a sign of commitment to their bond? Or worse, what if he'd felt the darkness in Dhani and wanted to have nothing more to do with him?

Dhani forced himself to step into the library. Tailor was using a saw to cut more shelves from a long plank of wood. Sweat glistened on his bare chest and a bandana was tied around his hair. The sharp definition of his muscles was plain to see in the light streaming in from the open windows. Once again, Dhani was struck by how magnificent the man was, and how much he paled in comparison. Quinn's words on the matter came back to him, yet they gave him little comfort.

Tailor must have sensed his energy because he stopped to look directly at Dhani. He took off his gloves and safety glasses then strode to Dhani and kissed him. The kiss was light yet passionate, just enough to remind Dhani of the delicious aches in his body from last night.

"Did you sleep well?" Tailor asked.

Heat rose in Dhani's cheeks. "Yeah."

"Did you eat?"

He rolled his eyes at that. "Yes, your highness. I ate."

Tailor grinned. "Good. We'll be finishing the shelves today. Can you grab some more supports? They should be in that box over there," he said, tilting his head toward the back of the room.

Relief washed over Dhani at the casual attitude of his mate. Perhaps Tailor thought Dhani had wanted him out of jealousy. If that was the case, Dhani was fine with that. After all, it was partly true. Before he could get the supports, however, Tailor stayed him with a hand on his wrist.

"Is more of your hair turning white?"

Alarm spread through Dhani as he reached up to touch the white streak. He'd forgotten to hide most of it after his shower. He quickly flipped his red hair over to mask as much of the white as he could. "I don't know. Guess I haven't noticed it." He held his breath, hoping his mate wouldn't detect the lie in his energy.

Fortunately, Tailor merely frowned and let him go.

They spent the entire day completing the bookshelves, stopping only for lunch and dinner. Although the work was exhausting, Dhani was thankful for the chance to exercise his body. He'd been trapped inside it for too long and working with his hands was something he'd always loved. Somehow, Tailor could sense when he was pushing himself too hard and would purposefully change what he was doing to give Dhani an easier task. Such as fishing the wires going to the ceiling fan or handing Tailor nails for the top shelves.

If Dhani wasn't so out of shape, he might have been offended that Tailor thought he couldn't keep up. But for now, he was only grateful.

Tailor also kept a conversation going throughout the long hours. He never once made Dhani feel uncomfortable or pried into the harsh realities of his past, even though Dhani was sure he had to be aware of them. In turn, Dhani found himself revealing more than he had to anyone other than his friend, Keenan. His likes and dislikes. Some of the challenges he had faced while living in Detroit as well as the few friends he'd had in the community he'd grown up in.

Tailor was so easy to talk to that Dhani had to catch himself several times from saying too much. He didn't want to tell his mate about his parents or the abuse he'd suffered during the two and a half years he'd spent in captivity with Keenan.

While he was aware of the abuse Tailor had gone through, and that Tailor probably wouldn't hold his past against him, he didn't want his mate to see him any differently. When most people heard of abuse, their attitudes changed to one of disdain or pity. Dhani couldn't stand the thought of his mate looking upon him with either one.

At the end of the day, Tailor walked him to his room and gave him a chaste kiss goodnight. Dhani showered again to wash off dust and sweat, then lay in bed. Every muscle in his body was sore and he was more tired than he could remember being in a long time. Yet, sleep wouldn't come.

His thoughts circled around his mate and how much Tailor had changed since they'd last met. He seemed happy now. Content. It was still hard to believe the man had spent the last year searching for him. And even harder to believe Tailor wanted him now as much as he wanted Tailor. It was like a fairytale come true.

Only this fairytale was an illusion.

Eventually, Dhani knew he would have to leave, and the illusion would be over.

He tossed aside his covers and went to the window. Outside, the moon and stars glittered brilliantly over the forest beyond. In a nearby tree, he spotted an owl resting on a low-hanging branch. When the owl looked his way, its yellow eyes sparked a memory Dhani had forgotten in the madness of the past year.

He had seen the golden eyes of a bird staring at him from the other side of a window before. He wracked his brain, trying to recall, then the memory came back to him swiftly.

When he had been rescued from the band of rogue *Vam'kir* and taken to this community for the first time with Keenan, he'd been sick with pneumonia. For days on end, he'd been confined to his room, restless but unable to shift and enjoy the forests that had been denied him for so long. Every night, he had stared out of his window, taking in the beautiful scenery. And every night, there had been an eagle sitting in one of the nearby trees, staring at his window as if watching over him.

When Dhani had learned that his mate's spirit was an eagle, he'd had no doubt it had been Tailor watching him. It was one of the reasons why he'd refused to give up on the man. If Tailor had truly wanted to dismiss him, he wouldn't have spent every night perched within view of Dhani's bedroom window.

The memory made Dhani shiver. He turned around to look at the expanse of his room. It was pleasant, well-furnished…and empty. Everything reflected the personal nature of his mate, but his mate wasn't there.

On impulse, he slipped into the hallway and went to the next door down. He raised his hand to knock then changed his mind. As quietly as possible, he crept inside and closed the door behind him. The room was dark with only the faint glow of moonlight coming in through the open curtains. Tailor's large figure stood in front of the window, staring out just as Dhani had a minute ago.

Tailor turned at the sound of the door closing and didn't move for several seconds. Then, without a word, he crossed the room and pulled Dhani into his arms, placing a kiss on the top of his head.

The anxiety Dhani felt at going to his mate was dispelled when Tailor led him to the bed and pulled the covers over him. Tailor climbed in next to him and wrapped him in a tight embrace.

There, in the silence of the room, Tailor murmured, "You are mine."

It was said with such possession that a shiver ran up Dhani's spine. Warmth flooded his chest and he curled closer into his mate's arms. A feeling of peacefulness encased him as sleep finally took hold and his head was filled with Tailor's comforting scent.

* * * *

Tailor glared at the directions on the pancake mix box then down at the concoction in the mixing bowl. Somehow, it had come out lumpy and slightly brown. It didn't appear to look like it should but he was sure he'd read the directions correctly. He shrugged and poured a good amount into the heated waffle maker. Pancake mix overflowed everywhere when he closed the lid, sticking to his fingers when he tried to scoop it back in.

He muttered a curse, then paused to sniff the air. Something was burning. Thin wisps of smoke were coming from the frying pan he'd filled with scrambled eggs. He cursed again as he grabbed a spatula to scrape them from the bottom of the pan. They stuck together when he flipped them like one large fried egg, soggy on one side and burnt on the other.

More smoke was coming from the oven door and when he opened it, billows rolled out, making him cough. The fire alarm blared to life and this time, he let out a string of invectives that didn't stop until he'd turned off the alarm. He opened the windows and snatched up a towel to wave the smoke out.

When laughter came from behind him, he turned to find Dhani standing in the doorway with amusement dancing in his eyes. His hair was pulled back into a ponytail, displaying the handsome angles of his face, and his clothes were snug on his lean body.

"Issues?" Dhani asked.

Tailor scowled at the strips of black bacon in the oven. "I'm thinking we should go out to breakfast."

With a smirk, Dhani walked over to look at the food. "Bacon, waffles and...what is that?" he asked, pointing at the eggs.

Tailor gave it some thought, then answered, "A charred egg pancake."

Dhani laughed again. "Why did you buy this food if you can't cook it?"

"I didn't," he grumbled as he washed his hands. "Quinn did. He threatened to maim me if I didn't feed you real food."

"Quinn?"

"That little man can get mean when he wants to." Tailor wasn't joking in the slightest. Quinn had always been small like Dhani, and timid, but being around Manning's confidence had given him a steel backbone. Tailor had a feeling Dhani would turn out to be the same way and find his confidence if Tailor could just get his mate to come out of his shell. Dhani already had no trouble displaying his anger, as Tailor's jaw could attest to.

"So if you can't cook, what do you usually eat, aside from the sandwiches we've been living off of for the past few days?" Dhani moved the dishes to the side then began rummaging through the fridge.

"I can live off the land and use a microwave better than anyone I know. It's the rest of the kitchen that has a problem with me."

Dhani cast him a derisive glance with one eyebrow raised. "I don't get it. Why did you buy all this incredible, antique cookware and appliances if you never use them?"

Tailor sat at the small breakfast table and watched his mate prepare another batch of eggs and pancake mix. "My guests love it. Makes them want to cook for me."

When Dhani raised both brows, he lifted his hands in defense. "Just friends, I swear." He grinned after Dhani went back to the stove. Yeah, that backbone was coming along nicely. Maybe he should teach his mate how to fight, or at least defend himself. It would boost Dhani's self-assurance and give Tailor a little peace of mind when he decided to go back to work.

"So how did you learn to cook?" Tailor asked.

"There was an old woman in my neighborhood of the community I grew up in. She would invite me over to eat when she knew my...when she thought I might be hungry."

When his foster parents refused to feed him, Tailor heard between the lines. He knew well the shame that came from having to accept charity when you were starving. On more than a few occasions, his own father had forbidden him to eat until he'd learned how to hunt on his own. He'd been seven when his father had started enforcing that rule, years before he'd been able to shift and track animals easily in his spirit form.

"She taught me how to cook," Dhani continued with a reminiscent smile. "She was really nice."

Tailor knew he probably shouldn't broach the subject, but he had to know. "This woman was aware that your foster parents were starving you, wasn't she?" The stiffening of his mate's back gave him his answer. "Why didn't she report it? The Alpha of your community would've found a new home for you immediately. That's part of their job."

Dhani whirled around and thinned his lips in anger. "Did anyone report the abuse your father put you through?"

He waited patiently for his mate to calm down. They both knew this wasn't about him. Besides, he'd been just enough of a stubborn idiot in his youth to be determined to handle anything his father dished out. He hadn't wanted help.

Dhani sighed and went back to cleaning the waffle maker. "I told her not to. Throughout the years, my foster parents took in other kids temporarily. I was the only one they kept permanently. I knew if I wasn't there, my foster parents would beat them as well. So long as I stayed, I could make sure I was the only one who...suffered."

The last word was hesitant, and it was all Tailor could do to keep his rage from bleeding into his energy. He was well aware of everything the word 'suffered' entailed for his mate.

Cy walked in and instantly covered his nose with one hand. "Whoa, what died in here?"

Tailor dropped the conversation and slanted a glance at the man. "My ego."

Cy peered over Dhani's shoulder at the fresh food cooking. "Your ego should be glad you have a mate who knows how to cook. Especially since he's willing to cook for you."

"Is there a reason you're bothering me?" Tailor asked in annoyance.

"It's fun?" Cy replied, taking a water bottle from the fridge. "I'd love to go on, but there is actually something I need to discuss with you. Dhani, mind if I borrow your mate for a minute?"

When Dhani nodded, Tailor went to the living room with Cy. "What is it?"

Cy sat on the arm of a recliner and took on a grave expression. "Rowan called me an hour ago. He said his men have reported some activity at *Roh Se Kahn's* castle."

Tailor narrowed his eyes. *Roh Se Kahn's* castle in Ireland had been abandoned ever since the *Ba'Kal* and *Vam'kir* had teamed up there to defeat his minions, and Keenan had cast the dark God out of this realm. Rowan and Manning had assigned two small teams to watch over the place in case *Roh Se Kahn's* son, Vane, decided to pick up where his father had failed. "What kind of activity?"

"Nothing concrete. They said they've seen shadows and heard sounds, but they weren't able to find anything."

"With Vane's ability to teleport, he could be in and out of there before the guards could catch him."

"My thoughts exactly," Cy agreed.

"Does Rowan think Vane might be looking for something there? I know Keenan took everything he could find that could be of use to his brother, but there's a possibility he might've missed something."

"He's not sure. He and Manning have decided to triple the number of guards there just in case."

"Maybe I should investigate it."

"No!" Cy exclaimed. "Rowan didn't even want me to tell you. He didn't want you to worry when you have more important matters to take care of." He pointed his bottle in the direction of the kitchen. "Only reason I did tell you is because I thought you deserved to know. I don't believe in coincidence, and activity at the castle so soon after Dhani's sudden appearance feels pretty off to me."

Tailor nodded. "I don't believe in coincidence either. Thanks for letting me know. I owe you one."

"Just take care of that mate you've got," Cy said. "He's a good man. Managed to keep your ass from killing anyone for a whole week."

Tailor scoffed.

"No, seriously," Cy went on in a sarcastic tone. "That's got to be some kinda record for you."

"I will kick. Your. Ass," Tailor growled, punctuating his words.

"I don't think it's *my* ass you want," Cy said with a wide grin.

Tailor restrained the urge to deck the man and went back to the kitchen.

"Everything all right?" Dhani asked.

"Fine." He wasn't going to let the news spoil his reunion with his mate. As they sat down to eat, he marveled at the breakfast Dhani had made. His mate had added spices to the eggs and the pancake batter had been mixed with a can of blueberries he didn't even know he had. Dhani really was a great cook.

After they cleaned the mess, Tailor suggested they run into the human town nearby to pick up more supplies for the library. While there were plenty of shops in the community, he had a feeling exposure to the outside world would benefit his mate more. Each community was extremely tight-knit and Dhani's presence could stir up questions from the locals neither one of them were ready to answer. Like who Dhani was and where he'd come from.

Dhani hesitantly agreed and rode with Tailor in a beat-up old pickup Tailor hadn't been able to bring himself to replace. In town, Dhani was quiet at first and stayed close to Tailor's side. Then, as the day progressed, he gradually loosened up in the relaxed ambiance of the town. Tailor was familiar with many of the shop owners, having visited them regularly whenever he needed supplies for his cabin. They greeted him warmly, and Dhani as well.

Tailor also took him to the furniture stores, wanting to browse them for possible pieces to put in the library. He asked Dhani's opinion on everything and was surprised to find his mate familiar with many of the antiquated styles. When he inquired about his mate's knowledge, Dhani smiled in embarrassment and replied, "I used to spend hours reading Victorian magazines. I always thought the furniture from that era held more character than the modern styles."

Happiness filled Tailor's chest and without thought, he pulled his mate in for a passionate kiss. To his relief, Dhani didn't shy away.

An elderly woman passing by in one of the store aisles cleared her throat and stopped to stare at them blatantly. Tailor met her gaze, expecting disgust, but she merely smiled. To Dhani, she said, "You're a lucky one, you are." Then her eyes shifted to Tailor, glinting with delight. "A man like that can kiss me anytime."

It was Tailor's turn to feel embarrassed and his face flamed ever so slightly. Dhani simply erupted into laughter and thanked her. As soon as she was gone, Tailor smacked his mate on the ass. Dhani spun around with a wide grin. "What? It's not my fault. You are sexy."

As Dhani continued down the aisle, Tailor took a moment to breathe in those words and the sight of his mate's joy. He couldn't believe he'd ever wanted to keep Dhani out of his life. The man had been made for him. He was so different from Dominic, yet so similar. Both seemed to be just what he needed at the right times in his life.

They packed the truck with several supplies and arranged delivery for what they couldn't take with them. Tailor took his mate to a café for lunch and afterwards, walked with him down the main street of town where the shops catered mostly to tourists. When Dhani paused at a store selling hats with an eager look on his face, Tailor insisted on buying him a few.

He suspected Dhani only wanted them to cover the increasing strands of white in his hair, and though he didn't comment, he knew it had something to do with *Roh Se Kahn*. Keenan, the God's son, had a full head of white hair and, from Rowan's description, the human body *Roh Se Kahn* had inhabited during his time on earth had also had white hair. It could be that Dhani's red hair would eventually bleed out as a result of his imprisonment in the alternate realm with *Roh Se Kahn*.

For now, though, Tailor would let him hide the change if that was what would help him adjust.

They made one last stop at the grocery store then left town. When they arrived back at the cabin, Tailor began taking the supplies from the bed of his truck while Dhani gathered the bags up front and headed inside. Cy came out to meet them with a grim expression. He pulled Tailor aside and said in a low voice, "Laya's here. I would've called you, but she showed up about three minutes ago. Have you told Dhani yet?"

Tailor cursed under his breath. He'd forgotten that Dhani's mother had promised she would return on this day. "No. Keep her busy while I—" He looked over at the cabin and saw Dhani already walking through the front door. "Dhani, wait!"

He ran inside and caught sight of Dhani in the living room. Laya was there as well, standing next to a window. Now that they were both together, the resemblance was striking. Laya's burgundy hair was swept back in a braid, displaying the elegant angles of her face, so much like Dhani's. She wore cargo pants and a loose-fitting brown top, making her small frame appear larger. Her hazel eyes mirrored the color of Dhani's and held a mixture of apprehension and excitement.

"Who are you?" Dhani asked warily.

Laya took a step forward. "You look so good, my precious son. I've waited so long to see you again."

Dhani sent Tailor an alarmed glance then looked back to Laya. "What's going on?"

"Dhani, I—" Tailor began.

"I'm your mother, Layzani. Or Laya," Laya interrupted, taking another step. "Don't you recognize me?"

Dhani dropped the bags he was holding and shook his head. "You can't be my mother."

"Of course I am! I sang to you every night since the day you were born. The same lullaby my mother used to sing to me. I kept you close and protected you. You always loved to smell my hair. It's the same color as yours. See?" She tugged her hair loose and held up a lock. "Yours is brighter, of course. There's some of your father's blond in you, but we have the same traits. Your eyes are hazel like mine. You even have my nose." Her lashes glittered with tears. "You're more handsome than I ever dreamed you might be."

Dhani's body was rigid and his tone deadpan as he said, "My mother is dead."

"No!" she exclaimed with desperation high in her voice. Her face contorted with guilt. "I did arrange for someone to tell the Alpha of the community I'd left you in that I had died shortly after giving you up, but only because I had to. I couldn't risk your father finding you, or me. It was too dangerous." She started forward with her arms held out. "I know it must've been hard for you to grow up without me. A child needs its mother."

Dhani lurched away from her. "Hard for me?" he rasped in anger. "No. I was too busy trying to survive to care about your death. You gave me up to strangers who made my life a living hell. Did you think of me at all after you abandoned me? When my foster father was beating the shit out of me and raping me? My foster mother did everything she could to make sure I paid the price for his attention. She was mad with jealously, because he preferred my bed instead of hers."

The rage and pain in Dhani's energy permeated the air and his body trembled with intensity. "I cried every night, trying to figure out why you hated me so much that you would give me to those monsters before you died. And now you expect me to be happy you're alive? To forgive you for giving me up while you went on with your life without me?" He turned an accusatory look on Tailor. "And you! What, did you find her thinking I would be grateful to see her again? How could you do this?"

"Dhani," Tailor said, layering his tone with warning. He had to get his mate to calm down. Dhani appeared ready to shatter from the emotions riding him. "Just take a breath. I don't think she intended for you to go through what you did."

"I had no idea," Laya said in earnest, her face ashen. "Oh, dear Mother, I'm so sorry. Please believe me. I told the Alpha to make sure you went to a good home. When I found out you'd been taken by *Roh Se Kahn*, I knew I had to find you again. I heard Tailor was looking for you and I sought him out. This isn't his fault. I'm your mother, and I'll always try to keep you safe."

"Safe?" Dhani's sudden laughter was laced with cynicism and a hint of hysteria. "Did you keep me safe when I ran away and prostituted myself to stay alive? Or how about when I was taken by the rogue *Vam'kir* during the war and held captive for two and a half years? Was I safe when *Roh Se Kahn* stole me from this earth and took everything from me?" His voice had risen to a shout by now and his cheeks were streaked with tears. Then, softly but with no less fury, he asked, "Why did you abandon me?"

Laya had taken a step back at Dhani's vehemence. Her hands covered her mouth and her eyes portrayed her horror. "I thought it was the only way to protect you from your father. He —"

Dhani cut her off with a sharp gesture. "Never mind. I don't want to know. I don't care why you're here, just leave."

"*Daishen*," Tailor said as he slowly approached.

But Dhani wouldn't listen. "Leave!" he screamed.

Chapter Seven

Before Tailor could react, Dhani shifted to his leopard form and bounded through the open front door of the cabin. Tailor looked to Laya, who was trying to hold in quiet sobs. He had no doubt at that moment she'd meant well for her son, but he couldn't bring himself to take pity on her. It was her actions that had inadvertently brought Dhani pain throughout his entire life.

"Stay here," he said forcefully, then shifted and flew out of the cabin in search of his mate. He rose high into the sky, following Dhani's scent. The feline form was easy to spot on the ground, racing farther into the forest, away from the community. Dhani's sleek form was beautiful even from Tailor's height. Tailor remained above the trees for a time to give Dhani space.

Half an hour later, Dhani stumbled and rolled to a jarring halt on the outskirts of a small clearing. Tailor swooped down to perch on the branch of a nearby tree. Dhani had shifted back to his human form and was kneeling on his hands and knees with his head hanging low. His hair had come loose and fell like a frayed red and white curtain over his face. When he finally stood shakily, he clawed both hands into his hair and braced his head as though in pain.

Tailor jumped down and shifted by the time his feet hit the ground. "Dhani," he started in a low tone.

Dhani jerked around to face him. For a brief moment, Tailor thought he saw bright silver eclipse the hazel in his mate's eyes. In the next, Dhani clenched his eyes shut and wrapped his arms around his waist, doubling over in obvious pain.

Panic seized Tailor and he took several steps forward. Something was wrong. He scanned his mate's body, looking for any signs that he'd been injured during his flight from the cabin, but there were none. Tailor's gaze widened in disbelief when more of his mate's hair turned white right there in front of him. Several strands of coppery red paled throughout Dhani's hair until it was all interlaced with full lengths of ivory.

Tailor was positive now the transformation was a result of Dhani's time spent with *Roh Se Kahn,* yet the change didn't seem to be happening gradually. It came in leaps and bounds. His mind raced back to the instances when the white in Dhani's hair had grown noticeably. The first had been outside the Alpha's house after Dhani's nervous breakdown. The second after Tula had shown up at the cabin, and now following Laya's appearance. Perhaps the correlation was in the strong emotions Dhani felt during each instance.

He moved closer and reached out to sooth his mate. "It's okay, baby."

Dhani reared back, tripping over his own feet in his haste. "Don't touch me!"

"I'm not going to hurt you." Again, he could've sworn Dhani's eyes flashed to silver when he looked up.

"You have that the other way around," Dhani said through clenched teeth.

The threat in his voice made Tailor's blood run cold, but there was something more. While rage still suffused Dhani's energy, torment lined his exquisite features. He was afraid, Tailor realized, and whatever had him scared had more to do with *Roh Se Kahn* than Laya. Tailor would bet his life on it. He forced his nerves to calm and stifled his emotions, hoping it would help Dhani regain control. "Tell me what I can do."

A minute passed before Dhani exhaled on a sob and charged into Tailor's arms, just as he had the night of Tula's arrival. He pulled Tailor down for a kiss, his body stiff and lips pressed a little too tight, as though he couldn't breathe in. There was none of the passion Tailor knew his mate was capable of. The kiss was mechanical, and at the same time, frantic.

Instead of pulling away, however, Tailor crushed Dhani close and took command, pushing his tongue into his mate's mouth and delving into his sweet recesses. Despite the gravity of the situation, arousal surged into him at the feel of Dhani's eagerness. He let it seep into his energy and felt an awakening response in his mate.

On the edge of his thoughts, he knew something wasn't right about Dhani's passion. Dhani was running away, trying to escape whatever held him in its grip, and was using Tailor for shelter. As before, his interest seemed to be born of desperation and need rather than desire. Tailor had felt it occasionally in the past with women who had lain with him only for a momentary chance to leave behind the stress of their lives. Even he had been guilty of using sex as an escape for several months before he'd come to terms with Dominic's death.

What he couldn't figure out, though, was what Dhani was running from. Instinct told him it was more than just memories and the nightmares that made him struggle in Tailor's arms when they slept together. It was as if *Roh Se Kahn* still had a physical hold on him, and Dhani wasn't strong enough to fight it.

Tailor firmed his resolve and tilted Dhani's head back, pushing deeper into his mate's mouth. The tension in Dhani's body lessened as he opened fully with a moan. Still, there was urgency in his response. His eyes as he glanced up reflected his spirit, the color of pale green on stained glass. He grabbed the front of Tailor's shirt and ripped it open, scoring Tailor's chest with claws that had emerged from his nails.

Tailor ignored the pain, focusing only on giving his mate what he needed. When Dhani dropped to his knees and raked his claws down Tailor's abdomen, trying to tear open his jeans, blood began to pound through Tailor's veins. The pain only added to his arousal and the sight of his mate so eager to take all of him pushed him past the boundaries of his concern.

Quickly, he unbuttoned his pants and lowered them, freeing his engorged cock. Dhani showed no hesitation. He grasped Tailor's thighs and engulfed him, surrounding the whole of Tailor's length with the searing heat of his mouth.

Tailor rocked back on his heels with a grunt. It was like nothing he'd ever experienced, not even with his first mate. He and Dominic had never had the chance to become truly intimate with each other. Not in the way lovers did when desire overcame reason. And no other woman or man had ever evoked the kind of attraction he felt for Dhani.

Dhani was like a storm. Timid at first, then staggering in his ferocity. He sealed his lips around the base of Tailor's erection, creating intense suction as he raised his mouth to the tip then went back down, over and over again. His tongue rasped along Tailor's sensitive skin, curling around his head and flicking across his tip.

Tailor could feel his cock pulsing with need, begging for more attention. He took hold of Dhani's head and thrust with his hips, gasping at the feel of Dhani's throat constricting around him. It took all of his restraint to keep from slamming into his mate's willing mouth and seeking out his release. He wanted more, needed more.

A part of him became aware of Dhani's influence over him. The potency of lust permeating Dhani's energy was obscuring Tailor's rationality. This wasn't the way he wanted their relationship to progress. He wanted to make love to his mate. To prove to him through gentleness and acceptance that he would always be there for the right reasons. Not simply because of the pleasure Dhani gave him.

But as Dhani hummed his eagerness, causing vibrations to ripple along Tailor's flesh, he lost all concentration and self-control. The drive to sink himself into his mate's warm hole was overwhelming.

He yanked Dhani up and claimed his mouth as he kicked off his shoes and pants. Dhani pulled away only long enough to shed his own clothes, then jumped onto Tailor, wrapping his legs around Tailor's waist. Their mouths fused together again and Tailor pressed the tip of his hard shaft firmly against his mate's entrance. Anticipation raced like electric currents through his blood, goading him to take what Dhani offered, but his protective instincts flared, making him pause.

He was a large man, and taking Dhani without preparation would hurt him. Tailor drew back and panted heavily into Dhani's mouth. "We can't do this here. I won't hurt you."

Dhani merely smiled in understanding and pulled at one of Tailor's arms. Tailor shifted his mate's slight weight to his other arm, holding him easily. For a brief second, he marveled at the way Dhani's slender body fit so perfectly against his. The way Dhani's slim curves molded around his corded muscles like their bodies had been made for each other.

Dhani drew Tailor's hand to his mouth and sucked in two of his fingers. He lathered them with saliva, sliding his tongue evocatively around them as he had with Tailor's cock. Tailor stared, enthralled at the erotic sight, until Dhani let go. He brought his fingers to his mate's entrance and eased them in, rolling them to stretch Dhani's entrance as much as he could.

Dhani buried his face in Tailor's neck and whimpered, "Please. Please, I need you."

The stark craving in his mate's voice stole the last of Tailor's reserve. He lined up the head of his dick with Dhani's ass and sank himself into the depths of his mate's hole. The sensation of Dhani's hot ridges squeezing him tightly drove every other thought from his mind. He encircled his mate's smaller frame in his arms and used the leverage to pump into him in long, deep strokes.

Dhani clung to him, pressing his face into the curve of Tailor's neck and groaning with panting breaths. The brace of his arms around Tailor's neck strengthened, yet it didn't counter the authority of Tailor's control. The way he yielded to Tailor's dominance, giving him all the control, caused tendrils of excitement to spiral throughout Tailor's being.

He pummeled into his mate harder and felt the demanding need of Dhani's energy rise. It made his head swim and his cock throb with increasing pressure. Then Dhani threw his head back and shouted. Ropes of cum spurted from his rigid length, bathing them both.

Tailor felt the force of his climax crest as Dhani's muscles clamped down around him. He yelled out his own release as he impaled his mate onto his thick length one last time. His body shook with the tremors of his aftermath and he held fast to Dhani's warmth until his legs threatened to give out.

Without letting go, he knelt down then lay back onto the cold ground, smiling when Dhani curled up on top of him.

Time passed with only their soft breaths and the sounds of nature surrounding them. Tailor closed his eyes, giving in to the tranquility in his soul. He surrendered to the feel of his mate encasing him and forgot about what the future might hold. Dhani was safe, in his arms, and that was all that mattered.

* * * *

A cool breeze wafted over Dhani, waking him from his slumber. He stirred and immediately felt a band of arms tighten around him. Tailor's reassuring scent filled him, making him smile. He snuggled into his mate's hold, tempted to go back to sleep, until a pang of hunger hit his stomach. When another draft of cool air made him shiver, he pushed himself out of Tailor's grasp.

Tailor lay underneath him, gazing up with infinite patience. It was an expression Dhani was becoming familiar with, yet one that still confused him. When had the asshole from his past turned into the knight in shining armor of his present?

He instantly berated himself for that thought. Tailor didn't deserve his anger, and Dhani was tired of clinging to the pain of his mate's betrayal. That part of his life was over. Tailor had shown him nothing but acceptance since his return, and that alone was more than he ever could've hoped for.

Tailor lifted a hand to thread his fingers through Dhani's hair. Dhani leaned into the soothing gesture, until he caught sight of the deep furrows in Tailor's chest. Four long claw marks had been scraped into Tailor's flesh on each side, deep enough to leave marred trails of dried blood painting the skin over his ribs. Farther down were more lacerations in the same formation running from the top of Tailor's abs to his lower midsection. It appeared as if a wild animal had tried to gut him.

"How did you get these?" Dhani breathed as he brushed his fingers over the wounds. They were dark in the fading sunlight and flushed by swollen, red skin on the outer edges.

Tailor frowned, then shook his head dismissively. "Nothing. How do you feel?"

The question caught Dhani off-guard. He felt fine. It was his mate he should be worried about. Then the memories of what happened crowded into his head.

His mother, Layzani, appearing out of nowhere. His blind rage and escape into the woods. The power of *Roh Se Kahn's* soul rising up in response to his anger and challenging him for control.

He'd been wild with the need to contain it. To keep it from devouring him. The more he'd resisted it, the more it had fought back with a cold so intense, he'd felt like he was burning alive from the inside.

Then Tailor had shown up with his kindness and steel fortitude. He'd been the rock Dhani knew he could cling to. The only protection he could trust to drive away the fury of *Roh Se Kahn's* madness with the emotions Tailor evoked in him. Even when he'd learned Tailor had kept Layzani's presence a secret, he'd known his mate hadn't meant to hurt him.

Yet, he couldn't say the same for himself. He recalled the threat he'd made when Tailor had tried to touch him. Only it hadn't been his threat. By that time, the darkness in him had grown so powerful, it had temporarily slipped past his control. *Roh Se Kahn* had taken over and spoken through him. It had taken all that he had to reclaim his soul to keep *Roh Se Kahn* from harming his mate.

He ghosted his fingers over Tailor's wounds, too afraid to touch them. "I did this," he whispered. The dark God may have taken control for a few brief seconds, but it had been his frantic need to take what his mate offered that had harmed Tailor in the end.

Tailor took his hand and placed it on his chest above his beating heart. "You didn't hurt me. I've suffered far worse, love. I know what's going on. *Roh Se Kahn* still has influence over you. I don't know how hard this must be for you, but I swear, I'll be here to help you through it."

Dhani stilled in dread. Was it possible Tailor knew about the trade *Roh Se Kahn* had forced? That he'd taken a part of Dhani and replaced it with a piece of his own soul? More importantly, what had Tailor meant when he'd used the term 'Love'?

"What is it, *daishen*?" Tailor asked after a period of silence.

Dhani frowned, unsure of what to think. "You used the word 'Love'."

Tailor shifted his gaze to the side uneasily. "I know this isn't the time, and I have no right to feel the way I do." He took a deep breath then looked directly at Dhani. "I love you. I have since the day I met you."

Warmth bloomed in Dhani's chest and his lips slowly curved up in a smile.

"And not just because we're mates," Tailor continued. "You're kind and forgiving in spite of everything you've gone through. I was a fool to push you away. An idiot. I was just scared of losing you like I'd lost Dominic. Not that I think you're Dominic. I loved him, but you're the one I want to be with. I love—"

Dhani shut him up with a kiss. Excitement made his heart pound and his body soar with pleasure. So long… He'd waited so long to hear those words and had no doubt in his mind they were meant only for him. He'd never been jealous of Dominic. It had been Tailor's unshakable love for his first mate that had made Dhani certain Tailor was worth waiting for. Any man who could love that completely could love again, if he was given the chance to.

He sat up and blinked the tears from his eyes. "I love you, too."

Tailor met his gaze unwaveringly and gave a small smile. Dhani could feel the truth of Tailor's conviction in his energy, yet it felt like there was something else Tailor was hiding from him. As though Tailor was purposefully suppressing a part of his emotions just as he had in the past.

When Dhani shook with a chill from the wind, Tailor tapped him on the thigh. "We should get back."

Dhani hesitated at the sudden distance of his mate, but decided to let it go for now. He found his scattered clothes with Tailor's help, then paused again while dressing when his thoughts veered back to Tailor's previous statement. "What did you mean when you said you know *Roh Se Kahn* still has influence over me?"

Dhani pulled on his shoes, avoiding his mate's gaze and holding his breath. As thrilling as it had been to learn that his mate loved him, Tailor's knowledge of the truth behind *Roh Se Kahn's* scheme would put an end to their relationship faster than Dhani had foreseen. Duty was everything to Tailor. Dhani knew that. There was no way Tailor would ignore the fact that *Roh Se Kahn* would eventually overpower Dhani's will and force him to carry out his plans.

Tailor knelt to take Dhani's face in both hands. "No one can go through what you have and come out unscarred. Being around him has changed you. It's why your hair is turning white. I'll never forgive myself for making you feel like you couldn't trust me. I respect the sacrifice you made in giving your freedom for Keenan's life, but I should've been there. I swear on my life *Roh Se Kahn* will never touch you again."

More moisture sprang to Dhani's eyes as relief swept through him. So his mate didn't know. He still had a little more time. Yet, how much was that time worth with the threat of *Roh Se Kahn's* darkness looming over his head? Even now, he could feel the dark God's soul hanging on the precipice of his tentative control. One more bout of rage and Dhani didn't know if he would be able to come back from the edge of *Roh Se Kahn's* insanity.

I'll just have to control my anger, Dhani told himself. He didn't want to let his mate go for a second longer than he had to. Tailor was his sanctuary, his freedom, his love — if only for a short while.

They shifted and headed back toward the cabin. Tailor led the way, streaming swiftly through the shaded trees. Sometime later, he cut in front of Dhani's path to snatch up a field mouse peeking from its burrow. After snapping the mouse's neck, he peered over at Dhani with an eloquent expression. Dhani rolled his eyes and mewled, then sought out a rabbit to feed on.

When Dhani was done, he took off at a lope in the direction of the cabin. Tailor gave a shrill cry of displeasure at Dhani's poor appetite, but Dhani couldn't force himself to eat any more. His stomach was tied in knots over the prospect of seeing his mother again. With any luck, she'd heeded his sharp request and left, though he highly doubted it.

At the steps leading to the cabin, he stopped and shifted back, frozen with trepidation. The lights were on inside and a slim profile paced in front of the windows.

Tailor took back his human form beside him and took his hand. "You don't have to do this. I can tell her to leave."

The temptation to let his mate take care of it was strong. The yearning Dhani had felt to see his mother again had died years ago, along with his innocence. It was so easy to hate her — to blame her for the misery of his life — but he couldn't give in to that. Not with *Roh Se Kahn's* soul hungering for the chance to feed off his anger and take control. "No. I have to do this."

They went into the cabin together and simultaneously flinched from the miasma of odors that assaulted them. On the coffee table in the living room was every food item known to man. The table was littered with pizza, chicken, sushi, Mexican food and several different varieties of Asian food he couldn't begin to identify.

Cy was chugging a beer when he walked in from the kitchen and almost choked in surprise at the sight of Dhani and Tailor. "Thank the Mother you're both here. This woman ordered every Gods-damned meal from every restaurant she could find in the human town, then made me pick it all up. Have I eaten? No, of course not! 'Cause she wouldn't let me!"

Laya flashed him a menacing glare. "This is for my son."

Cy glared back. "I'm just sayin', tip the driver. When did that custom become outdated?"

Dhani fought the grin twitching at his lips. Cy was so much like Tailor, it was scary.

Laya huffed then turned to Dhani in earnest. "I thought you might be hungry when you got back. I didn't know what you'd like so...I got a little bit of everything."

Quinn came in from the kitchen waving a fried chicken T.V. dinner in his hand. "This is why humans are obese and why we're following in their footsteps. When did fat become the main ingredient in convenience? We're shifters, for fuck's sake. We can feed off the— Dhani!" He dropped the dinner and ran to Dhani, pulling him into a tight hug. "Your mom told me you'd left. I had to come over to make sure you were okay."

Dhani returned Quinn's hug, grateful for his concern. At the doorway to the kitchen was Quinn's mate, Manning, who was pouring whiskey into the three glasses he held. He strode to Quinn and gently pushed him aside, saying, "Let the man breathe." He handed a glass to Dhani. "Drink this. Trust me, it'll help." The second glass he gave to Tailor and the last he offered to his mate. When Quinn wrinkled his nose and averted his face, he shrugged and kept the glass for himself.

Quinn reached out to touch a lock of Dhani's hair. "Did you bleach your hair recently?"

Dhani pulled his hair over his shoulder, noticing with dread that more of it had turned white. Fortunately, Laya interrupted before he could think of a lie.

Laya cleared her throat, looking around at everyone nervously. "I appreciate the support all of you are showing my son, but I'd like to speak with him alone."

As one, all eyes turned to Dhani. He looked around at the familiar faces, seeing the worry and protection they all held for him, and was awed by their commitment to his safety. In their energies, he could feel their caring sentiment, even in Cy, who he trusted the least. It humbled him, and at the same time, gave him confidence.

However, their presence couldn't quite diminish the anger he felt over what his mother had done. Air rasped through his lungs as his throat constricted with pain. The darkness inside him surged forth and threatened to swallow him whole. He reeled around, gave the glass to Tailor then clasped onto Tailor's bare midsection, pressing his forehead onto his mate's solid chest. His palms sparked with the spitting electricity of *Roh Se Kahn's* power fighting for dominance, causing Tailor's body to jerk spasmodically.

At any moment, Dhani expected Tailor to shove him away in suspicion or shock, or at the very least, fear. But Tailor didn't. Instead, he pulled Dhani close and held him in the circle of his arms. Dhani knew he had to be causing his mate pain, yet Tailor refused to let go of him. The knowledge somehow brought Dhani back to his senses and gave him the courage to push down the darkness.

He gulped in several deep breaths of air, trying to compose himself, then looked up to find the same infinite patience gazing down at him from his mate's clear blue eyes.

Tailor leaned down and whispered in his ear, "I'm not going anywhere."

Dhani nodded then took back his glass of whiskey and swallowed half of it. "I'm okay." He walked to one of the recliners and sat down. To Laya, he said, "I want them here."

Laya gave a disapproving look. "Son, I don't think—"

"I'm not your son," Dhani snapped. He took another calming breath when Tailor squeezed his shoulder then sat in the chair beside him. "Anything you have to say to me, you can say to them."

She paused, her lips twisting in an awkward smile. "Are you hungry?" When Dhani only gave her a deadpan stare, she straightened with a cursory nod. "All right then, I'll get to the point."

She was silent for minute and walked to the fireplace as if gathering her thoughts. Quinn, Manning and Cy sat on the couch opposite Dhani. Cy looked at Tailor then down at the welts on his chest, wiggling his brows with a knowing grin. Tailor merely narrowed his gaze in warning.

"When I found Tailor," Laya began, "I told him why I had to give you up. You father and I were bonded mates by the time I became pregnant with you. I loved him very much, but I learned later that he wasn't the man I thought he was."

She went on to say that she'd discovered her mate was in league with many other *Ba'Kal*, *Vam'kir* and humans who all worshiped *Roh Se Kahn*. How they had devised a plan to free *Roh Se Kahn* from his prison with a dark spell that had been preserved and hidden for more than two millennia. By the time she'd found out who her mate truly served, it had been too late. The group had already started the incantation, testing it on several *Ba'Kal* needed for the light of their spirits.

She claimed she'd tried to run away, but her mate had refused to let her leave. He couldn't risk her telling anyone and was convinced she would eventually come to accept the dark God as the rightful ruler over all the races. For six years, he'd held her and Dhani captive at *Roh Se Kahn's* castle until she'd managed to escape to the United States.

Dhani frowned. "I don't remember my father or growing up in a castle." In all honesty, he barely remembered his mother. He had only vague snatches of his youth. The only thing he recalled clearly was the day she'd left him.

"Of course you wouldn't," she said sorrowfully. "Your father kept us secluded and didn't want to have much to do with you until you were older. I'd tried numerous times to escape, killing a few of the guards during my attempts. At that point, I think he would've killed me if our life forces hadn't been tied together by our bond. I knew he would come looking for us and try to raise you as a follower of *Roh Se Kahn*. I had to give you up to keep you safe. It was the only option."

It made sense, though Dhani couldn't imagine being so utterly clueless about one's mate. He glanced over at Tailor, certain he would be able to tell if the man were keeping secrets that important from him. Then again, wasn't he keeping a secret far worse? He harbored a sliver of the dark God's soul, essentially putting everyone around him in danger. All because he couldn't bear to let his mate go yet.

I'm no better than my father, he thought with frightening realization.

Laya wrung her hands nervously. "What I haven't told Tailor yet is what happened when my mate and the other followers succeeded in the incantation. When the spell was performed on the fifth *Ba'Kal* and his spirit was ripped from his body, it didn't die. You see, it wasn't the spirit they needed, necessarily. It was the separation of the spirit from the man that released the power of the light in the *Ba'Kal*. When the man died, the spirit was forced to find a new home to avoid dying."

She paused for long seconds, then said, "The spirit entered my womb and joined with you, Dhani. I think it was only able to do that because you were still unmolded and innocent. That's why you've always felt two spirits inside of you when all other *Ba'Kal* have just one. The joining sent me into labor immediately and you were born a month premature."

Dhani felt the blood drain from his face. He'd never told anyone about his second spirit, not even Keenan. He'd been too afraid of what it might mean. That he was abnormal, a freak. To him, however, his falcon had been as much a part of him as his leopard. They'd kept him sane during the torture and loneliness of his childhood.

Now his falcon was gone, perhaps forever. It was the piece of him *Roh Se Kahn* had taken in exchange for a part of his own soul. The perfect solution for the dark God. By leaving Dhani's leopard inside him, no one would suspect he'd been changed. It was also what had given *Roh Se Kahn* the ability to send him back to the human realm.

Just as Dhani's father had done, *Roh Se Kahn* had ripped Dhani's second spirit from him and used the light from the separation to open a rift to the human realm. The dark God would've passed through himself if it were possible, but to create a large enough rift would have required the dormant light of several others, as the group of *Roh Se Kahn's* followers had provided during the first incantation that had freed him.

Although Dhani had lost all communication with his spirits upon being dragged into the alternate realm, he'd felt the separation of his falcon keenly. It had almost driven him insane when *Roh Se Kahn* had performed the spell to send him back. After Dhani's failed attempt at suicide, however, he'd had no choice except to deal with it.

Tailor creased his brow. "You have a second spirit? Why didn't you tell me?"

Dhani took another drink and winced as the liquor scorched his dry throat.

"Because it's hard being different," Quinn replied for him, a note of sympathy in his voice. "You can be afraid of what others might think, even when you know they love you."

Dhani nodded, surprised again at the way Quinn could read him so easily. He supposed they both had more in common than he'd originally thought. Quinn had been the *Aucinthe*. The one person in the world with the power to bring about the rebirth of the *Bassen'kir*. In a similar fashion, Dhani was the only *Ba'Kal* ever born with two spirits.

Quinn then turned an accusatory glare on Tailor. "And you weren't exactly the most receptive person when you met him."

Tailor twisted his lips wryly. "I was an asshole."

Quinn snorted his agreement.

"That's not all," Laya cut in. She looked from Tailor to Dhani and back again, then said slowly, "The fifth *Ba'Kal* my mate used for the spell, the man whose spirit entered my son" — she took a hesitant breath — "his name was Dominic."

Silence filled the room. Dhani frowned in confusion at the significance of that name. It was oddly familiar. Then it hit him, and the room seemed to tilt around him. Nausea rolled through his stomach as he turned to look at his mate in horror.

His second spirit had belonged to Tailor's first mate.

Tailor's skin turned ashen and his muscles strained with tension. There was no emotion in his energy or on his face. Nothing to portray what he was feeling.

No one moved or said a word until Tailor rose stiffly and left the room. Dhani flinched when he heard the front door open and close. His mind was blank at first, trying to grasp the concept of what he'd just been told.

He carried, or had carried, the spirit of the man who'd originally been chosen by *Miel Se Luuda* to be Tailor's mate. He'd never been meant for Tailor after all. They were only tied together because of some sick twist of fate. A cruel joke devised by the Mother to give them both the fantasy of happiness.

It wasn't real. None of it had ever been real. Tailor's attraction to him had only been the call of Dominic's spirit reaching out to him through Dhani. Once again, his life had wrapped him up in another lie.

First, his mother had faked her own death to get rid of him. Then, when he and Keenan had been rescued from the rogue *Vam'kir*, he'd thought things could only get better, only to be sucked into an alternate realm by *Roh Se Kahn* to save his friend's life. Now, he was learning that the connection between him and his mate had nothing to do with him at all. On top of everything, he had no right to be there. Evil dwelled inside him and he'd been hiding it from the start.

He was nothing more than a minion. A living lie.

He looked around at the faces staring back at him, all holding a mixture of disbelief and pity. It was more than he could handle.

Barely reining in the sobs suffocating him, he ran from the room and took the stairs two at a time to his bedroom. He slammed the door behind him then went to the closet and began rummaging through the boxes on the top shelf. It was there somewhere. It had to be. He'd seen it before when he'd been going through the clothes Tailor had bought for him.

Hastily, he swiped at the blurring moisture in his eyes, growling in frustration. He had to do this. It *had* to be possible. The universe had no right to demand that someone should live with so much pain. The mounting pressure in his chest threatened to rip his heart apart, unable to contain the agony.

His hands shook violently as he reached for the last box on the shelf. Twin sparks of electricity bolted from his palms, exploding the box before he could grab it. Bits of cardboard rained down around him and the heavy objects inside clattered to the floor. One was the leather-hilted dagger he'd found two days ago.

He snatched it up then went to stand in front of the dresser mirror. His hair was almost completely white now and streaks of tears stained his flushed cheeks.

He was an abomination. The darkness in him was beating against his will, trying to drown him. When he'd been sent back to this realm, his only hope, the only thing that had taken away his despair, was the thought of seeing Tailor again. All he'd wanted was to find that brief moment of happiness he'd been searching for his entire life.

But Tailor wasn't his anymore. He never had been. The dream Dhani had been clinging to was still just that—a dream. Without Tailor, there wasn't any reason to keep fighting.

At the same time, though, he couldn't simply give himself over to the dark God. He refused to be the instrument of Tailor's destruction.

Dhani gripped the dagger in both hands and pressed the tip to his chest. He took one last breath then jerked the blade toward him with all his strength. It nicked his shirt before it flew out of his hands and embedded itself into the nearest wall.

Waves of anguish crashed into him and he let out a wild scream, punching the mirror in front of him. He turned and sank down, his back hitting the dresser. The sobs he'd held in came pouring out beyond his control. His mind raged at the injustice of his life. How could he be so damned? How could he have been such a fool, striving to live through so many obstacles only to be the tool used to carry out *Roh Se Kahn's* plans of genocide?

He wept until there were no more tears left in him. Eventually, his thoughts emptied and his mind went blank, eyes staring into nothingness. When the door opened, he didn't have the energy to move or even blink.

Quinn appeared in front of him and sat down. His face was grim, though Dhani couldn't muster the curiosity to figure out why. Quinn then poured liquid onto a cotton swab and daubed it over the knuckles on one of Dhani's hands. It stung, but the pain was distant. Through his peripheral vision, he watched as Quinn wrapped his hand in gauze then moved to sit beside him.

He didn't resist when his head was pulled down to rest on Quinn's shoulder. His body felt numb, like the shell it had been in the alternate realm. Faraway words sounded in his ears, murmured softly in gentle voices. He didn't recognize any of them, but they didn't matter. His eyes closed as the heavy weight of exhaustion bore down on him and he surrendered willingly to it.

A single thought entered his mind just before sleep overcame him. A simple thought. A prayer for death.

Chapter Eight

The silver cast of the moon drew deep shadows from the forest around Tailor. He lifted his eagle's head to the slight breeze, listening to the rustle of nature and breathing it in to clear his thoughts. Ahead of him, a dim light shone through the lace curtains of his mate's bedroom window on the second floor of his cabin. He stared at it, hoping to catch a glimpse of Dhani.

When he'd left the cabin, he had shifted immediately and taken to the skies, his only thought to get away from the confusion and turmoil of his emotions. After years of being forced to suppress them, he still had a hard time processing them. He hadn't been prepared to take in the revelation Laya had disclosed. His mind was still trying to make sense of the situation.

From the beginning, he'd known there had to be a reason why he'd been given a second mate. Another chance at happiness. Come to find out it wasn't a second chance at all, but a new beginning with his first chance.

The intricacies of it all made his head hurt, but in the hour he'd spent flying, searching for reason in the absurdity of the situation, one thing had become clear. He was tied irrevocably to Dhani.

A shadow blacker than the night drifted out from the tree line and he grudgingly flew down from the branch he was perched on. He took back his human form at the same time Manning shifted from his panther spirit and met his gaze. Manning held two swords in his hands and tossed one to Tailor.

Tailor caught it by the hilt, curving his lips in a private smile at the fact that his friend knew him so well. The temptation to work out his anger and confusion as he always had — in combat — was strong. However, it wasn't what he needed this time. He drove the blade into the cold ground. "How did she know?"

Manning didn't need an explanation for the question. Tailor knew his friend wouldn't have left without getting every unsaid piece of information from Laya, just as he would have if their roles had been reversed.

Manning pushed his own sword into the ground. "She researched you before she went looking for you. Found out the spirit that had entered Dhani had belonged to your first mate. She was able to come to her own conclusion that you two were mates because of that spirit."

Tailor nodded. It changed nothing. His thoughts were still reeling in confusion and the pain in his chest only grew stronger.

"Do you want him?"

"What?"

"Do you want him?" Manning repeated. "Dhani. Do you still think of him as your mate?"

The question took Tailor by surprise. It was so far from the subject his thoughts had been circling around that it took him a moment to answer. Yet, it had everything to do with the problem he faced. In a ragged voice, he said, "I love him."

"Then why are you out here instead of in there with him?"

Tailor raked a hand through his hair and turned his back to Manning. "It doesn't matter to me that Dhani has Dominic's spirit. I mean, yeah, it matters. It explains a lot, but it's not the only reason I fell in love with him. Dhani is…mine. He's the kind of person that makes me feel like the luckiest bastard on earth just for knowing him. He was willing to love me even after I hurt him. Hell, he sacrificed himself to save a friend. I can't imagine my life without him. Again."

"So what's the deal?"

Tailor whirled around, his hands balled into fists and teeth clenched. "Don't you get it? I didn't just kill Dominic. I served him up on a silver platter. When I led that group of *Vam'kir* into our community, I thought I'd been responsible for his death. Fuck, it would've been preferable!"

He laughed almost hysterically. "Only he wasn't killed. He was taken and used for a spell that ripped him apart to free our enemy. I should've been there to protect him! I should've looked for him when I couldn't find his body. All these years, I've blamed myself for his murder when I should have searched for him. He suffered a fate worse than death because I was too consumed with grief to remember one of the first rules my father taught me! Never believe without proof."

He spat out the last words, nearly retching over the foul taste they left in his mouth.

Manning's expression remained impassive. "You couldn't have known."

"No? *No?* I searched for Dhani, didn't I? I chased after the impossible, knowing I had about the same chance of finding him as a neutered squirrel has of busting a nut."

Manning furrowed his brow. "*What?*"

"The point is…I found him. I never gave up on him. Where the hell was I when Dominic was taken?" he shouted. The rage and self-hatred he'd felt when Laya had revealed the truth came rushing to the surface, so strong he couldn't see straight.

"All our lives," Manning ground out, "I've seen you follow meekly in the steps of your father. You were like a dog begging for scraps, doing anything to please a man who could never be satisfied. He beat the shit out of you on a daily basis and you just stayed there and took it every time. The first time I've seen you do anything for yourself was the day you met Dominic. Then Dhani came along and gave your life meaning again.

"Tell me you want to throw him away just because you can't get over your past. Tell me he's not worth your pride and I'll put you out of your misery right now."

Fury consumed Tailor and he lunged for Manning, rearing back to throw a punch. Manning dodged it then wrestled him to the ground. They went at each other viciously until Tailor pinned him down and raised a fist to strike him. Manning caught it in his palm before it could hit his jaw, meeting Tailor's gaze with the same ferocity. "We can go at this all night. It wouldn't be the first time, but I'm not the one you should be focusing on."

Tailor vibrated with the emotions flooding him. There was so much guilt and shame crushing in on him, tearing him apart, he didn't know how to take back control. It was only the hard tolerance on Manning's face that brought him back to awareness.

He fell into a sitting position at Manning's side and dug his elbows into his knees, burying his head in his hands. Tears stung his eyes for the second time in his life. The only other time he'd cried had been after losing Dominic.

Manning sat up and spoke in a low voice. "I've lost a lot of friends and good men in the battles we've had to fight. I don't want to lose another. Dhani needs you as much as you need him. So quit dickin' around and show him that you love him."

Tailor laughed on an exhale and dried his eyes. Manning was right. He had more important things to do than wallow in self-pity. He stood and clasped Manning's hand to pull him up. "I really hate you sometimes."

Manning grinned. "Shut up and go to your mate."

Inside, they found Cy standing at the foot of the stairs with his arms crossed and an implacable expression on his face. Laya was arguing with him and apparently getting nowhere.

"I have a right to see my son. Now get out of my way," she demanded.

"Not 'til my man says it's okay."

"He's not even here!"

"I am now," Tailor said as he strode toward them. He clapped Cy on the shoulder in thanks then turned to face Laya. While he believed she had the best intentions for her son, he didn't want to deal with her yet, and he doubted Dhani wanted to either. "Take one of the spare rooms down the hall. I'll let you stay here only on the promise that you give Dhani space until he's ready to talk to you again."

She glared defiantly. "I'm his mother."

"And I'm the one he trusts," he said, meeting her defiance evenly. "Take the offer or get out."

Her lips pursed in indecision, though she didn't argue further. Instead, she walked stiffly down the hall he'd indicated and chose one of the bedrooms.

Manning went upstairs with Tailor. In Dhani's room, Tailor looked around in alarm at the mess. The closet had been ransacked and bits of a cardboard box lay scattered over thrown paraphernalia, as if it had exploded from the inside. Tailor recognized the box as the one he'd stored a few old daggers in and found one of them embedded in the wall next to the closet door.

The contents on top of the dresser had been knocked to the floor and the mirror was shattered. Splatters of blood painted the shards in the center and the few that had fallen down. Leaning against the dresser on the floor was Quinn, fast asleep with one hand in Dhani's hair. Dhani was also asleep, lying with his head in Quinn's lap and his thin body curled into a ball.

Tailor noticed cotton swabs and a bottle of peroxide beside them before he saw the bandage covering the knuckles on one of Dhani's hands. Blood had seeped through the bandage and dripped onto the floor at Quinn's knee. Tailor shook his head, almost afraid to ask. "What the hell happened in here?"

Manning shrugged. "We heard him banging around up here, then he screamed. We found him like this, collapsed on the floor with his knuckles bleeding. I think he tried to use that knife on himself and got pissed when he couldn't go through with it."

Another wave of guilt hit Tailor. He should've been here. He never should've left Dhani alone. Still, it didn't feel right. The Dhani he knew wouldn't have resorted to suicide, no matter how bad things seemed. *Roh Se Kahn* had changed him, of that there was no doubt, but they hadn't been discussing Dhani's time with the dark God. They'd been talking about Dominic's spirit and the new home it had found in Dhani.

"This doesn't make sense," he murmured. "Dhani wouldn't do this." There were too many missing variables. It felt like he was staring at a puzzle, his mind trying to see the picture clearly when it was obvious pieces were missing.

"Maybe he thought he'd lost you. Suicide doesn't make him weak. Not after everything he's gone through."

"No," Tailor said, shaking his head again. He told Manning about the whitening of his mate's hair following each of his bouts of anger. About the electric shocks he'd felt earlier when Dhani had grabbed his waist, and even how Dhani seemed to use sex to calm himself down. He expected Manning to try to explain it all away with common logic, but his friend only nodded grimly.

"When Quinn was tending to his hand," Manning said quietly, "Dhani didn't move or speak. His eyes were…dead. Like he was somewhere else entirely. And his scream… I've never heard anything like it. I wouldn't think it had come from him if I hadn't known for certain he was alone in this room. Do you think *Roh Se Kahn* might still have some kind of hold over him?"

Ice crept into Tailor's veins. "It's possible." Entirely too possible for his liking. "Cy told me about the reports Rowan's received from his men of strange movement at *Roh Se Kahn's* castle. It's too close to Dhani's appearance."

"Agreed."

"If Dhani doesn't improve soon, I'm taking him to see Keenan. For some reason, he doesn't want to go, but if anyone will know what's happening to him, it'll be Keenan."

"If that becomes necessary, Quinn and I will go with you." Manning raised a hand at Tailor's protest. "Dhani is family to all of us. I'd protect him as I would my own mate."

Tailor nodded in gratitude. He gently shook Quinn awake to thank him, then picked up his mate. Dhani didn't stir once as Tailor carried him to his own room and laid him down in the bed while Manning left with Quinn. He replaced the bandage on his mate's right hand then lay down beside him, pulling him close.

For hours, he watched Dhani, brushing his hair softly and hoping to Goddess he was wrong about *Roh Se Kahn's* hold on his mate.

* * * *

Over the course of the next week, Dhani's condition only worsened. He became distant, withdrawn. The day after his attempted suicide, Tailor had asked him if he'd tried to take his own life. He had smiled and denied it, not even bothering to hide the lie from his energy or come up with a cover story.

Over the following days, he continued to help build the library and engaged readily in conversation. Although his attitude wasn't quite friendly toward his mother, he appeared to have accepted her presence and treated her cordially. He'd also warmed up to Cy and laughed occasionally at his jokes.

Everything seemed to have returned to normal, or as close to normal as they'd ever been, yet Tailor could tell his mate's behavior was forced. All of it, down to the way his body responded when Tailor kissed him and held him at night. He was rigid and hesitant, his smiles lacked true joy and when he looked at Tailor, it felt like he was looking right through him.

Laya was convinced she was the cause of his distance. She admitted it might have been better to hold off on the truth of her mate and Dominic's spirit for a while, but she hadn't wanted to rekindle her relationship with Dhani on a lie. Tailor had to concede his respect for her choice. If he'd found out later she had kept Dominic's spirit a secret, he would've had no trouble kicking her out.

To her credit, she didn't let Dhani's cool attitude deter her efforts to befriend him. Each day, she thought of new, heartfelt stories to tell him about his youth spent with her, such as the stories she used to read to him and the trouble he'd gotten into. She also told him of what she'd done with her life afterwards and how she'd thought of him every day.

Her love for her son was genuine, and her regret for abandoning him even more so. Despite the abuse Dhani had gone through as a result, Tailor was beginning to admire her. She'd done the only thing she could think of to save her son and had tracked Tailor down years later to try to save him again.

Tailor also did everything he could think of to pull his mate out of his apparent depression. He'd reassured Dhani repeatedly that Dominic's spirit wasn't a justification for his attraction. It was only the force that had driven Tailor to realize he could love again. Not all mates chose to bond, and some of those who did never truly fell in love, as Laya could attest to. Whenever he told Dhani this, however, Dhani would merely smile and say he understood.

It was going on day seven now and Tailor's apprehension was bordering on full-blown panic. Dhani had given up all pretenses of normalcy and spent most of his time alone in his room. He barely spoke and ate only when Tailor reminded him to. The only deliberate action he took was going to Tailor's bed and curling up next to him every night.

Tailor scrubbed his face and downed more of the whiskey in his glass. He stared out of the kitchen window at the night sky, mulling over the plans he'd made.

Cy came in and poured himself a drink. "I think more of his hair is turning white."

"It is," he confirmed with a sigh, taking a seat at the table. "I'm losing him. I know it has to do with *Roh Se Kahn,* I just can't figure out how the God is still affecting him."

"Whatever you decide to do, I'll be here."

Tailor creased his brow. "I value your friendship, but you've fulfilled your duty to Rowan in watching out for me. I'm sure you must have some family you wish to return home to."

Cy deliberated for a minute, then said, "I lied when I said Rowan sent me. I asked him to give me leave so I could help you."

His frown deepened. "Why would you do that? We hadn't even met."

Cy upended his glass, refilled it, then sat down across from Tailor. "My brother died in the battle against *Roh*

Se Kahn's minions. He left behind a mate, six children, the whole white picket fence dream. It should've been me," he said tightly.

"When I found out about what Dhani had done to save his friend and that he'd been taken by the dark God, I had to do something. We all played a part in that battle, but Dhani showed more courage than almost anyone else that day. I couldn't let another good man be taken forever by *Roh Se Kahn* if I could help it. Your mate deserves a chance at happiness, no matter what he's going through right now."

Tailor felt a whole new appreciation for the man come over him. He raised his glass in salute and tapped it against Cy's.

Cy cleared his throat. "So what are you going to do?"

He let out a heavy breath. "I'm going to take Dhani to see Keenan, whether he wants to or not. Hopefully, Keenan will know something about the changes he's going through. I've booked a flight for all of us, including Laya. She'd have my head if I didn't bring her along."

Cy grinned. "Mothers-in-law. Gotta love 'em. Just make sure she doesn't take your balls, too. They've been known to do that."

Tailor scoffed then finished his glass and put it in the sink. "I'll see you in the morning. We leave at eight."

He went to his room where Dhani was already sitting in bed waiting for him. He sat down in front of his mate and took his hands. Dhani's gaze remained far away and his body listless. Tailor didn't bother to couch what he was about to say in evasive words. "I'm taking you to France tomorrow to see Keenan."

For a brief moment, life flickered back into Dhani's eyes and his energy reflected a mixture of joy and fear.

Then it was gone. He gave the same apathetic smile he'd been giving for days and went back to staring into nothingness.

A spark of anger pierced Tailor before he could tamp it down. He felt so utterly helpless. This wasn't his mate anymore. It was a living, breathing shell with Dhani's soul trapped somewhere inside. Dhani's imprisonment was starting all over again and there was nothing Tailor could do to free him.

"We'll leave in the morning. I'm going to pack our bags then I'll come to bed."

There it was again. That hated smile. Tailor kissed his mate's forehead then packed their things. Dhani nestled into his side when he lay down sometime later, though Tailor couldn't sleep. He spent the rest of the night trying to shove a single thought from his mind, refusing to dwell on what he had no answer for.

What if they couldn't bring Dhani back?

* * * *

The next morning, they boarded the plane to France. Manning and Quinn had left their son with Quinn's sister, Mara, and her mate, Cherrie, to babysit for the next week. Dhani remained silent for the entire trip, staring out of the window. He barely acknowledged Laya when she tried to offer him the in-flight meal. It took a stern command from Tailor to get him to eat. They gathered more than a few stares, but Tailor ignored them.

At the airport terminal in Florac, France, Rowan and Keenan were waiting for them. Rowan was similar to his brother, Quinn, in appearance. They both had the same pale skin, black hair and angular features. The only differences were Rowan's trim cut hair and the fact that he was twice Quinn's size.

As soon as they passed through customs, Keenan caught sight of Dhani. His face lit up with joy and he ran toward him, only to pull up short a yard away. Shock replaced his joy and a telltale sign of horror spilled out of his energy. He looked up at Tailor who nodded. Tailor had described Dhani's condition to Keenan the night before, but he knew Keenan hadn't quite been prepared for it.

Keenan looked back to Dhani and yanked him into a fierce hug. Though Dhani didn't lift his arms to return the gesture, his gaze was fixated on Keenan when Keenan pulled away to run a hand through the white strands of Dhani's hair. It was almost a perfect match for Keenan's own platinum hair now. "I don't care," Keenan whispered. "I'm just so glad you're here." He hugged Dhani again and this time didn't let go for a while.

Tailor, Quinn and Manning greeted Rowan, then Tailor introduced Laya.

She shook Rowan's hand. "Thank you for rescuing my son from the rogue *Vam'kir* and for keeping him safe…for a time. Tailor's filled me in on what I've missed of Dhani's life. I'm grateful your mate was, and is, such a good friend to him. I know they've both gone through a lot."

Rowan wore the same expression Tailor had when he'd first met the woman, distrustful and wary. "You could say that."

Keenan refused to let Dhani go as they picked up their luggage then headed to the parking garage. Tailor was glad to see that Dhani didn't pull away once.

Lately, Tailor had been the only person Dhani would allow to touch him for more than a second or two.

Outside, Rowan tossed a set of car keys to Tailor. "I brought your favorite. Go ahead and take them," he said, tilting his head to indicate Dhani and Keenan. "I'll meet you back at my place."

Tailor recognized the keys to the classic Pontiac Firebird he'd constantly borrowed when he had lived with Rowan for six months to help get the treaty between their races in order. He was somewhat of a thrill-seeker and loved the hum of a fast car. It would have put a big, sloppy grin on his face to drive it again if his mind wasn't preoccupied with the reason he was there.

He recalled the way to Manning's place, having driven it many times to and from Florac, and navigated the scenic roads easily. The palace of Manning's birthright was majestic even at night. The turrets at its four corners were lit against the night sky and rose high above the buildings of Manning's clan which surrounded it. An outer circle of several other clans made it almost impossible to lay siege to the palace.

When they drove through the gates at the same time Manning arrived, a host of servants came out to take the cars and their luggage. Inside, Tailor took a moment to marvel at the changes Rowan had made. Gone was the cold feel of the iron fortress Rowan's father had designed the palace to be, and in its place was warmth and comfort. The furnishings were modern yet cozy and the concrete walls had all been smoothed over and painted. A vast improvement.

Tailor frowned and glanced at Rowan. "This is Keenan's doing, isn't it?"

Rowan snorted. "He banned me from decorating after I suggested a pool table in the living room. *I* thought it was a good idea."

"Of course you did," Keenan said derisively. "You also thought a full bar in the kitchen and a bouncing castle in Adreanna's room were good ideas."

Tailor grinned. Adreanna was Rowan's two-year-old daughter from his ex-wife, Deirdra, and Keenan was more protective of her than any parent he'd met.

"You thought of that, too?" Manning asked. "I wanted to put a castle with a ball pit in my son's room, but Quinn wouldn't let me."

"And a little inflatable pool next to it."

"Yeah!"

They carried on for a good minute, one-upping each other with their ideas and building their excitement. It wasn't until Quinn tapped his foot on the floor and cleared his throat loudly that they finally quieted. Quinn glared at them. "Could we?"

"Right, sorry," they said in unison.

Tailor shook his head, thankful he hadn't lost his mind to parenthood.

Keenan started for the staircase leading to the second floor. "I'll take Dhani to his room." He paused to look back at Tailor. "Do you two want to share one?"

"Yes!" Dhani exclaimed, surprising them all. It was the first word he'd spoken in nearly two days.

Xenessa, the *Vam'kir* historian, entered the foyer. She was exactly as Tailor remembered her, dressed in her usual conservative clothing with her brown hair swept up into a severe bun. Her timeless features softened her strict appearance, made even more welcoming by the large smile on her face. "You're all here! I'm so—"

She stopped abruptly to stare at Dhani. Her face paled and eyes widened. "Oh, sweet Mother," she breathed, pressing a hand to her breast and swallowing convulsively.

Seconds later, Cy came in through the front door. "Damn, I've missed home." To Rowan, he said, "If you don't mind, I want to visit my sister-in-law and her kids later to—" He paused abruptly as well to look over at Xenessa sharply.

Xenessa's mouth gaped as she stared at Cy, then glanced from Cy to Dhani repeatedly. "I...I..." she stammered.

"I'm going to take Dhani up now," Keenan said, each word stretched out to emphasize his perplexity over Xenessa's strange behavior.

Tailor didn't bother to hide his confusion, either. He'd never seen Xenessa flustered. It was weird and oddly frightening. "I'll bring him something to eat." He went to the kitchen where Rowan's cook already had a hot meal prepared for him. It was the same elderly, plump woman he'd met on his previous stay. She had a great, motherly nature about her and Tailor hadn't been ashamed to flirt mercilessly to get her to cook his favorite meals.

She handed the tray to him then patted his arm. "It's good to see you again. My lord let me know you were coming and thought your mate might be hungry. Give Dhani my best, will you? He's such a good boy."

He thanked her with a kiss on the cheek, to which she giggled. As he headed upstairs, a part of him was stunned that she remembered Dhani from the few days he'd spent at the palace before he and Keenan had run away to take on *Roh Se Kahn* by themselves a year ago. Then again, that Dhani had been the man he'd fallen in love with. The one who could make anyone feel good just by being himself.

When he entered the room Keenan had taken Dhani to, he saw Dhani sitting on the side of the bed and Keenan taking off his shoes. Tailor put the tray on the nightstand then took his mate's jacket off and stacked pillows against the headboard for him to lean back on. He took his mate's face in both hands and said, "It's time to eat, Dhani. Can you hear me?"

Again, that hated smile met him. Almost mechanically, Dhani began eating the food Tailor had placed next to him. Tailor's chest tightened the way it always did at the emptiness in Dhani's eyes. His mate appeared so fragile, as though he might fall apart or waste away if Tailor wasn't there to take care of him.

Keenan tugged on Tailor's arm and leaned in close to whisper, "We need to talk."

Tailor kissed his mate on the temple then left with Keenan. As soon as they were in the outer hallway, Keenan clamped a hand around his wrist and pulled him downstairs to the living room. Everyone else was there, filling their plates with the food the cook had brought out for them.

Keenan politely dismissed the cook then promptly went to the liquor cabinet and poured a drink, downing the entire glass. He screwed up his face, exhaling in disgust. "Damn, I hate this stuff, but I need it. We all do. Rowan, please," he said, holding a bottle of gin out to his mate.

Rowan cocked his head in confusion, but proceeded to fill a glass for everyone, giving them to Keenan to pass out. When he was finished, he sat down on the couch and looked at Keenan who was now pacing in front of the fireplace. "What is it, love?"

Keenan took another gulp of his gin then clawed a hand through his hair. "That isn't Dhani!"

Chapter Nine

Keenan waved his glass in the direction of Dhani's room with a wild look in his eyes. "I mean, it is Dhani, but it isn't. The Dhani I knew, he's...well, he's gone. I don't know how the hell it happened." He began to pace again with agitation in every step, shaking his head. "All I know is, that's not my Dhani. It has to be some kind of spell. Some kind of exchange. I'm not sure, maybe a possession or something –"

"Keenan!" Rowan said firmly. "Calm down. What are you talking about? If that's not Dhani, who is it?"

Keenan stared at his mate, then at Tailor. Hesitantly, he said, "My father."

As the room filled with silence, Tailor thinned his lips in frustration. "I already told you *Roh Se Kahn* has some kind of hold over him. I need to know –"

"No," Keenan interrupted. "I mean, *that's my father*! I would recognize him anywhere. Dhani doesn't just have darkness inside him like me. He's literally a host for my father's soul."

"He's right," Xenessa chimed in. "When I met Keenan, I was misled by his darkness. At first, I'd thought he was *Roh Se Kahn,* but when I saw Dhani earlier, I felt the difference. Keenan inherited his darkness whereas Dhani, quite literally," she said, using Keenan's word, "*is* darkness. I believe he's the living embodiment of *Roh Se Kahn.*"

Everything within Tailor stilled. His mind repeated Xenessa's last sentence over and over again, unable to grasp the significance. It couldn't be. Every kiss, every breath and sensuous emotion he'd felt from his mate over the past two weeks had been all Dhani. He was sure of it. Past the dryness in his throat, he said, "I know Dhani's in there somewhere. He has to be."

"He is," Xenessa assured him. "I could feel his spirit, although it was very faint. I just don't know how much of Dhani is still in control. From the information Keenan relayed to me about what you told him yesterday, it seems *Roh Se Kahn's* soul was only gradually taking over. You told Keenan that Dhani's hair had only a single streak of white in it at first, right? Then the white became more and more prevalent in his red hair."

Tailor nodded.

"I would surmise that the white signifies *Roh Se Kahn's* growing power over him. If I recall correctly, the human host *Roh Se Kahn* was using during his recent time in this realm had also grown a full head of white hair after the God's possession of him."

"That's right," Rowan said. "but it was whiter than Keenan's or Dhani's, and his skin was nearly translucent."

"Because of the amount of time *Roh Se Kahn* had spent using his body. From what I saw, Dhani's hair still retains a small portion of its original color. That must mean *Roh Se Kahn's* soul hasn't been able to corrupt his completely yet."

"Yet?" Tailor said through clenched teeth, feeling rage boil in his blood. How could he not have seen what Keenan and Xenessa had so easily recognized in his own mate?

"This is my fault," Keenan said frantically, bracing his head between both hands. "I shouldn't have taken him with me to fight my father. I should've made him stay here where it was safe."

Rowan strode to his mate and pulled him into a tight embrace. "Shhh. Don't do this to yourself. No one could've predicted what happened, and you can't tell me Dhani would've stayed if you had told him to. He loved you. He still does. We'll find a way to save him."

Tailor watched the best friend of his mate cling to Rowan's larger build as if his life depended on it.

His life and freedom...

Tailor's mind went into overdrive, trying to put together the missing pieces of the puzzle eluding him. "Dhani came back," he said slowly. "He appeared out of nowhere at a *Ba'Kal* community."

"So...?" Cy asked.

"So he couldn't have been released by *Roh Se Kahn's* followers. They would've kept him with them if that was the case."

"Is it possible Dhani could've found a way out himself?"

"No," Xenessa said. "Dhani had no darkness in him when he was pulled into the alternate realm. The spell to open a rift between the realms would require both light and dark, such as Laya's mate used, as you told Keenan over the phone," She said to Tailor, her excitement matching his. "*Roh Se Kahn's* darkness from the other realm and the light from the separation of your first mate's spirit."

Tailor nodded. "Which means *Roh Se Kahn* had to be the one to free Dhani."

"I don't understand," Keenan said. "I read up on the alternate realm I sent my father back to. Only essences of darkness dwell there. The only light would've been in Dhani's spirit and he still has it."

"Or not," Laya murmured, her face blanching. "At least, maybe not both of them."

Keenan drew his brows down. "I know you told me he has two, which I still can't believe Dhani didn't tell me about, but… Oh." His eyes rounded as realization set in.

"The spell would require only one spirit," Tailor said, finishing Keenan's thought. "*Roh Se Kahn* could've taken the spirit of my first mate and replaced it with a part of his soul. That would leave Dhani with his leopard and we would've been none the wiser if Laya hadn't shown up and told me the whole story."

Xenessa leaned forward, her face animated as the pieces of the puzzle were finally beginning to come together. "Dhani's leopard may be the only reason he's been able to resist *Roh Se Kahn's* control for so long. I understand now. The rift *Roh Se Kahn* created by taking one of Dhani's spirits would only have been large enough for Dhani to pass through."

Tailor tipped his head in agreement. "If I were the dark God, I would command Dhani to gather my followers to perform another incantation to free myself, using the power of the light in them to make the rift big enough."

"Dhani's a ticking time bomb," Manning concluded. "Once *Roh Se Kahn* has full control over him, there's no telling what he might do to complete the God's plans or whether we'll even be able to stop him."

"I can," Keenan said with grim determination. "I still have the spell I used to cast my father out of this realm. Maybe if I can find a way to alter it, I can draw my father's soul out of Dhani then send it back. I'll start looking through the books I took from my father's castle. There has to be something in them that can help us."

Cy stood up. "I'll go with you. There might be a spell in there we can use to inhibit *Roh Se Kahn's* control over Dhani."

"And me." Laya spoke up, standing as well. "I have to do something. I can't just keep sitting around watching my son fade further and further away from me. I won't let him down again."

Keenan smiled with a look of newfound respect. "Okay, then. Let's get started."

Tailor put his glass down. "I'm in, too."

Keenan shook his head. "You need to stay with Dhani and let us know of any changes. From now on, we can't let him out of our sight for a single moment."

He acknowledged the truth of Keenan's statement grudgingly. In all honesty, he wanted to stay by Dhani's side to keep an eye on him as he had been for the last several days. Yet, the futility of doing nothing was starting to test every ounce of patience he possessed. He forced himself to stack a plate with food despite his lost appetite then bid everyone goodnight.

In the room, he found Dhani asleep above the blanket, still dressed in jeans and a T-shirt. Quietly, Tailor kicked off his shoes then went to his luggage by the closet doors. He took his weapons out immediately, the only ones he'd had permits to enter France with, and put them in the bottom drawer of the dresser. His gun he placed in the top drawer of the nightstand. In the bed next to Dhani, he ate his food then shifted Dhani to pull the covers over them. Without waking, Dhani instinctively curled up next to him and settled his head on Tailor's shoulder.

Tailor's mind still raced with the new discoveries he'd made, but his recent lack of sleep clouded his thoughts and pulled him under. He drew his mate into the circle of his arms and closed his eyes, telling himself he would sleep for only a short while. Just a few hours…

* * * *

Apprehension filled Dhani when his eyes sprang open. His body stirred and he shuffled quietly out of his mate's arms to sit up in bed, only it wasn't him controlling his actions. It was *Roh Se Kahn*.

For the past three days, he'd been a passenger in his own body. Watching everyone around him from the cage of *Roh Se Kahn's* control. He was a prisoner again, held hostage by the force of the dark God's essence, so much stronger than his.

The night he'd learned his falcon spirit had once belonged to Tailor's former mate, something had snapped. All the despair and pain that had consumed him had been the leverage *Roh Se Kahn* needed to push his way past Dhani's resistance.

The God was more devious than Dhani had given him credit for. Instead of using the weakness of Dhani's anger, *Roh Se Kahn* had broken through his will using the force of his grief. In that moment when Dhani had given up hope, thinking he had lost Tailor forever, *Roh Se Kahn* had pounced. He'd shattered the barrier of Dhani's will and staked his claim, making it only a matter of time before Dhani could no longer stave off his domination.

So many times since then, Dhani had tried to reach out to his mate. To scream at him and tell him of *Roh Se Kahn's* presence inside him, but the words wouldn't come out. *Roh Se Kahn* had taken his speech first, then his sight and finally the whole of his motor skills. It had been the God who had boarded the plane to France to set his plans into motion. The God who had hugged Keenan and stayed close by his side while traveling to Rowan's palace.

All the while, Dhani had raged inside to give even the barest hint to his mate and best friend that he wasn't who they thought he was anymore. The most he'd been able to manage for the past several days was pressing himself into Tailor's warmth at night. To show his mate that he still loved him. That he was still there.

And his smiles…

He could see how much Tailor hated them, as if he thought they were false when they were just the opposite. They were the only truths aside from their closeness at night that Dhani had been able to give him.

He padded on bare feet around the bed to the dresser, his vision clear in the pitch black of the room. A glimpse in the mirror showed him *Roh Se Kahn's* silver eyes staring back at him. It was strange and terrifying to see his own familiar face, yet know that it no longer belonged to him. Dhani could only watch helplessly as he flashed his teeth in a malicious grin.

The God was up to something. Although Dhani couldn't read his thoughts, he felt every emotion in *Roh Se Kahn's* soul. At that moment, *Roh Se Kahn* was feeling…exultant.

Dhani took one of the daggers from the bottom shelf where he'd seen Tailor place it earlier, then stepped lightly back to the bed. He firmed his grip on the hilt and it was only when he raised the blade, preparing to bring it down viciously, that he realized *Roh Se Kahn's* intent.

No! he screamed within, throwing all that he had into seizing command of his own body again. Relief shot into him when his arms obeyed and halted their downward motion, but his control was tentative. His arms shook as *Roh Se Kahn* fought him, the blade hovering mere inches from Tailor's chest. Inside, he could feel the God laughing at him, taunting him.

Dhani used the last of his energy to yank his arms back and force his fingers to release the hilt. *Roh Se Kahn* reclaimed control in the next instant and caught the dagger before it could fall to the floor and wake Tailor. It all happened so fast, it took a moment for his mind to catch up.

He'd actually stopped *Roh Se Kahn*! But his solace in that act was short-lived. The strength of his will was depleted and he didn't know if he could go another round if *Roh Se Kahn* tried again.

Fortunately, the God seemed to lose interest in Tailor. His sick humor gave way to impatience as he set the knife on the nightstand then called forth the power of his darkness. Dhani felt it rise swiftly within him, a cold force suffocating in its potency. His vision blurred and stomach lurched at a horrible sensation of displacement.

Suddenly, he found himself in a different room. *Roh Se Kahn* must have teleported him—one of the God's many abilities, Dhani recalled, from what Keenan had told him years ago.

This room was decorated with lavish furniture in soft, pastel colors. A four-poster bed stood at the far end on which sat two figures masked by a sheer curtain of silk gauze. They spoke quietly, their words muffled. Dhani didn't recognize the pair until his mouth opened and he said in an imperious voice, "Vane."

Dhani's thoughts reeled in alarm. *Roh Se Kahn* was finally going through with his plan. He'd known all along it was inevitable, especially after Tailor had taken him to see Keenan, inadvertently reassuring the God that the object of his hatred was alive and available for him to use. Yet, Dhani couldn't quite believe it was happening. In the back of his mind, he'd foolishly clung to the hope that he would succeed in taking his own life before *Roh Se Kahn* could force him to go through with what he intended for Keenan.

Vane, the only one of Keenan's half-brothers still alive after the battle a year ago, surged to his feet. His sleek, tailored suit fit his tall frame well and enhanced his aristocratic features, though his short, blond hair was mussed. He pulled a knife from a holster hidden by his jacket and flung the blade straight at Dhani's head. With a simple flick of Dhani's wrist, the knife was knocked from its path and clattered harmlessly to the floor several yards away.

Vane stared in disbelief, then narrowed his eyes. "I know you. You're the boy who brought my brother back to life. The one my father took with him to his prison when he was cast out of this world. How did you get in here?"

The other person on the bed pulled aside the gauze and rose to stand next to Vane. It was a woman with long, auburn tresses and a full figure concealed by an ivory, satin robe. Her pale skin glittered with diamonds hanging at her ears and neck, and the slant of her chestnut-colored eyes was shrewd.

It was Deirdra, Rowan's ex-wife and the mother of his daughter, Adreanna. The last Dhani had heard, she'd been pregnant with Vane's child during her marriage to Rowan. She and Vane had conspired to overthrow Rowan's throne with the intent of making Vane the proxy *Magnique* until their son was old enough to rule as king over the *Vam'kir.*

Confusion filled Dhani. The one and only time he'd ever seen her was when he and Keenan had snuck into *Roh Se Kahn's* castle to defeat him. She had been in Vane's room, arguing and crying over broken promises. Vane had revealed to her that he'd never cared about her or their child. That she had only been a tool in his scheme to get rid of Rowan and take control over the *Vam'kir.*

What was Vane doing here now?

Dhani didn't believe for a moment the demigod had miraculously grown a conscience in the past year and had gone back to Deirdra out of any semblance of love. And the child, if it had been born, would be obsolete. It was not of Rowan's blood and therefore had no ties to the throne.

Deirdra pulled tight the lapels of her gown in a false attempt at modesty. "What's going on?"

Vane ignored her, sneering with contempt as he advanced on Dhani. "Tell me, boy, did my father make you beg for mercy when he had you in his prison? Did he make you pray for death as Keenan did when I tortured him like the slave he was?"

Without any effort, *Roh Se Kahn* drew on his darkness and raised Dhani's hand, shooting a bolt of lightning at Vane's chest. The demigod flew backwards onto the bed and Deirdra jumped away with a shriek.

Dhani approached Vane, meeting his shocked gaze with contempt. "You disappoint me. How can you expect to win a fight when you can't even recognize who you're fighting with?"

Vane rubbed the scorch marks on his suit then sat up, staring at Dhani in consternation. "Father?"

"I see your wits haven't improved during my absence...or your tastes," he said, curling his lip in Deirdra's direction.

"How is this possible?"

He paced to the other end of the room. "This boy has two spirits. I'm not sure how that came to be, but it has worked to my advantage. I was able to open a portal to this realm by taking one of them and replacing it with a part of my soul. However, there was only enough light for the spell to send him through. The rest of my essence is still trapped in that prison. We'll need to gather my worshippers so I can perform the spell again and free myself completely."

"That may not be an option." Vane flinched when Dhani rounded on him. "Yet! I mean, it'll take time. Your followers who were still alive scattered after the battle. In your absence, they fled. I've only been able to track down a few. They're scared of Rowan's retribution if he were to find out who they truly served."

Dhani could sense through Vane's energy that he was lying, though *Roh Se Kahn* didn't seem to notice.

"And this one's mate," Vane went on, gesturing to Dhani's body, "has been searching for him ever since you stole him. He's been killing every follower of yours he can find. It'll make things harder. There's no telling where they've gone into hiding."

"Then find them!" Dhani roared. "Recruit more. Do whatever is necessary or I'll no longer have a use for you."

"Y-yes, sir." Vane stammered.

"Where are your brothers?"

"They didn't survive the battle."

If that saddened the God in any way, Dhani couldn't feel it. There wasn't even a hint of hesitation in his threat to Vane. The only emotion Dhani could feel in him was a slight annoyance at the setback to his plans. "You'll have to do, then. Find my followers and have them meet us at my castle."

Vane stood with a frown. "Rowan and Manning are having the castle watched by their guards. It's why I haven't returned to it."

"No," Dhani sneered. "You haven't returned because you're a simpering coward. I'd have thought you would've found a way to free me yourself by now. I'll take care of the guards. You have one day to gather enough people for the spell."

When Vane nodded, Deirdra ran to him and clutched his arm. "You have to take me with you, and Sevrick. You promised you would take us with you when a chance arose."

"Who is Sevrick?" Dhani asked.

Vane glanced at him nervously, as if he hadn't intended his father to find out about Sevrick. "He's my son. I can teleport him and Deirdra to the castle now. They won't be a distraction, I swear it."

Again, Dhani was confused. Why was Vane bothering to care for a child he'd never wanted?

The God's ire hitched up another notch, but he didn't argue. "Get him now. We have no time to waste."

Deirdra's face lit up with elation. "Sevrick's room is just down the hall. I can have his things packed in two minutes," she assured Dhani as she rushed through the door.

Vane and Dhani followed her, only to halt when they caught sight of a group of three men coming up a flight of stairs at the far end of the hallway. Judging from their uniform pale skin and dark hair, Dhani guessed they were *Vam'kir*. Rowan must've assigned a guard to keep watch over his ex-wife.

As one, the men drew guns from their holsters and shouted at Vane and Dhani to identify themselves.

Dhani growled in the God's irritation. "What is this?"

Vane glanced at him. "They're Rowan's men, charged with making sure I have no contact with Deirdra. Nothing more than a nuisance. I'll take care of them."

"You'll take care of the task I gave you," Dhani ordered. "Take your child and whore to the castle then get started. I'll meet you there."

As Vane headed in the direction Deirdra had gone, the guards yelled at him to stop and fired several rounds. Dhani lifted a hand, the darkness rising within him, and created an invisible barrier that deflected the bullets. The men continued to fire, emptying their guns, then froze in disbelief when they saw Dhani still standing.

In that brief period of silence, Dhani effortlessly sent crackling bolts of lightning at two of the guards. They were thrown back into the wall behind them and crumpled to the floor without so much as a single scream. Dhani strode to the third man, who was staring down in terror at the corpses of his companions, and grabbed his neck. Although Dhani was only half the man's size, *Roh Se Kahn's* power gave him the strength to lift the guard and slam him against the side wall, holding him there.

"Tell your king to prepare for the funeral of his mate," Dhani said in a low voice. "It won't be long now."

Within, Dhani scrambled to summon what little strength he had left, using that of his spirit's, as well. This would be his last chance. His only opportunity to get a message to Keenan. He took *Roh Se Kahn's* control by surprise and forced his lips to form the words he needed to get out. "To bring about the end, one must return to the beginning."

While Dhani knew the message was vague, he couldn't risk being any more specific without *Roh Se Kahn* comprehending the meaning. His only hope was that the guard would relay it to Rowan who would, in turn, tell it to Keenan. Keenan would know what it meant. He had to.

In the next instant, *Roh Se Kahn* reclaimed his possession over Dhani and slammed the guard's head into the wall, knocking him out. The dark God's rage swept through Dhani with a vengeance. "Try that again, *boy*, and we'll pay another visit to your mate. One he won't live through."

Despite the God's promise to kill Tailor if Dhani defied him again, Dhani allowed relief to sweep through him. He knew there wouldn't be another opportunity to warn Keenan or his mate in the next day, but at least he'd been able to get his message out.

Over the next half hour, he watched, helpless and horrified, as *Roh Se Kahn* used him to take out the men

Rowan and Manning had appointed to watch over the castle. He sank into the refuge of his mind, thinking of Tailor and hoping Keenan would understand his message and find him…or find a way to kill him.

Chapter Ten

Light seared the backs of Tailor's eyelids. In one smooth move, he pulled his gun from the nightstand and aimed it at the door. "Rowan," he grumbled, lowering his gun. "Sorry, guess I'm a little on edge."

"You should be," Rowan replied. "I take it you didn't hear Dhani leave."

He looked at the space where Dhani should've been at his side, then at the alarm clock. It was three in the morning. Dhani wouldn't have wandered off without waking him. Then, he took in the sight of one of his knives on the nightstand, which caused his apprehension to spike. "Where is he?"

"I have my guards searching the palace and grounds now, just in case."

"Just in case of what?"

Rowan hesitated, then said, "I received a call fifteen minutes ago from one of my men at Deirdra's house. There's been a break in. Two men fitting Vane and Dhani's descriptions left with her and her baby."

He stilled as the news sank in. It didn't seem possible. When Rowan had returned from the battle at *Roh Se Kahn's* castle, he had remanded Deirdra into forced seclusion on a remote island off the coast of France. Technically, since their marriage had been dissolved, she would've been free to live her own life if not for the fact that she had instigated Rowan's attempted assassination and carried Vane's child.

With Vane still alive, the risk that he might join with Deirdra again and raise their child to use the darkness in him for evil had been too great. The only choice had been for Rowan to surround her with his guards at a spot where transportation was limited.

The bay leading to the island was a six-hour drive, let alone the two-hour ferry ride to get there. Yet, Tailor had gone to sleep with Dhani in his arms just two hours ago. Despite all this, there was no doubt on Rowan's face that the information from his call was true.

Tailor jumped out of bed and began arming himself.

"Tailor, what do you think you're doing?"

"What the *fuck* does it look like I'm doing?" he yelled, barely containing his anger. How could he have slept through Dhani leaving? His one job had been to watch over his mate and he'd failed, just as he had a year ago when Dhani had run away with Keenan to *Roh Se Kahn's* castle. "I'm going to find him. Have you checked your garage for missing cars?" He pulled on his shoes, noticing that Dhani's were still on the floor where Keenan had placed them.

"My guards are on it, but I don't think that's how he left. Tailor, wait. We need to think this through." When Tailor tried to brush past him, Rowan grabbed his shirt and shoved him against the wall. "I said stop!"

Tailor fisted Rowan's wrists and bared his teeth, emitting a feral growl. It was only their close friendship that kept him from decking the man. "Dhani is my mate! I can't lose him again. Not to *Roh Se Kahn*. Now get out of my way!"

"I'm trying to help you!" Rowan yelled back.

"Tailor," said a soft voice. Keenan entered the room, twisting his hands anxiously. There was so much stark fear in his eyes, reflecting Tailor's own frenzied turmoil, that it forced Tailor to pause. "I think I know what happened. The best thing we can do right now is come up with a plan. I need you to focus, for Dhani's sake."

After a few seconds, he nodded curtly, seeking that inner place where he could divide his emotions from logic. Keenan was right. If they had any hope of finding Dhani, they had to do it rationally.

"I've woken up the others," Keenan said. "Come with me."

Downstairs in the kitchen, Manning sat on a barstool at the island in the middle of the room with Laya. Quinn was making coffee and Xenessa stood at the wall near the fridge. Beside her was Cy, who was talking on his cell phone. As Tailor sat on the other side of Manning, his attention was drawn to Xenessa's hand firmly holding onto Cy's. Her gaze constantly flitted up to Cy and each time their eyes met, they both gave a secretive grin.

The sight was so incongruous that it took Tailor's mind off Dhani's situation for a brief moment. Then he saw Xenessa stand on the balls of her feet to kiss Cy's neck.

It couldn't be. Cy was covered in tattoos and piercings. He was the quintessential rebel. A man who fit Tailor's own image and didn't give a damn about anyone or anything past what he thought was worthy of his respect. Xenessa, on the other hand, was more conservative than a nun at a human Sunday mass.

Tailor's mouth fell open and a small part of his faith in the grand scheme of things died.

"Scary, isn't it?" Manning said.

"They can't be," Tailor murmured. "*Mates*?"

"Kinda makes you wish you were blind, right?"

Tailor shuddered and averted his eyes. "What the hell was the Mother thinking in pairing them together?" He'd always thought Xenessa was incapable of sexual interest. While he had to admit she was beautiful in spite of her strictness about proprieties, the first and only time he'd flirted with her, she had threatened to cut his balls off.

"About the same thing she was thinking when she paired you with Dhani." Manning merely laughed at Tailor's menacing glare. "Come on. You can't tell me if it weren't for the fact that you and Dhani are mates, you would have a chance in hell with him."

Tailor had to shrug grudgingly. It was true. Dhani had always been out of his league. Handsome and good-hearted with the kind of innocent virtue that kept him wondering why Dhani had ever looked twice at him.

Cy ended his call then looked around the room. "That was the guards. They've found no trace of Dhani. No one passed through the gates since we arrived and none of the cars are missing."

Quinn frowned as he began passing out mugs of coffee. "How did Dhani leave, then? Someone had to have seen him."

"Not necessarily," Keenan said, glancing at his mate. "You should tell them first."

Rowan's expression hardened. "The guard who called me from Deirdra's house said he and two others encountered men fitting Vane and Dhani's descriptions coming out of her bedroom with her. When they opened fire, the two men with the guard were hit by bolts of lightning and he was later knocked unconscious. Another group of my men responded to the sound of gunshots but by the time they got there, there was no sign of Vane, Dhani, or Deirdra and her son."

Rowan inhaled deeply, meeting Tailor's gaze. "The two guards that fell were charred beyond recognition. It would've taken great power to carry that out. More than we know Vane has."

"We can't know that," Tailor argued, feeling a heavy weight bear down on the pit of his stomach. "Vane would have more reason to kill the guards than Dhani — *Roh Se Kahn* — would."

"Maybe," Keenan said quietly, "but Vane doesn't have that kind of power. He can teleport and cause destruction in nature, rip apart the earth and destroy its elements like I can, but he can't create bolts of lightning. Only my father can do that."

Keenan clawed his fingers through his hair. "We have to accept the possibility that my father has full control over Dhani. With *Roh Se Kahn's* power, he likely teleported out of here to find Vane. My brother is the only one who might know where the rest of *Roh Se Kahn's* followers are hiding. The humans in service to him that we captured after the battle admitted there were a substantial number of followers who weren't at the castle. From the number of men in league with my father that Cy told us you found, there are still a good portion of them left.

"I know the way my father thinks. He'll want to perform another spell to release the rest of his soul and he'll need the dormant light of his followers to make the rift between our realms large enough for him to pass through. With Vane at his side, he'll succeed."

Xenessa stirred. "We may yet be able to stop him, but how will we find him?"

A hush fell over the room, then Rowan turned to Keenan, his brow creased. "The guard that was knocked unconscious…he had a message for me."

Keenan scoffed. "Yeah, *Roh Se Kahn* used Dhani to tell me he wants to kill me. It's not as if he hasn't tried a million times before. You don't have to worry about me," Keenan assured his mate. "He didn't succeed then and he won't now. We should be more worried about Dhani."

"Not that message," Rowan said, shaking his head. "The one after that. Dhani told the guard, 'To bring about the end, one must return to the beginning'."

"The beginning?" Manning asked.

Laya gasped suddenly. "The castle!"

Quinn frowned. "What?"

"The castle!" she repeated. "*Roh Se Kahn's* old base of operation, where he put everything into motion. That has to be the beginning he was speaking of! He had to have taken my son there."

"Damn," Rowan muttered. He took out his cell phone and dialed a number, leaving the room for privacy.

Tailor's thoughts whirled at the implications of Dhani's message as the others continued to speculate. It had to have come from Dhani himself, not *Roh Se Kahn*. The dark God was too smart to give them such an obvious clue. Yet, what Keenan had revealed earlier was just as invaluable. *Roh Se Kahn* needed a shifter to complete the spell to bring him back. Who better to fit that role than his *Ba'Kal* son who had led to his demise?

When Rowan reentered the kitchen with a stricken expression, Tailor already knew what he was going to say. "Your guards at the castle are dead."

Rowan dipped his head absently. "I called three of them, including one of yours," he said, nodding to Manning. "None of them answered their phones."

"Dhani's already killed them," Tailor said in a deadpan voice. "He's preparing for the incantation. If it were Vane making his move, he'd have done so months ago." His fury at the way the dark God was using his mate beat at the wavering control he had over his emotions, though he refused to give in to it. This was the crux of all he'd feared since meeting Dhani. That he wouldn't have the strength to protect another mate, but with his fear came pure determination.

He wouldn't let Dhani down. Not this time.

Keenan's face flamed in outrage. "How can you believe Dhani would do that?" Pain and betrayal came through strong in his energy and moisture glistened in his eyes.

"I don't," Tailor replied. His tone was cold and vicious, though none of his animosity was meant for Keenan. "The man that killed those guards wasn't Dhani. It was all *Roh Se Kahn*." He looked to Rowan, ignoring every protective instinct that pounded at his conscience. Even the yearning of his spirit begged him to deny what had to be done. "We have to find a way to send *Roh Se Kahn* back before Dhani releases him."

Rowan tilted his head in acknowledgment. "Give Manning and me time to gather our forces. We can be in Ireland at *Roh Se Kahn's* castle by the next nightfall." Then, with an edge to his tone, he asked, "If there's no way to release Dhani...if we can't find a way to separate his soul from *Roh Se Kahn's*, what will you do?"

Tailor swallowed heavily. Rowan was testing him. The love and fear everyone held for Dhani was like a thick miasma smothering the oxygen in the room, yet no one could contest the validity of Rowan's question. If Dhani went through with the spell to release *Roh Se Kahn,* millions of innocent lives would be put in jeopardy again. Their very existence could be wiped out.

He looked to Keenan and said, "You'll find a way to stop this and save Dhani. I know you will."

Tears gathered in Keenan's eyes, spilling down his cheeks.

"And if you don't, I'll take care of Dhani myself, and I'll die with him. No one, *no one,* will touch my mate other than me," he commanded past the tightening of his throat.

Silence reigned until Keenan nodded perfunctorily. "I'll find a way. When I do, I'm going with you." He stared at Rowan as if challenging him to object, though it was Tailor who denied him his wish.

"You can't go. *Roh Se Kahn* will want to use you to open the portal to this realm. His pride and revenge won't let him take anyone else. You're more important than Dhani right now. As long as you're here, *Roh Se Kahn* isn't. Not all of him. You want to help? Find a way to free Dhani. That's what you can do."

He stood and left the room, feeling the icy stares of everyone in the room at his back. He knew what they were thinking. That he was a stone cold bastard unworthy of his mate, but he didn't care. While Keenan may believe he knew his father, he was too vulnerable to emotions. Tailor knew the mindset of a sociopathic killer better than he did. He'd been raised by a monster and taught to think like one.

The only way to defeat evil was to beat it at its own game, which meant he had to become as ruthless as *Roh Se Kahn*. Dhani's death may be inevitable, he knew that now, but it wouldn't be at the hand of their enemy. If that time came, he alone would be the one to take his mate's life, and end his own in the process.

There would be no continuing after Dhani. He was done — with life and love. Dhani was his second chance at forever, and he refused to live it without him.

On the cultivated grass in the backyard of Rowan's palace, Tailor fell to his knees. He threw his head back and let loose his fury in a defiant roar. All of his despair, his hopes and fears, crested in a fierce cry that escaped his control. He pressed his head to the ground and wept, craving the one person who could bring him peace. The only person who made his life worth living.

After a time, a hand settled on his shoulder and he sat up to find Laya kneeling at his side. They looked at each other, sharing the depth of their despair, then stared out into the night.

It wasn't until the light of dawn emerged over the horizon hours later that Tailor was able to come to terms with his conviction. He was going to save his mate, or he would die trying.

* * * *

Fading rays of sunlight filtered in through the long windows spanning one side of the great hall in the castle. They painted the statues and murals of war lining the walls in muted colors of pink and blue-grey. Many of them had been destroyed during the battle. What had remained intact was now decaying from exposure to the elements. Large chunks of the outer walls had been blasted apart and rubble littered the floor where no one had bothered to clean it.

Dhani sat down on the seat of *Roh Se Kahn's* inlaid marble and cast-iron throne as the God stared out through his eyes on the ruins of his once majestic great hall. The God's anger had been seething inside him since they'd arrived and *Roh Se Kahn* had seen for himself the evidence of his downfall.

All because of his firstborn son.

The doors at the far end of the hall opened to emit a shifter of average build with short blond hair and a leering smile. Behind him, several humans came in carrying a long hardwood table which they placed in front of the dais. They nodded to the shifter then left.

"My Lord," the shifter said in greeting, "it's good to see you again, even if it is in a…different form. It's an honor to help you cross over from your prison realm as I helped you the first time."

Dhani narrowed his gaze. "I don't recall you. What is your name?"

"Achilles." He bowed low then moved to the steps of the dais. "I was the one who led the team to kidnap the shifter used in the spell when we first released you. I've been in command of your human forces and," he paused and licked his lips, "I'm the father of the boy you're using now."

Within, Dhani recoiled in horror. *My father*, he thought. The traitor who had held him and his mother captive, giving her no choice except to abandon him

171

after their escape. The man responsible for the death of Tailor's first mate.

All the animosity and pain of betrayal Dhani had held for his mother paled in comparison to the hatred that rose in him now. There was no regret or even the slightest trace of concern for his son on Achilles' face. In fact, he appeared to be glowing with pride.

I've been hating the wrong person, he realized. At least Laya had loved him — wanted him in spite of her mistakes. The man in front of him held no kindness in his piercing blue eyes. Only a look of avaricious satisfaction.

"It was always my hope that he could be of use to you," Achilles went on.

"Yet, you obviously couldn't hold onto him," Dhani said, peeling his lips back in the God's disgust. "If you had, my firstborn wouldn't be alive right now to defy me. This pathetic boy is why Keenan still lives."

Achilles' pride faltered. "Th-that's not my fault," he stammered. "Dhani's mother stole him from me before I could teach him to serve you."

"I remember you now. You kept your mate and son locked within my walls for six years, then you lost them. Did you know your son had two spirits?"

"No. Well, I suspected, but — "

"Enough!" Dhani snapped. *Roh Se Kahn's* patience was wearing thin. "Where is Vane? Why is he taking so long to teleport Keenan here? We need to perform the spell tonight."

Inside, Dhani's anger was stifled by a wave of apprehension. He couldn't let *Roh Se Kahn* go through with his plan to activate the spell by ripping Keenan's spirit from him and taking the ultimate revenge.

Keenan's life for the release of the rest of his father's essence.

It had been *Roh Se Kahn's* intention all along, and the reason Dhani had been reluctant to visit his friend from the start. He'd foolishly thought he could delay the God's plan by staying away. A part of him hadn't wanted to give up the time he'd spent with Tailor and the other part had hoped he would've found the strength to kill himself before *Roh Se Kahn* took control of his body.

He'd underestimated the God's power, and it was going to cost Keenan his life.

Achilles glanced at the doors then back again. "Vane wanted me to tell you it'll take a few more hours to gather the rest of the *Ba'Kal* needed and to decide which human's body you will inhabit. He doesn't want to take Keenan and alert the *Magnique* to our plan until everything is in order. Meanwhile, I thought we might go over how you intend to take over *Miel Se Luuda's* creations, or destroy them, if that is your wish."

Dhani stared at him warily. "I will go through with my original arrangement. Since Vane is the only one of my worthy sons still alive, he will take control of the *Ba'Kal* and *Vam'kir* once we crush their forces. I see no reason to deny what I promised him years ago."

The lie was so thick in *Roh Se Kahn's* energy, Dhani wanted to yell at his father to see the truth. Vane was nothing more than an instrument to bring about *Miel Se Luuda's* demise, along with that of all her children. During the time he'd been trapped in the alternate realm, his soul assaulted and tortured by the God, he'd come to know *Roh Se Kahn* intimately. It had never been the God's intent to allow Vane to rule. His only desire was for the death and destruction of everything *Miel Se Luuda* stood for.

In the end, not even those who served *Roh Se Kahn* would be given his mercy. So long as they had the power of light in them, however renounced, they would perish.

Dhani listened, helpless, as *Roh Se Kahn* spent the next few hours going over his false strategy, all the while reveling in his deceit. The shattered windows were sealed with plastic sheeting and a fire was lit in the hearth for warmth. Several lanterns were placed in sconces along the walls to give light as the sun set over the horizon.

Eventually, Vane entered the great hall followed by a group of three dozen men and women comprised of humans, *Ba'Kal* and *Vam'kir*. One of them was carrying a second, folding table which he hurried to set up beside the wooden table several feet from the dais.

Deirdra walked in at Vane's side. She was dressed in a form-fitting gown with diamonds dripping from her ears, neck and waist. Her stance was regal and her expression serene as triumph glinted in her chestnut-colored eyes.

Dhani shuddered within, appalled at her blindness. She truly thought she was going to rule at Vane's side as she'd wanted to all along. However, his dismay wasn't for her. It was for the innocent child she carried wrapped in a blanket in her arms. Her son, who was a victim of circumstance just as much as Keenan was.

"Father," Vane began in a voice filled with anticipation, "the moment is here. I will give us our victory and make you proud. After I bring you back, I'll reign over *Miel Se Luuda's* children in your name."

Suspicion flickered in *Roh Se Kahn's* energy. Vane's words were a little too couched in ambiguity. "Where is Keenan?"

"He'll be here, when the time comes. I swear to you, his death will be brutal. I'll make him pay for daring to think he's anything more than the slave you made him." He gestured for the followers to fan out in a wide circle around the tables. Two of them flanked Deirdra while a third unrolled an aged parchment then nodded to Vane.

Vane strode to Deirdra and gently took his son from her. When she protested, he merely smiled. "Don't worry, my dear. I promise you, I have only Sevrick's best interests at heart." He laid his sleeping baby on the surface of the folding table.

Roh Se Kahn's alarm heightened, mirrored by Dhani's. Vane was changing the game. There could be only one reason why he was putting his son on the table.

"What is the meaning of this?" Dhani demanded imperiously, gaining his feet.

At the same time, Deirdra surged forward but was restrained by the two men at her sides. "What are you doing? You told me that table was meant for the human your father would use as his new vessel." Her voice trembled as she struggled against the men at her sides. Whatever Vane was intending, he apparently hadn't deigned to inform her of it.

"Vane!" Dhani bellowed. "I gave you an order to find a human for me to possess. It has to be willing. Your bastard son has no part in this."

"Oh, but he does." Vane tipped his head in the direction of Achilles, who was at Dhani's side.

Dhani turned just in time to see the flash of steel in the man's hand before a knife was plunged into his gut.

Searing pain drove him to his knees, and it was all he could do to stay erect when the blade was wrenched out. He stared in shock as his wrists were bound in cuffs behind his back and a strip of leather was tied around his mouth to gag him. Achilles turned him then yanked on his hair, forcing him to meet Vane's malicious gaze.

Roh Se Kahn's fury swamped Dhani in torrents that refused to let Dhani's body give in to the rending pain.

Deirdra began to scream and curse Vane in righteous fury until Vane slapped her harshly. "Keep her quiet," he ordered the men. He turned back to Dhani and slowly began to approach. "Did you really think I would fall for your lies again? That I would play your puppet while you took away every promise you made to me? I knew, when you took Keenan's blood a year ago to complete your army of minions, that you would betray me. Your hatred for *Miel Se Luuda* is so blinding that you can't even see the greater picture. Why destroy this world when you can rule it?"

Vane clenched Dhani's jaw to the point of bruising, yet *Roh Se Kahn* refused to act. Dhani could feel the God's rage smoldering, waiting to find out what Vane's true intentions were.

Vane struck him hard across the cheek. "It was never Keenan you should've worried about. It is I who will surpass you. Ever since your failed attempt to take power, I've been here, turning your followers against you. Their allegiance belongs to me now."

On the other side of the hall, the doors flew open again and two men came in dragging an unconscious *Ba'Kal* male. They took him to the hardwood table and tied him down using thick rope.

"I knew you would find a way out of your prison," Vane continued as he strolled to stand between the two tables. "I've been preparing for it. The only hope I had was that you would come back before my son grew too old. You see, I don't need you to carry out the promises you made to me, and I don't need Keenan. I'm going to perform the incantation on this *Ba'Kal* and send your essence into my son's body. Being too young to resist you, he's the perfect, *willing,* vessel. Once you're inside him, I'm going to trap your powers with the same collar you made for Keenan."

He brought up his hands to dangle a thin, metal collar from one and a key from the other.

Dhani recognized the collar dangling from Vane's fingers as the same one that had been locked around Keenan's neck when *Roh Se Kahn* had spilled Keenan's blood to complete his army of minions. The same collar the God had fashioned to trap Keenan's powers when he was nine years old. The metal was enchanted to inhibit the forces of light and dark in the person who wore it, and only responded to those with darkness in them.

With that collar around Sevrick's neck once *Roh Se Kahn's* essence was transferred to the baby, Vane would have complete control over him.

"After Keenan defeated you, he took all of your texts on the dark arts, but not before I got what I needed from your own chambers. I knew you kept the strongest of your spells there, and I found one that can separate your powers from your essence. Most of them, at least. The relocation spell will take your powers and give them to me. As soon as I have them, you will become obsolete, *father,* and I'll send your essence back to your prison where you'll spend the rest of eternity regretting your betrayal of me."

Deirdra kicked one of the men holding her in the groin, making him stagger back long enough for her shout out, "You'll kill our son! He can't survive that." Two more men wrestled her under control.

Vane merely smiled. "I'm counting on it. I won't make the same mistake as my father by trusting in my son. I don't need an heir when I can rule forever as a God."

Roh Se Kahn's rage peaked and he drew on every ounce of darkness he'd forced into Dhani. It exploded in a blast at Vane's feet, shattering the floor and upending both tables. One of the followers caught the baby before it could hit the ground while Vane flew back and skidded several yards away. The collar and key were knocked from his hands and skittered across the floor.

Vane was on his feet seconds later, shouting out orders. "Start the spell!" To Achilles, he yelled, "Take him down but keep him alive. The boy can't die until all of my father's essence is in Sevrick." He pointed at the followers closest to the waking *Ba'Kal* still tied to the hardwood table and said, "Hold the shifter down. I need to get the collar on the baby once the incantation is done."

The darkness in Dhani swelled in another overwhelming crest. It disintegrated the cuffs at his wrists and the leather strip in his mouth, then flowed outward to attack Achilles. The knife Achilles brought down in an arc turned to ash with rapid decay that spread from the hilt to his hand in a single heartbeat. He let out an earsplitting screech and scrambled away, clutching the blackened stump where his hand used to be, tightly to his chest.

Dhani lurched up and stumbled down the dais steps. His strength was fading fast. He was teetering on the edge of death, could feel it in every fiber of his being.

Although the blade had missed his vital organs, the blood loss was becoming too much. Within, he prayed for the finality *Roh Se Kahn* had denied him through suicide, yet the God kept him going.

He lifted a hand and cast out a blazing stream of fire to his left, bathing five of the followers in coruscating columns of flame. Their shrieks echoed throughout the hall in an agonizing chorus.

Vane tripped over his own feet in his rush to get away. "Finish the Gods-damned spell!" he shouted over the chaotic noise, sending out his own bolt of power toward the ceiling above Dhani.

Dhani raised a forearm to block the debris that rained down on him with an invisible shield. He clapped his hands together then drew them apart, creating a spitting ball of electricity between them so immense, it scorched his palms. He lifted his hands over his head and prepared to cast it toward Vane when a piercing jolt hit his shoulder. The electric ball dissipated as he spun on his heels and fell onto his side. More pain radiated through his muscles and he glanced down to find a weeping bullet wound an inch below his right clavicle.

Further weakened, Dhani couldn't summon the strength to stand, no matter how much *Roh Se Kahn* demanded it of him. Instead, he set his sights on the mass of newcomers who swarmed into the great hall. Hope surged up within Dhani when he saw Tailor run in at the head of a group of warriors. His mate had a gun aimed at him and was shouting words that were drowned out in the commotion. At his sides were Manning, Cain, Rowan and Keenan.

Dhani wanted to warn them all to get back but *Roh Se Kahn* was still in full control. He compelled Dhani to wave his hand and use the darkness in him to fracture the ceiling above the warriors. Huge chunks of mortar and brick tumbled down and surrounded Tailor and the others in a cloud of dust.

Dhani cried out inwardly against the God even as he was forced to send a second blast of destruction in Vane's direction. Vane was thrown into the air, then came down hard on the floor. In the next heartbeat, Dhani looked to the follower who was still reading from the parchment and sent out a violent peal of lightning that ensconced the man in white light. Close to him, the two followers holding Deirdra cowered away, allowing her to lunge for the man still holding her baby.

With the last of his strength, Dhani pushed himself up to a sitting position and searched for Vane. The demigod was defending himself against two warriors with his powers, but blood coated the side of his face and he staggered to one knee. Dhani lifted his good arm and prepared to cast another bolt of lightning, only to reel from a vicious punch across his jaw. His head hit the floor, dazing him, and he looked up.

Tailor stood over him with a gun aimed at Dhani's forehead. Dust covered his hair and his eyes blazed a bright golden hue, face frozen in an unyielding expression. "Don't think for a second I won't kill my mate to send you back to hell," he said through clenched teeth.

Within, Dhani silently cried out in joy. Tailor was still alive, and he was aware of *Roh Se Kahn's* presence. At that moment, Dhani's fear of death was replaced by a sense of gratefulness. He knew he was going to die regardless of what happened, and was glad — *so glad* — that his mate was there with him. He didn't want to die alone.

Somewhere in the distance, Keenan shouted above the commotion. "Tailor!"

Dhani and Tailor looked to their left where Keenan was running toward them with the collar and key in his hands. Behind him, one of the followers was giving chase and pulled out a gun. In one fluid motion, Tailor unsheathed a dagger at his belt and flung it at the woman. She went down instantly, the blade buried deep in her throat.

Dhani used the distraction to raise his hand for a second blast of power toward Tailor, but he was impeded again, this time by Keenan. Relief swept through Dhani as his friend sent a burst of funneled wind so strong, it felt as if Dhani's hand had been knocked aside by a bat.

"Hold him!" Keenan yelled.

Tailor tackled Dhani and pinned his wrists to the floor just as Keenan arrived. Keenan's eyes were wild with fright, yet at the same time, stark with fierce determination. He closed the collar around Dhani's neck and locked it with the key.

Dhani peeled his lips back in a feral growl. "This isn't over."

"No," Keenan replied vehemently. "It's not. Sleep."

The metal warmed around Dhani's neck and molded to his skin. The feel of *Roh Se Kahn's* insidious darkness was extinguished, trapped beyond Dhani's senses by the collar, along with the light of his spirit. His eyes closed and mind shut down. The last thing he heard was his name whispered in the ragged voice of his mate.

Chapter Eleven

"Wake."

That single word penetrated the fog eclipsing Dhani's mind and brought him into consciousness. The first thing he felt was a profound emptiness so much like what he'd experienced in the alternate realm that fear consumed him. The light of his spirit was gone without a trace. He had to be back in that prison, defenseless and vulnerable without the comfort of his leopard and falcon.

A scream was wrenched from his throat and he sat up in terror. Though his eyes were open, he couldn't make sense of what he was seeing. He fought against the hands that pushed him down until a shout broke through his craze.

"Dhani! Dhani, wake up! You're safe. Look at me."

It took a while for his mind to register the deep tenor of his mate's voice. Tailor was hovering over him, holding him down in a gentle but firm grip. Tailor's eyes were bloodshot with dark circles beneath them and stubble covered his jaw, as if he hadn't slept in days. He looked nothing like the carefree, composed warrior Dhani had known, yet the sight was so welcoming that moisture pricked Dhani's eyes.

Tailor's demeanor was hesitant and cautious as he continued to stare down at Dhani as though searching for something. "Is it really you?"

Dhani stilled as he realized what his mate was asking. He reached inside himself, seeking out the cold darkness of *Roh Se Kahn's* energy, and came up empty. It was gone, or rather seemed to be obstructed by whatever force was also blocking his leopard. It felt like half of his soul had been stripped away just as when *Roh Se Kahn* had taken his falcon. While the sensation was unnerving and almost painful, he couldn't help the relief that flooded through him at the absence of the God's darkness.

It was him spiritless and aching from the emptiness, but all him.

He nodded as tears spilled down his temples.

An indecipherable expression crossed Tailor's handsome features before he grabbed Dhani in a crushing embrace, then brought their mouths together. The torrent of emotions coming through strong in his energy swamped Dhani, overwhelming him and, at the same time, narrowing his world down to only the feel of his mate holding him.

Tailor was everywhere all at once. He delved his fingers into Dhani's hair and pressed the solid mass of his upper body down, surrounding Dhani with the invigorating weight of his heat and passion. Need, heavy and intense, poured into Dhani with the demand of the kiss. He opened fully and drowned in the way his mate took control, swallowing his every breath as if his life depended on it. Desire surged within him as his cock swelled and he thrust his hips up almost involuntarily.

He was on the verge of begging for more when somewhere in the background, a throat was cleared loudly.

Tailor withdrew to stare down at Dhani, their faces inches apart. "I've missed you."

A grin tugged at Dhani's lips. "I've missed you, too." His grin deepened when Tailor rumbled and closed his eyes as if fighting for restraint.

"Do you feel up to talking?"

"I think so," he replied with a frown. Only when Tailor helped him sit up did he become aware of the deep aches in his body. His abdomen and right shoulder flared as his muscles stretched, causing him to wince and bite back a curse. Both hands were wrapped in thin gauze and what he could see of his right palm was covered in bruises.

He was in the bed he'd shared with his mate for a few hours at Rowan's palace before *Roh Se Kahn* had teleported him out. Around the room stood everyone else, their gazes fixed on him in concern. Rowan and Manning held guns discreetly at their sides, their expressions guarded.

Keenan stood between them with tears streaming down his cheeks. He ran to the bed and flung his arms around Dhani's neck, squeezing until Dhani began to cough. With a soft chuckle, he pulled back and smiled. "I knew you were in there somewhere."

Dhani swallowed past the lump in his throat. "I never thought I would see you again." Then a tide of fear shadowed his joy. "You have to get away from me. Your father's going to make me kill you and I can't —"

"No," Keenan hushed him, pulling him in for another quick hug. "You don't have to be afraid anymore. We've figured it all out. When I saw you at the airport, I knew I was looking at my father. He's not as clever as he likes to think. As soon as Rowan got a call from the guards at Deirdra's place, we put two and two together. Your mom knew *Roh Se Kahn* was taking you to his castle from the message you gave that guard. That's how we knew where to find you."

Dhani looked to Laya and, for the first time, saw his mother instead of the woman who had abandoned him. "I met my father," he said in a strangled voice. "I'm…sorry that I blamed you. I thought you were the monster." He glanced at Tailor, seeing the love he had for his mate reflected in the man's eyes, then back again. "I was wrong. You did what you could to keep me away from him. I don't know if I could've been as strong as you."

Laya's chest heaved in a small sob and she pressed a hand to her mouth in an effort to keep her composure. She cleared her throat several times as her eyes glistened, then said, "You are my son. A woman needs no greater strength than that."

Dhani nodded then brushed the moisture from his own eyes. As much as he wanted to close the rift between him and his mother, there were still a hundred questions crowding his thoughts. To Keenan, he asked, "How am I here? *Roh Se Kahn* was in me. He had full control and now, I can't feel him anymore. I can't even feel my spirit—"

"I had to put this on you." Keenan lifted a hand to Dhani's neck.

With shaking fingers, Dhani touched the warm collar and shuddered. He recalled it all, now. Vane's betrayal of *Roh Se Kahn* and the appearance of Tailor and the others just as the incantation had begun.

"The collar inhibits my father's power over you. It'll buy us some time. I took a chance that Vane would have it on him at the castle. Since I'm the only one of us who can activate it, I couldn't sit behind and do nothing. No matter how dangerous it could've gotten." He slanted Tailor a meaningful glance.

But it had been dangerous, Dhani thought. At least for him. He recalled his mortal wounds and stripped out of his shirt to find two livid scars on his shoulder and abdomen. "I was dying."

"You probably would have if we'd arrived two minutes later," Rowan said as he and Manning holstered their weapons. "We've had to keep you asleep for the past two days while my blood healed you. Do you remember anything about what *Roh Se Kahn* is planning to do?"

He shrugged. "Just that he wants to go through with his original plan of annihilating the *Vam'kir* and *Ba'Kal*, then go after *Miel Se Luuda*. He talked for a while with Achilles, my father, but he didn't go into specifics. He only wanted to know what had happened over the past year, whether the races were still united, their numbers. Things like that. He tried to lead Vane on again by telling him he would let him rule, but Vane saw through his father's lie. Vane turned all of the followers against him and was going to use the baby… Oh no, the baby!"

"It's okay," Rowan said, holding up a hand. "We have Deirdra and Sevrick here with us. She told us Vane had planned on sending his father's essence into the boy before trapping it with the collar. Did you see what spell he was going to use to steal *Roh Se Kahn's* power?"

Dhani shook his head. "Achilles might have. He knew more about what Vane was planning than anyone else."

"Too bad we can't ask him," Manning grumbled. At Dhani's confused stare, he explained, "Vane teleported himself and all of the followers out with him. We have no idea where they could be."

"Well, that shouldn't matter anymore, right? Vane was waiting for *Roh Se Kahn* to come back. He needs his father's powers. It's why he hasn't done anything 'til now. As long as I keep this collar on, *Roh Se Kahn* will stay trapped." A twinge of anguish pierced his chest at the possibility that he might never again commune with his leopard or regain his falcon spirit, but it was a small price to pay. When Manning looked at Tailor grimly, Dhani repeated, "Right?"

"It's not that simple," Tailor said hesitantly.

Keenan stirred uneasily. "The collar is only a temporary fix. Since it's inhibiting your spirit, it could also prevent you from shifting during the full moons every month. I can't be certain because I stopped wearing it when I was sixteen. I hadn't matured yet so I wasn't forced to shift. I don't think it's going to be possible for you to live the rest of your life without shifting."

Dread coursed through Dhani's veins. "It might be possible. We don't know for sure. Quinn told me once he went for four years without shifting. If he can do it, so can I. Besides, my leopard isn't dead, it's just trapped."

Quinn's brows drew down in sympathy. "I was beaten during each full moon. The pain took my mind off the shift, but it was still…excruciating. It would've driven me insane if Mara hadn't rescued me. Trust me, if there was any way I thought it could work, I'd tell you."

Despair seized the air in Dhani's lungs as he looked to his mate. "Then you have to kill me. There's no other way."

"No!" Tailor said vehemently. "We've made it this far. I'm not going to give up now."

"We have some time," Keenan said. "The full moon isn't for another five days. There has to be a spell or something in my father's books that can tell us how to get him out of you. He traded your second spirit for a piece of his soul, didn't he?" At Dhani's nod, he sighed. "I don't know if I'll be able to return your other spirit, but I'll try."

"We all will," Laya said. She stepped forward to kiss Dhani's forehead. "I didn't let your father take you from me and I damn sure won't let *Roh Se Kahn*, either. I love you."

Dhani nodded again in a daze. When everyone began to file out, he said, "Thank you."

They gave him quiet reassurances then left.

"How are you doing?" Tailor asked after he closed the door.

Dhani stared down at his wrapped hands. They might as well have been covered in blood with the amount of deaths he'd caused. "I killed all those people. They're dead because of me. I almost killed you."

"*Roh Se Kahn* killed those people," Tailor corrected.

"With my hands!" he exclaimed, feeling his anger rise. This was all his fault.

"He killed them with his power. Rowan and Manning had the bodies of their guards inspected. Every one of them was with killed by lightning, not a weapon."

"I should've warned you before he took control."

"Damn it, Dhani!" Tailor ground out. "Don't do this. Do you really think *Roh Se Kahn* would've allowed you to warn me or anyone else? If it were that easy, he never would've released you. He knew exactly what he was doing."

Grudgingly, Dhani had to admit he might be right. *Roh Se Kahn* had known about his attempted suicides, and each time the thought of revealing the truth to his mate had crossed his mind, he'd been overwhelmed by fear. Could *Roh Se Kahn* have been behind that?

Still, he couldn't shake his guilt. His emotions and the hope Tailor was trying to give him were too disparate. His thoughts were a jumbled mess and his heart was conflicted. "You don't understand. You shouldn't even care. We're only mates because my father killed Dominic and his spirit entered me. No matter how much we might love each other, it's built on pure coincidence."

"You just don't get it, do you?" Tailor let out a growl and raked his hands through his hair. "You are the most impossible, frustrating, dumbest smart man I've ever met!" He strode to the window and stared out for a minute, then whirled around. "Your leopard is the spirit trapped inside you now with *Roh Se Kahn*. Which means your falcon is the one he took to replace it with a piece of his soul."

Dhani frowned. "How did you know my other spirit is a falcon?"

"Because that was Dominic's spirit. If you think our attraction as mates stems only from Dominic's spirit, then why have we still been able to feel that attraction? Your falcon has been in an alternate realm this whole time, yet I can feel the draw toward you even with that collar on."

He felt his anger begin to fade as comprehension dawned.

"You can try to push me away all you want," Tailor said softly, "but I'm not going anywhere. We're mates as much because of your leopard as we are Dominic's falcon. We can fight over it or blame fate or whatever else you can think of, but I'm not your father. I won't leave you and I won't turn on you."

The conflict of Dhani's emotions swelled, filling his eyes with more tears. "I don't know what to do. I can't help feeling responsible—"

Tailor was there in an instant pulling him into a strong embrace. "It's okay. We're going to get through this." He rocked Dhani in silence for a time, then lifted his chin until their eyes met. "No matter what happens, I won't leave your side. Not even in death."

The force of his mate's conviction staggered Dhani. What if it did come down to his death in the end? He couldn't stand the thought of inadvertently taking Tailor with him, yet his gut told him his mate's conviction was more than a just promise to keep Dhani alive, even at the cost of his own life.

Tailor was a proud warrior with unflinching principles. Would he really take his life if Dhani didn't survive? Dhani didn't want to think it, but neither could he deny that if their roles were reversed, he would choose the same path.

He clung to his mate and prayed, pleaded with the Mother, that it wouldn't come to that.

* * * *

The next two days passed by in a blur. It was the morning of the third and all Tailor could think about was time. The time he'd lost with Dominic and the countdown of hours until he might lose his second mate. They were going to attempt to rid *Roh Se Kahn's* soul from Dhani tonight. If they failed, they would still have another couple of days before the full moon to try again. Only problem was…Keenan hadn't yet found a spell to perform the act safely.

Tailor poured himself a mug of coffee in the kitchen then added a few fingers of Amaretto to it. Cy entered minutes later wearing the same clothes he'd had on the day before. His eyes were bloodshot and his waist-length hair was mussed around his pale face. He squinted at the bottle of amaretto, glanced at the coffee, then snatched the bottle and took a long swig.

Tailor chuckled. He knew that look—had worn it many times in the past, and always after a night of passion and sin. Cy was suffering bad, so Tailor did what any friend would do. He slapped Cy on the back and yelled, "How's life treating you?"

Cy yanked a knife from the back of his belt and snarled. "Talk again and I will slit your throat and use your tongue to slap you with."

Tailor laughed. "Now who's chasing the sheep when he should be hunting the wolf?"

Cy scowled darkly. "This *sheep*" — he said, holding up the bottle—"is doing a damn good job of saving me from the wolf."

"You're scared of Xenessa, aren't you?"

"I'm not scared of that wolf—*woman*," he tacked on quickly. When Tailor only narrowed his eyes, Cy's shoulders slumped in defeat. "Scared. Terrified like a little bitch. How the hell do you do it?"

Rowan strolled in with Laya beside him. "Do what? What are we talking about?"

Tailor grinned. "Cy's afraid of his mate."

Rowan paused then burst out laughing. At the deadly glare Cy shot him, his laugh turned to a choking cough and he banged his fist against his chest. "Sorry, I, uh...can see how that might be an issue. You two having problems?"

Cy took another swig then glowered down at the bottle. "She wants me to bond. Says her biological clock is ticking. She wants to have kids! I mean, yeah, sure I want to have kids someday, and the woman is amazing in bed. She can do things with her body that defy—"

"Whoa!" Rowan said, holding a hand up. "This is the woman that used to wipe my nose when I was a kid. Spare me the details. Please."

"I'm just saying," Cy drew out with punctuation, "Things are going a little fast for me."

Tailor shrugged as he took back the bottle to pour more into his mug. "Well, it's not like you've been playing hard to get. And you two *are* mates. I don't really see what the issue is here."

"Talk to me again when you've been a bachelor for three and a half centuries," Cy grumbled. He flicked a glance at Rowan, his lips forming a cagey grin, then canted his head. "Although, maybe you're right. She is a hell of a woman. She does this thing in bed with her hips that hits me in just the right—"

"Stop!" Rowan yelled, lifting his fingers to his temples to massage them. "It hurts."

Keenan stomped into the kitchen and threw a pair of white gloves onto the island counter. "There's nothing!" he yelled. "Not a damn thing in any of those books on how to get my father out of Dhani."

Cy cringed. "Keep it down! Some of us are trying to have a hangover."

Keenan ignored him and looked to Tailor. "Should you be drinking that? We need to be focused for tonight."

"This was Dhani's idea," Tailor said, twisting his lips. "Said I was driving him crazy hovering over him all the time, which is why I left him with you in the library. Where is he?" He hadn't wanted to leave his mate alone on the off chance *Roh Se Kahn* managed to break through the power of the collar supressing his soul.

"He's fine. Manning and Quinn are with him and Sevrick."

"Are you sure it's a good idea for him to be around the baby?" Rowan asked.

Keenan waved dismissively. "If the collar wasn't holding up, we'd have known by now. Besides, my father never wanted to have anything to do with Sevrick. Dhani, on the other hand, really seems taken with the boy. I haven't seen him smile and laugh so much since... Well, it's been a long time. I think their time together is good for both of them, especially considering Deirdra won't have anything to do with him now."

Rowan poured a cup of coffee for Keenan and handed it to him. "I don't think she's doing it out of spite. I spoke with her yesterday and I have to admit, she's changed. She truly believed Vane would've carried out his promises to make her his queen when he came into power, but she didn't realize he would do so by killing Sevrick. Honestly, I'm proud of her. She was willing to give up everything she'd ever wanted to save her son.

"On top of that, she actually trusts Dhani with Sevrick despite *Roh Se Kahn's* presence. She said the few times Vane came to see their child on the island, Sevrick couldn't stand for Vane to hold him. She thinks now the boy must've sensed his evil intent and I have to agree. Sevrick hasn't cried once around Dhani."

"I suppose you're right," Keenan replied dubiously. "Anyway, I still don't know what to do about Dhani. The only information I've been able to find is how my father was able to sire me and my brothers. Apparently, he retained a residue of the light used to free him from his prison in the first place and he used that light to procreate. However, that's not going to help us with Dhani."

"So what do you think we should do?" Cy asked.

Keenan sighed heavily. "If I still can't find anything by tonight, I'll just have to use the same spell *Miel Se Luuda* gave me a year ago to send my father back and hope it doesn't kill Dhani in the process. I know it won't kill me—"

"Are you sure about that?" Rowan's tone was angry, but the depth of concern in his eyes was unmistakable.

"I'm positive. What killed me last time was a stake to the heart." He chuckled lightly. "I'm like a modern day vampire."

"Yeah, well, who wouldn't that kill?" Rowan muttered.

Keenan rolled his eyes. "Like I was saying, the spell won't harm me but I'm not so sure about Dhani. There's also the fact that we'll need to take the collar off for the spell to work. My father's soul has to be free at the time I send it to the other realm. Problem is, as soon as the collar is off, my father will take control of Dhani again. He could kill us all in seconds."

Laya stirred. "What about a tranquilizer? When we were at the castle, Dhani was struggling from his wounds. He might've died if Rowan hadn't given him his blood. That must mean *Roh Se Kahn's* soul didn't make Dhani's body as resistant to injuries as yours. Perhaps if we put him to sleep, the dark God won't be able to force his will."

Keenan pondered for a minute, then said, "That might work. So far, it's the best shot we have." He met Tailor's gaze grimly. "I'm going to do everything I can to keep him alive. You know that. But I think you should prepare yourself for the alternative. If Dhani doesn't make it…" The rest of his sentence was choked off as his eyes glistened with unshed moisture.

Tailor simply nodded. He couldn't afford to give in to his emotions. His mate needed him to be strong, and until the outcome of the spell was final, he wouldn't fail to give Dhani every second of happiness he deserved.

Chapter Twelve

Later, Tailor found Dhani in the library where Keenan had returned to scour more of the books he'd confiscated from *Roh Se Kahn's* castle. Dhani was lying on the floor with Sevrick, playing with the toys Rowan's daughter, Adreanna, had outgrown.

While it was odd seeing the affection of his mate for the child of Deirdra's love affair, he had to agree with Keenan. The two really were good for each other. At five months old, Sevrick was a happy baby and had quickly grown attached to Dhani. Their relationship had also taken Dhani's mind off the future.

For a moment, Tailor let himself imagine what it would be like to start a family with his mate. He'd never wanted kids in the past, always too scared he might turn into the psychopath his father had been. But he was a different person with Dhani. His mate had a way of making him see the positive in every situation.

Though not the one they faced now.

There were too many loose variables. Too much risk involved to find any kind of solace in the present. The anger over the situation Tailor had been keeping at bay rose to the surface again, threatening to pull him under. Never once had he contemplated suicide in all the years of his fucked-up life, but he knew he couldn't go on living without Dhani. Couldn't face piecing together the shards of an empty life after the death of another mate. Not again.

He'd rather damn his soul for eternity than spend one more day knowing what he'd lost if Dhani were to die.

For a brief moment, the vise of his control wavered and he felt a sliver of his fear bleed out into his energy. It was only a second before he mastered his emotions again, though long enough for his mate to notice. Dhani looked up sharply to where Tailor stood in the doorway with an expression of such infinite understanding, it pierced Tailor's heart like a knife. Somehow, in the past few days, Dhani had come to terms with the possibility of his own death. Yet, it only served to fuel Tailor's rage over the circumstances.

Dhani deserved so much more than the role of pawn to be used and discarded in the war between their Gods.

Unable to bear the compassion in his mate's eyes, he pivoted and strode quickly from the library. As he reached the end of the hall, he heard Dhani shout behind him. Reluctantly, he turned to watch his mate jog toward him.

Dhani slowed his approach then placed a hand on Tailor's chest. "You don't have to hide your emotions. You can talk to me."

Tailor let out a bark of derision, taking a step back. "And what good would that do? You want me to tell you how scared I am, or the fact that I think this is all bullshit? Or how about how helpless I feel after a lifetime of training to deal with any situation? You think it'll make it any easier to talk about my feelings?" He knew it wasn't fair to take out his anger on his mate, but he couldn't rein it in.

"I just meant I understand what you're going through."

"Do you?" he growled. "Really? 'Cause if you did, you wouldn't expect me to go on living if you meet your death. I know that's what you want. You're so ready to sacrifice yourself again to save everyone around you that you refuse to see what I want." He swallowed heavily to steady his voice. "I won't stay in this world without you. I can't. And if I can't save you, the afterlife holds no meaning for me."

Dhani was silent for several seconds as a myriad of emotions radiated from his energy. Finally, what appeared to be acceptance shone from his hazel eyes and he closed the distance between them. "Then bond with me."

At first, Tailor was too stunned to respond. "Dhani—"

"Did you think I didn't already know you would seek your own death if I died?" He shook his head with a humorless grin. "When I was in that alternate realm, I wondered a thousand times if you were ever thinking of me. Then when *Roh Se Kahn* cast me out and I found you, I expected you to reject me again. A part of me wanted you to. It would've been so much easier, but you didn't. Every time I wanted to give up, you were there."

Dhani looked away and a single tear spilled down his cheek. "For the past two days, I've been asking myself if I could go on living if you were the one to die, and I can't keep lying to myself. I love you. There is nothing in this world for me without you."

For the first time in his life, Tailor tore down the walls caging his emotions and let them flow freely. He poured all of his anger, bitterness and love into his energy, holding nothing back. When Dhani sucked in a breath and met his gaze with wide eyes, he threaded his fingers through his mate's hair and tilted his head back, saying gruffly, "I love you, too."

Dhani released a breathless laugh then lunged into Tailor's arms. Tailor barely had time to catch his mate when his breath was devoured in a fiery kiss. Dhani wrapped his arms and legs around him and pressed their mouths together, flicking his tongue erotically over Tailor's.

Dhani's eagerness washed over him like a teasing inferno, scattering his thoughts and making him crave more. He took command of the kiss and backed his mate to the nearest wall. Fire burned in his blood and his dick thickened against the rough material of his jeans. He ground it into Dhani's own rigid length and felt his skin tighten at the rush of pleasure that shot up his spine.

Dhani moaned into him, submitting in the way he always did without giving up full control. The feel of his sinuous body yielding to Tailor's larger frame was utterly seductive, and one of the things Tailor loved most about him. Not many people could survive what Dhani had and come out with their sense of self intact. In bed, Dhani always surrendered to him, but it didn't diminish his strength. If anything, it gave him a power unlike anything Tailor had ever known.

The courage Dhani showed in the face of impossible odds was overwhelming and humbled Tailor like nothing else could. All this time, he'd been fighting to save his mate when it was Dhani who was saving him.

Tailor reached for the nearest door and shoved it open, uncaring of whose room he entered. When he saw it was a bathroom, he locked the door behind them then set Dhani on the counter next to the sink. Arousal surged through his system as Dhani ripped open his shirt then lowered his head to suck one of Tailor's nipples into his mouth. The stinging bite of Dhani's teeth sent a wave of pleasure to his groin, making him throb painfully with desire.

He kicked off his shoes and shed the rest of his clothes as Dhani jumped down to do the same. As soon as they were naked, he lifted Dhani back onto the counter and crushed their mouths together, not bothering to curb the wild hunger driving his instincts to stake his claim. To ravage every part of Dhani until there was nothing left to define them as individuals.

In the back of his mind, he knew he should slow down. This could be their last time together and he wanted it to be special, but he couldn't hold back. For more than a year, he'd been consumed with making Dhani his, and in Dhani's absence, he'd thought he had lost that chance forever. Now that the moment was here, the past no longer mattered. All that existed was the warm body against his, making him whole again.

He reached between them and fisted their cocks in his large palm, echoing Dhani's groan as he squeezed their steel lengths together mercilessly. The pressure made his adrenaline flare and he began to stroke them furiously even as he inhaled his mate's panting breaths.

Dhani clung to him and threw back his head on a loud moan, gyrating his hips in rhythm with Tailor's hand.

The sight of his mate's desire and the knowledge that it was just the two of them nearly pushed Tailor over the edge. There was no interference from *Roh Se Kahn* or hidden reason to Dhani's passion as there had been before — when Dhani had used him to quell the storm of his inner battle with the dark God. This was real, and the energy flowing between them made the need to bond with his mate fierce.

When Dhani's moans rose in volume, Tailor clamped his fingers around the tips of their cocks to stave off their orgasms. At Dhani's whimper, he smiled and kissed him lightly. "Not yet. I have to be inside you."

The haze of lust in Dhani's eyes changed to concern as he lifted his hand to touch the collar at his neck. "Are you sure we can bond? I can't even feel my spirit."

"The collar only inhibits its communication with you. It's still there. I can feel it reaching out to mine. Don't be afraid."

Dhani met his gaze clearly. "I'm not."

Tailor kissed him again then knelt down to search the cupboards below. He found a bottle of massage oil and poured it onto his fingers. With ease, he picked Dhani up and turned him around so that they both stood facing the mirror in front of them. He watched, mesmerized by the rapture on Dhani's face as he pushed two fingers past the tight ring of Dhani's ass, then another, stretching it to accommodate his thickness.

He twisted and hooked them to find his mate's prostate, grinning in satisfaction when Dhani braced himself against the countertop and let out a sharp gasp. After several torturous seconds, he grabbed the oil again and poured more onto his straining cock. The restraint it took to enter his mate slowly was nearly unbearable. Dhani's hot ridges against his sensitive skin, grasping him to the point of pain, drove all thought from his mind.

He wanted to be gentle, to draw out the moment as long as he could, but his control fled at the look of aching need on Dhani's face. He withdrew then slammed into his mate, going as far as he could go. When Dhani yelled, he hesitated, worried he might have hurt him.

Dhani shook his head and met his stare in the mirror. "No, don't stop. Please."

It was all the encouragement Tailor needed. He lunged in again and again, burying himself so deep, he could feel the pressure of Dhani's ring contracting around his root. Sparks danced beneath his skin as he clutched his mate's narrow hips and yanked him back onto every one of his thrusts. Dhani's mouth was open and his eyes glowed with the ecstasy of his spirit.

The primal urge that had been riding Tailor blazed to the surface and his canines exploded from his gums. He pulled Dhani's hair to one side then sank his teeth into the soft flesh of his mate's neck. Dhani's shout rang out in his ears as the sweet tang of his blood flooded Tailor's mouth, carrying with it the alluring scent and essence of his mate. It eclipsed Tailor's mind and filled him with more power than he could ever have imagined.

As he swallowed his mate's nectar, he could feel Dhani's spirit and soul intertwining with his own, melding together in a bond that not even death could sever. It was exhilarating and too much all at once.

With as much effort as he could muster, he pulled away to lick the puncture wounds on Dhani's neck. In one swift move, he spun Dhani around and lifted him until Dhani's arms and legs were wrapped around him. As soon as he'd lined up the head of his cock with Dhani's ass, he plunged in again, grunting at the searing heat that engulfed him.

For a brief second, Dhani paused and creased his brow.

"Do it," Tailor rasped as he pumped into his mate furiously. "You won't hurt me. You never could."

Dhani pushed aside the blond locks of Tailor's hair then bared his canines. The feral look in his eyes made Tailor shiver with anticipation. The moment Dhani's teeth pierced his skin, pain seized Tailor's muscles, only to give way to a tide of pleasure so strong, his entire body trembled. He felt his mate take several strong pulls before Dhani jerked his head up and stared at him with wide eyes.

"I can feel you," Dhani whispered.

A smile of triumph stretched Tailor's lips. "And I, you. You are *mine*."

He began to thrust into Dhani again with rapid deep strokes, holding him close in the band of his arms. The friction between them increased, setting fire to his nerve endings. His balls tightened as his imminent climax swelled, bringing him to the peak of his rapture.

As one, he and Dhani tipped their heads back and shouted out their orgasms. Ropes of cum spurted from Dhani's hard length even as Tailor filled him with his seed. The bond tying them together burned white-hot in Tailor's soul, encompassing him in the brilliance of Dhani's emotions. All the love and yearning of his mate wove into his own until he no longer knew where Dhani left off and he began.

They clung to each other in their embrace as aftershocks shook them, prolonging the strength of their release. Finally, Tailor lowered his mate and asked softly. "Can you still feel me in you?"

Dhani turned his head sadly. "I felt your soul for a moment, but it slipped away."

Tailor kissed his forehead then pulled him close. "When this is all over, you'll feel me again. I promise."

They stepped into the shower and took their time bathing one another, in no hurry to return to the reality of what had to be done that night. Tailor caressed every inch of Dhani's body as if he were exploring it for the first time. He could feel Dhani's emotions inside him, rising to his touch and flitting across his mind like sensuous feathers.

As they made love again in their bedroom, it was with all the gentleness Tailor should've shown him when they'd first met. And when nightfall finally came, they dressed wordlessly and left to meet their fate as one.

* * * *

Dhani pulled out a clean outfit from his luggage and got dressed, trying to ignore the trembling in his hands. He'd known this time would come all along, yet he felt completely unprepared for it. It wasn't just his life he could lose anymore. Tailor would follow him into death if the spell didn't work. So much was riding on the unknown and his faith was dwindling fast.

He turned as his bedroom door opened and his mate stepped in. Tailor looked every bit the blond, unyielding warrior he was. Black leathers hugged his long legs and a black shirt strapped with a weapons harness defined his muscular chest. His hair was pulled back into a ponytail, sharpening the handsome angles of his face and regal countenance. Everything about him screamed of a potent savageness contained only by his strength of will.

Dhani held his breath, still unable to believe the man was his. In all his life, he'd never imagined he would be so lucky as to find a mate like Tailor, or to have a future with him. At any second, he expected it all to be ripped away. *And it still might be,* he reminded himself. The night wasn't over yet.

Tailor strode to him and pulled him in for a passionate kiss. "Are you ready?"

"No!" Dhani said emphatically, then sighed. "But I guess I can't put this off."

"I'll be with you the entire time. We're going to get through this," Tailor reassured him.

They walked to Rowan's parlor room, where Keenan would perform the incantation. Everyone was there, including twenty of Rowan's personal guards. They lined the walls and each was armed with a small arsenal of weapons. Dhani's apprehension spiked at their stone-cold expressions. While he knew they were necessary should *Roh Se Kahn* break through the effects of the tranquilizer, it still shook him to know he was, quite literally, facing a firing squad.

Keenan approached him first and paused when he saw the puncture wounds on Dhani's neck. He glanced at the identical wounds on Tailor then back to Dhani. "You two bonded?" At Dhani's nod, concern creased Keenan's face and he looked to Manning.

Manning's face took on an expression of surprise that quickly changed to sorrow. Dhani knew what they were thinking. They would both lose Tailor if things went south. He expected them to yell at him for being so reckless with Tailor's life, but Manning simply nodded in acceptance.

Keenan's smile was bittersweet as he hugged Dhani tightly. When he didn't let go after a while, Dhani tapped him, saying, "I'm not dead yet." He laughed nervously as Keenan pulled away. "Besides, haven't we been here before?"

Keenan's face grew somber and his lips thinned. "I'm not going to let that bastard take you from me again. This ends tonight."

"I know you'll succeed," Dhani replied, putting as much false bravado as he could into his voice. Unfortunately, his friend wasn't buying it.

"The tranquilize will put you out for hours, but I'll only need a minute to recite the spell and contain my father's essence long enough for it to leave this realm. Oh, and I'll need you to drink this." He reached behind him to the glass Rowan proffered then handed it to Dhani. "It's a concoction I found in one of the spell books that'll put you into a deeper sleep."

Alarm spread through Dhani. "The tranquilizer won't be enough?"

"Maybe. Better safe than sorry."

Dhani took the glass and upended it, then immediately started coughing. "What the hell's in this?"

"Other than the rum I spiked it with? You don't want to know. Trust me, it's better with the rum."

He forced the rest down then handed the glass back. Quinn hugged him next, offering words of encouragement, then Tailor led him to a bare, cast-iron table situated in the center of the parlor. With steel wrist and ankle cuffs welded to its sides, it was utterly out of place among the modern furniture.

On their way through the gathered crowd, Dhani caught sight of Deirdra holding her son and hesitated. "Should she be here?" he asked, his gaze flitting down to Sevrick with worry. *Roh Se Kahn* had no compunctions about killing his own sons, and Dhani knew the God didn't feel any differently toward his grandson. Sevrick could die if *Roh Se Kahn* took control.

"I don't know. I'll—" Tailor started, but Deirdra had overheard and cut him off.

"I want to be here. I was wrong about Vane and I'm…sorry for what you're going through." Her words were stiff and filled with hatred instead of remorse. "That coward is nothing without his father's power and I want to watch it taken from him forever. Besides, Vane could teleport in at any time and take my baby, anyway. This is the safest place for me to be." She looked to Rowan and asked, "Right?"

Rowan sighed. "Deirdra, we've been over this. I can have my men take you far away—"

"No," she said adamantly. "I need to be here."

Dhani wanted to argue, he couldn't stand the thought of inadvertently hurting Sevrick, but Tailor urged him toward the table. "Come on, love. Let's get this over with."

Dhani lay down on the cold surface of the table and watched as his mate and Cy shackled him, keenly aware of the eyes on him. With each steel cuff they locked into place, the reality of what was happening bore down on him. An uncontrollable tremble started in his hands and spread to the rest of his body.

Tailor leaned down to smooth his hair and kiss his forehead. "It's going to be okay. I promise."

Though his words held strength, Dhani could feel no emotion in his mate's energy. He knew Tailor didn't want him to feel the fear distantly reflected in Tailor's eyes.

Laya moved to the table as Tailor and Cy stepped back and held up a syringe. "This is a heavy sedative, so you should be out in seconds." At Dhani's nod, she kissed his cheek and smiled sadly. "I'm so proud of you, my son. I'll see you when you wake up." She tied a tourniquet around Dhani's bicep then pierced his vein to inject the liquid. "Count backwards from one hundred."

Dhani looked at his mate and focused on Tailor's unerring gaze, unable to keep a tear from falling down his temple. "One hundred, ninety-nine, ninety-eight, ninety…" He felt his eyes droop as warmth flooded his body. Gravity shifted, pressing him down until he was paralyzed, and the world fell away.

Chapter Thirteen

Awareness slammed back into Dhani when he felt someone pull the collar from his neck, followed swiftly by *Roh Se Kahn's* darkness. It sprang forth with a vengeance, carrying all the rage of the dark God and searing Dhani's insides with its magnitude. A scream ripped from his throat and his body arched as if he were being split in two. The agony crested, wracking him mercilessly, until it suddenly dissipated. He dropped back down onto the table, twitching from the residual effects.

Dhani's mind was sluggish, but his body was filled with tension. *Roh Se Kahn* writhed within him, taking over and elevating his senses. Dread coursed through Dhani as he realized the sedative and concoction he'd been given hadn't affected *Roh Se Kahn* in the slightest. Once again, he was a prisoner of the God and powerless over his actions.

Roh Se Kahn was confused, as if the collar had kept him blind and deaf. With the collar gone now, however, he was in full control and smart enough to assess his surroundings before making a move. He forced Dhani to keep his eyes closed, listening instead to the commotion around them. Dhani recognized Tailor's raised voice suffused with alarm and several others arguing.

Two fingers were pressed to Dhani's jugular vein, then he heard Keenan shout, "Quiet, all of you! He's still alive and unconscious, but I need to do this quickly. My father could awaken in him at any time."

Silence fell around them until Keenan began to recite the spell to evict *Roh Se Kahn* from Dhani's body. *Roh Se Kahn's* fury rose and he snapped Dhani's eyes open. Tailor's face came into view, hovering above him. Just as the God became aware of the shackles binding Dhani, Tailor yelled, "Keenan, he's awake!"

Roh Se Kahn used his darkness to send blinding sparks through the locks on the cuffs, shattering them and burning Dhani's skin in the process. Dhani jerked up and shoved Tailor in the chest, sending him hurtling backwards with a blast of power so great, it knocked down all those in Tailor's path. When Cy grabbed Dhani's throat, Dhani sent him flying with another blast then cast out a coruscating wave of fire toward the rest who were closing in.

The room erupted into screams as several tried to escape the flames burning them alive. A female voice rose above the chaos, shouting, "Shoot him!" but *Roh Se Kahn* had already spotted the weapons on the guards. He erected an invisible shield around Dhani that deflected the barrage of bullets aimed at him. A few of the guards fell from the ricochets and, somewhere in the background, Tailor commanded a ceasefire.

"Father!" Keenan's yell caught *Roh Se Kahn's* attention at the same time a bright ball of pure energy was flung from Keenan's hand.

Dhani had no doubt it could penetrate the shield, but somehow the dark God had anticipated this. He drew on the light of Dhani's spirit and formed his own energy ball made more powerful with the darkness he spliced it with. Dhani threw the ball and watched as it impacted Keenan and created a shockwave that threw Keenan back and all those surrounding him. Keenan crashed into a large, glass cabinet then fell to the floor.

Dhani stalked over to him and yanked him up by his hair. "Did you really think you would win this time? The light in this shifter is just as powerful as yours."

"No!" The shout came from Rowan who drew a dagger from his belt and hurled it at Dhani.

Instead of deflecting it with his shield, *Roh Se Kahn* made Dhani move Keenan to intercept it. The blade buried itself hilt deep in Keenan's shoulder and he staggered with a pained grunt. Dhani wrenched Keenan's head up and said in a low voice, "Say goodbye to your precious mate."

From the corner of his eye, Dhani saw Cy aim a gun at him and fire just as Tailor tackled the man. The bullet never made its mark, however. The room shifted and blinked out of existence as *Roh Se Kahn* used his power to teleport Dhani and Keenan from the parlor.

Dhani's stomach lurched from the displacement and when his vision cleared, he found himself in what appeared to be a lavishly decorated living room. While he'd never been there before, he knew the dark God had. *Roh Se Kahn's* comfort in their surroundings made him sure of it.

He shoved Keenan to the floor then pressed the sole of his shoe to Keenan's throat, pinning him. Keenan struggled weakly, glaring up at him.

"Save your strength, slave," Dhani sneered. "I won't let you die yet."

"And I won't let you get away with this," Keenan rasped. "I defeated you once and I'll do it again."

Dhani laughed with *Roh Se Kahn's* cynicism. "You're no match for me anymore, *boy.* It seems your friend has bonded with his pathetic mate, giving him twice the amount of light as before. I can feel it like a beacon in his soul, infusing me with more power."

Inwardly, Dhani's mind seized in panic. Had he really empowered *Roh Se Kahn* by bonding with Tailor? He felt the truth in the God's elation. Horror sickened him as he stared down on his best friend. After all of this, he was still going to be the death of Keenan.

He knelt and fisted the hilt protruding from Keenan's shoulder. "I should be thankful to you. I took my power of darkness for granted before, but you can be sure I won't make that mistake again. In fact, I'm growing rather fond of this shifter. I think I'll keep him. Once I open the portal to that hell realm, I'll reunite him with his second spirit, giving me three times the amount of light to match my darkness. I'll be unstoppable. And you, slave, will be the catalyst that begins my reign over this realm."

When Dhani yanked the blade free, Keenan screamed then slumped down with sweat beading his brow. "Not today," Keenan whispered.

A loud crack came from the ceiling and Dhani glanced up to see a wide seam parting the plaster above. The ground started to shake violently and the walls creaked in protest. Keenan was using his power.

The entire room was about to cave in on itself. Dhani had seen Keenan do it before.

He pressed a hand to Keenan's chest and sent a bolt of lightning into him so powerful, Keenan screamed again as sparks ignited all over his body. Dhani watched, incapable of stopping himself, as Keenan writhed for countless seconds before the pain became so great, he passed out. Afterwards, two men and a woman, all *Vam'kir,* ran into the room and stared in shock, then pointed their guns at Dhani.

"Who are you?" the woman demanded.

Dhani lifted a hand and this time, felt only pure darkness emanate from him. The trio froze as if held in suspension. "I am your one true God, *Roh Se Kahn.* This is my dwelling and so long as I inhabit this earth, I will not suffer traitors at my side. If any of you choose to continue worshipping my son, Vane, I will end you now."

To Dhani's surprise, they all fell to their knees in obeisance as soon as *Roh Se Kahn's* power was lifted from them. They weren't innocents, Dhani realized. Wherever this place was, it harbored the God's followers.

"Take him," *Roh Se Kahn* commanded through Dhani, gesturing to Keenan. "Bind his wound. I need him alive to carry out the spell that will free the rest of my essence from the realm it was banished to. Go nowhere and tell no one of my presence. I'll return after I've procured everyone else I need." When the trio didn't move right away, he barked, "Now!"

Dhani stared as Keenan was dragged roughly away, then raged against the God's will. *Roh Se Kahn* flexed Dhani's muscles and spoke to him softly. "Don't fight me, shifter. You should be grateful my plans for you have changed. I'm going to make you immortal. Your face will be the last one every *Ba'Kal*, *Vam'kir* and *Bassen'kir* on this earth sees before they perish. We will bask in the blood of their destruction."

Within, Dhani felt himself die a little. There would be no one to stop *Roh Se Kahn* now and no hope of Tailor finding him when he didn't even know where he was himself.

Roh Se Kahn laughed through him, then cast out his senses to blanket hundreds of miles in every direction in search of his wayward followers. When he detected several within range, he teleported out, reveling in Dhani's anguish.

* * * *

Tailor hit the floor with Cy then reared back and punched him. When Cy blocked the next punch and rolled out from beneath him, Tailor hauled him up and slammed him against the nearest wall. "What the *fuck* were you thinking?"

"I wasn't going to kill him!" Cy shouted. "Just slow him down. And you should've let me. Now he has what he came for."

"I should rip out your throat right here."

"Try it and you'll be sipping your food through a straw for the rest of your life."

"Enough!" Rowan shouted from across the room. "This isn't going to bring our mates back." He looked around the parlor at the damage done then scraped a hand through his short hair. "Cy, call the clan doctor and tell him to come immediately. You three," he said, pointing to a group of the guards, "take the wounded and do what you can for them until the doctor shows up."

"This one is dead," Cain said from where he knelt beside a guard with two bullet holes in his chest.

"This one, too," Laya called out from a corner of the room where a female guard lay across a shattered end table, eyes staring out into emptiness.

Guilt conflicted with the anger on Rowan's face as he flexed his jaw. "Get them out as well," he said to the remaining guards. "Don't contact their families yet. I don't want it made public that *Roh Se Kahn* is loose in our realm again. We need to take care of this with as much discretion as possible."

Tailor waited impatiently as Laya and Quinn helped take the wounded and the dead were carried out. When only a handful of the unharmed guards remained, he turned on Rowan. "Screw discretion. We have to figure out where Dhani and Keenan are."

"I want to get them back as much as you do," Rowan fumed, "but I can't risk an uproar. Not so soon after the last battle with *Roh Se Kahn*. We barely contained our exposure to the humans then. If my people find out *Roh Se Kahn* is back, there could be rioting among my clans." To the handful of guards, he ordered, "Leave us."

"No, wait," Manning said. He narrowed his gaze on two of the guards standing near Rowan. "Why didn't you open fire with the rest of the guards when Dhani attacked us?"

The two men looked at each other, then shook their heads in denial. The man with the buzz cut spoke first. "I don't know what you're talking about."

"We hesitated," the other said a little too quickly. He looked to Rowan. "Sorry, *Magnique*, but we didn't want to take the chance of killing the kid. We know how important he is."

They were lying. Tailor could feel it in their energy like an oppressing veil.

Fortunately, Rowan sensed it, too. "Mark, Jermain, what are you hiding?"

The pair glanced around at the other three guards spread throughout the parlor, then the one called Mark gave up his innocent act and raised his gun to Rowan's head. "Fuck it. Now's as good a time as any."

Rowan's eyes turned crimson in outrage at the same time Manning lifted his gun to the betrayers, but before either of them could make a move, the female guard near Manning yelled, "Don't." Her own gun was aimed at Manning's head, just far enough out of arms' reach to prevent Manning from knocking the weapon out of her hands.

As one, the remaining guards pulled their guns even as Tailor, Cain and Cy drew theirs. Deirdra gasped and shrank behind the cover of a tall recliner, holding Sevrick close to her breast.

Tailor braced his fury at the unseen standoff as his mind raced to make sense of what was going on. It wasn't likely the guards were in league with *Roh Se Kahn* or they'd have left with him. Which could only mean they were working for Vane. Either way, he didn't have time for this shit. Dhani was somewhere out there, trapped again by *Roh Se Kahn's* power, and Tailor's gut told him the God was going to go through with his plans in the next twenty-four hours.

"What is the meaning of this?" Rowan seethed.

"Call him," Mark said to Jermain without looking away, then twisted his lips in a mocking grin. "Did you really think you could put an end to everything my lord worked for and spent years cultivating? Did you think you were so impervious that you could escape his retribution? We have always been here, serving him, while you sat on your so-called throne and chose your pitiful compassion for the shifters over taking power."

Rowan's heated gaze flicked to Jermain, who was talking animatedly on his phone. "I trusted you. You helped me track down dozens of *Roh Se Kahn's* followers after the battle."

"They were weak!" Mark shouted. "It was Vane they should've been serving, not his father. *Roh Se Kahn* would've destroyed us all, and he still might, unless Vane takes his power for himself."

"And you think Vane will reward you for your service once he has that power? You're a fool! Vane won't stop until there's nothing but sheep for him to lead among the humans and our kind. He won't need you to stand at his side once he takes control. He'll destroy everything—"

"You're wrong! I hold more value to him than I ever have in your court. Our people need a leader, not a coward who hides behind the walls of his palace. You'd see that if you weren't so busy taking the advice of your precious council."

Just as Jermain ended his call, Vane appeared in the center of the parlor along with a mixed dozen of humans, *Ba'Kal* and *Vam'kir* armed with various weapons. His pale blond hair was slicked back and the expensive, designer suit he wore was at odds with the combat fatigues of his followers. He surveyed the room then focused on Deirdra with an avaricious gleam in his eyes. "You've done well, Jermain. How long ago did my father leave with his slave?"

Mark spoke up, overriding Jermain's response. "No more than ten minutes ago, my lord. I made sure *Roh Se Kahn* was gone before he knew of our involvement. What would you have us do with the *Magnique* and *Jaes'din*?"

Vane flashed his teeth at Rowan in a feral smile. "Kill them. Kill them all."

At that moment, a black fox darted into the room and sank its teeth into the tendon at the back of Mark's knee. Not a second later, Laya sprang through the open doorway and let loose a throwing knife that pierced the back of Jermain's neck, taking him out instantly.

"Stand down!" Rowan roared, ignoring the bullet that flew over his head from Mark's gun and charging Vane with deadly intent. His voice resonated with the power of the *Magnique*, paralyzing those followers who were *Vam'kir*. Manning called out his own command, freezing the *Ba'Kal* followers with his power of the *Jaes'din*, but neither order lasted long. An invisible yet tangible force pulsed outward from Vane which seemed to negate Manning and Rowan's powers.

Once again, the room exploded into chaos. Laya barely had time to retrieve her knife before Mark rounded on her, striking her hard across the face. Mark reached behind him to snatch Quinn in his fox form and flung the fox toward the bay windows of the parlor. Cy leapt to catch Quinn and rolled with him safely to the floor. Simultaneously, Laya came up behind Mark and slit his throat, her eyes blazing bright green with the ferocity of her spirit.

Tailor smashed the butt of his gun into the guard's nose beside him then hooked an arm around the man's neck and used his body as a shield. With no hesitation or emotion, he aimed his gun and fired, taking out the female guard threatening Manning first, then the five closest to where Rowan wrestled with Vane. Each one fell with a bullet to the head.

"Tailor," Manning shouted as he dodged the swing of another guard, "on your left!"

Tailor swung around and shoved the man he held into the follower racing toward him. He emptied the last of his rounds into them then grabbed the gun his living shield had dropped. In the middle of the room, Cain and Rowan fought viciously with three others, but Tailor couldn't find Vane among them anymore. He glanced around, unable to spot the demigod, until a high-pitched scream drew his attention on the opposite side of the room.

Deirdra was stumbling away from Vane in terror, clinging to her baby. When Vane wrenched his son from her arms, she tackled him, biting his ear and jerking her head from side to side like a rabid animal. Vane cried out then withdrew a blade hidden by his suit jacket and stabbed Deirdra in the stomach.

Tailor shifted to his eagle form and flew toward the demigod, but he wasn't fast enough. His talons curved to claw at Vane's eyes, only to grasp at thin air. In the next instant, Vane reappeared several yards away next to a bookshelf where Keenan had placed the collar and key that had bound *Roh Se Kahn* within Dhani. Tailor shifted back and fired his gun too late. Vane had already vanished again, taking his son and the collar and key with him.

Tailor's vision clouded with rage, but his bloodlust was cut short when Deirdra collapsed onto him. Instinctively, he caught her in one arm and lowered her gently to the ground. She stared up at him through wide, stricken eyes as she clutched at the knife in her belly, trying futilely to hold onto life. Blood flowed freely through her fingers and trickled from her pale lips.

Despite his hatred for her, a sliver of pity slipped past the wall caging in his emotions. She had sacrificed herself to protect her son. No matter her sins, she deserved his respect, if only for that single act.

When he lifted his gun, expecting to kill any followers who remained, he found the attack was over. Cain and Cy were securing the four followers left alive and Laya was checking to make sure the rest were dead.

Quinn sat on the floor with tears streaking down his face and Manning's head in his lap. A pool of blood was gathering beneath Manning's body from a knife wound on his right leg and a bullet in his chest just inches from his heart. "Rowan!" Quinn screamed. He rocked frantically, cradling his unconscious mate in the circle of his arms.

Rowan ran to them, tore open his wrist with his fangs, then pressed it to Manning's mouth. After he'd massaged Manning's throat to make sure he'd swallowed enough blood, Rowan ripped open Manning's shirt and allowed his blood to trickle onto the gaping wound in Manning's chest.

"He'll be all right," Rowan assured Quinn. "He's a tough son of a bitch. He'll pull through."

Quinn let out a tortured sob. "He took the bullet to save me. Please don't let him die. I can't lose him."

Rowan licked his wrist to stem the flow of his blood then took Quinn's face in his hands. "He's *not* going to die, little brother," he said fiercely. "You hear me? Don't you dare give up."

Quinn nodded solemnly then stared back down at his mate.

As soon as Tailor was sure Manning would survive, he called for Rowan. Deirdra was fading fast and she was the only one who might know where Vane had taken Sevrick.

Rowan fell to his knees on the other side of Deirdra and cupped her face. Without looking away, he asked Tailor, "What happened?"

"She tried to keep Vane from taking Sevrick, but he stabbed her. Vane took the child, as well as the collar he means to use on his son."

Deirdra's gaze slowly found its way to Rowan's. "I'm so sorry," she breathed. "I never —"

"Shhh," Rowan hushed her, smoothing the frayed tendrils of her auburn hair. "I know you did everything you could to protect your son. I'll find him, I swear it, but I need you to tell me where you think Vane took him. Where would he go?"

She shook her head as her eyes welled with moisture. "I don't know. Please, Goddess, find him! Find my baby."

"I will," Rowan said quietly. He moved to reopen the wound on his wrist but Deirdra's body had already stilled with the finality of death. The light in her eyes was gone and her face was frozen in the longing plea for her son.

Tailor closed her eyelids then looked to Rowan. "She died as a mother and a warrior. You should be proud of that, at least. I'll help you get Sevrick back."

"We will," Rowan said tightly. "As well as our mates."

Chapter Fourteen

Tailor hissed as vodka was poured over the open cuts on his knuckles. When he tried to retract his hand, Mara held him still and dabbed the cuts with cotton.

"Stop being such a baby," she admonished briskly. "Besides, you deserve this. I can't believe neither one of you told me what you were planning to do. I should cut off your nuts and make rocky mountain oysters out of them."

Tailor grimaced and crossed his legs as she wrapped his knuckles. She was cut from the same cloth as her brother, Rowan, and he had no doubt she was capable of following through with her threat. When she hadn't heard from Rowan or Quinn about what was going on, she'd taken it upon herself to find out personally. Her mate, Cassie, had agreed to watch Quinn and Manning's son so she could fly to France. Two hours after Keenan had attempted the spell on Dhani, she'd arrived at Rowan's palace to find him and Tailor in his dungeon interrogating the four surviving traitors.

None of them had provided any information Tailor didn't already know, and his patience was bordering on nonexistent.

"It was best you weren't here," Rowan said from where he paced in front of the fireplace in his living room. "It was too dangerous."

"I'm a warrior," she snapped. "Not some frail thing that needs to be protected. Maybe if I had been here, Manning wouldn't be laid up in bed."

"And maybe you'd be dead," Rowan shot back. He scrubbed his face with a groan. "Mara, I don't need this right now."

"Well, you *do* need me since you're a man down. So what's the plan?"

Tailor grabbed the bottle of vodka and took a swig, standing as soon as Mara was finished wrapping his hand. To Rowan, he said, "You should let me kill all but one of those traitors to make him talk. A beating may not have worked, but fear will."

"Don't you think I want to do that?" Rowan shouted. "My mate was taken as well, but I can't override the laws I set in place. They have to go before the council for sentencing."

"That sentence will be death for treason! Why are you putting it off for some idiotic formality?"

"Rowan's right," Manning said as he limped into the room, held upright only by Quinn at his side. Although Rowan's blood had gone a long way in accelerating the healing process, he was still in bad shape. His skin was ashen and his breaths were labored.

As Quinn helped his mate to sit on the couch, Tailor straightened in concern. "*Jaes'din,* you shouldn't be out of bed."

"Now who's standing on formality?" Manning smirked. "I know this is hard on both of you, trust me, but Rowan has to follow the rules. When this is over, there will still be traitors out there willing to try to bring *Roh Se Kahn* back again. A public execution will make them think twice. It might also flush out whoever else among Rowan's guard is working for Vane."

Rowan shook his head. "I should've seen it. I thought Mark was a good man. I'd even considered appointing him as a third *Meraan*."

"You can't blame yourself," Quinn said quietly. "None of us could've known Vane's influence ran so deeply."

Xenessa and Cy came into the room with Laya and Cain. Cy frowned at Manning but didn't remark on his presence. To Rowan, he asked, "Did you get any information?"

"No. You?"

"Xenessa and I called in all the guards who have access to your palace. Of the fifty, we were able to ferret out two who were lying when we asked them if they were working for Vane or *Roh Se Kahn*. They refused to admit to anything, so we had them taken to a cell in the dungeon."

"Then we're right back where we started," Rowan growled in frustration. "*Roh Se Kahn* isn't going to put off the incantation to free the rest of his essence any longer than it'll take for him to gather what followers he can find. We're running out of time."

Tailor curled his fists, trying to keep his emotions in check. The answer to where they would find Dhani was right in front of him. He could feel it. He just needed to focus his thoughts. "We know that *Roh Se Kahn* plans to use Keenan to perform the incantation, and he needs the light in his followers to do it. Vane took his son to use as a host for his father's essence so he can drain his father of his powers. I'd bet anything he's going to need the light in his own followers for that spell."

Rowan shrugged. "Even so, what good does that information do us?"

"Every traitor started out with allegiance to *Roh Se Kahn*, then switched to Vane after *Roh Se Kahn* was driven back to the alternate realm. They don't care who they serve, they just want power. The followers are going to flock to whoever can give them that. They'll be playing both sides."

Laya raised her brows in understanding. "*Roh Se Kahn* would have to go to a location where he knows his followers will be, even if those followers are currently serving Vane. Which means Vane will also know the location."

Tailor nodded. "It can't be any of the places I've gone to over the past year and they wouldn't be stupid enough to return to the castle."

"I know where *Roh Se Kahn* is," Laya breathed with widened eyes. "The same place he was originally freed from his prison realm. When I was held in *Roh Se Kahn's* castle, Achilles would travel there often to meet with the humans in service to the God. It was a place Vane was familiar with. I'm positive Vane would've used it to hide some of those who stayed true to his cause after the battle a year ago."

"It's possible," Manning agreed. "Where is this place?"

"Near Dover, England. I remember that's why I became suspicious of my mate in the first place. He would leave for months at a time, claiming to fight in the war between the *Vam'kir* and us, but none of the other warriors stayed gone that long. I followed him to Dover after he'd taken Dominic and found him at a remote ranch that had been abandoned."

"Do you think you could find it again?"

"I'm sure of it."

Rowan sighed. "Then this is the best we've got. We'll take the forty-eight guards I know I can trust with us. My private jets can be fueled and ready within the hour."

Manning dipped his chin. "I can have a group of my warriors meet us there."

Rowan shook his head. "It'll take them too long to fly across the Atlantic Ocean, and there could be traitors among your men as well. We can't take the risk."

Grudgingly, Manning admitted Rowan was right.

Tailor mulled over the plan while the others discussed the preparations. He didn't like a single part of it. They had no way of knowing whether Dhani would be at that location or how many followers he might have gathered by the time they got there. Manning wouldn't be fit to go along and they'd already seen *Roh Se Kahn* counter the effects of Rowan's power as *Magnique* over the *Vam'kir* traitors. On top of it all, they no longer had Keenan to say the spell that would cast the dark God from Dhani's body.

When he interrupted the others to bring up that last point, Xenessa stirred uneasily. "If Keenan is unable to recite the spell when we get there," she began, "there may yet be another course of action we can take."

Tailor frowned at her cautious tone. "As long as it doesn't involve killing my mate, I'm in."

"No, of course not!" she said. Then hesitantly added, "I hope not. While you were all attempting to free Dhani from *Roh Se Kahn,* I was communing with *Miel*

Se Luuda. I asked her if there was any other spell we could use to banish *Roh Se Kahn* if the original one didn't work."

Rowan's eyes darkened. "Why didn't you ask her earlier and save us the trouble we're in now?"

"Watch your tone, boy," she said sternly. "I helped bring you into this world and it won't take me eighteen hours of labor to take you out of it."

Cy laughed, then hastily coughed and grumbled an apology when Rowan shot him a look that promised pain.

Xenessa huffed. "Communing with the Mother isn't exactly like making a phone call. She told me there's a…variation of the spell that might send both Vane and *Roh Se Kahn* to the alternate realm. However, it also requires someone with both light and dark in them. If Keenan can't say it, I'll have to channel the powers of light and dark in Sevrick to pull it off, and even then, I'll need to get Sevrick away from Vane first."

"So we'll need to distract Vane," Rowan surmised.

Xenessa nodded.

Tailor didn't doubt the historian truly wanted to save Dhani, but something in her energy told him she wasn't telling him everything. "Just how is this spell going to work?"

She hesitated, glancing at her mate, then at Laya. "I can't tell you. It's something only Laya and I can know about."

Laya, Tailor and Cy all spoke up at once. Tailor yelled, "What the hell does that mean?"

"You are *not* coming with us," Cy said to Xenessa in an imperious voice.

Laya creased her brow in confusion. "I don't understand. How can I help?"

Xenessa turned on her mate first. "I'm thirty years older than you and the historian of our race. I can damn well go where I please." To Laya, she said, "I'll fill you in before we leave." Then, finally, her gaze met Tailor's. "And you… Out of all of us, you know the dangers we face the most. It's why you bonded with your mate before Keenan tried to expel *Roh Se Kahn* from Dhani's body. You made peace with the possibility that Dhani might not survive, and you chose to follow him into death should that be his fate. I can't say I can guarantee Dhani's survival, but I'm asking you to trust in me…and in *Miel Se Luuda*."

Just as Tailor was about to argue further, Manning spoke up sharply. "*Ketai!* As your *Jaes'din,* I order you to stand down."

The authoritative command stopped Tailor like nothing else could have. He saw the sympathy in Manning's eyes and swallowed his protest. "I'm sorry," he said to Xenessa. "I know your intentions are true. I'll distract Vane myself when the time comes."

He helped Quinn take Manning to his guest bedroom then left to prepare for the coming battle. All the while, only one thought circled his mind endlessly. If Dhani died, Tailor would kill everyone responsible before he met his own death. God or otherwise.

* * * *

The first silver rays of dawn crested over the evergreen treetops by the time *Roh Se Kahn* was satisfied with the small army he'd gathered. He materialized Dhani's body just in front of the porch of the ranch, then released his hold on the last man struggling in his arms.

Achilles stumbled awkwardly in vertigo, clutching to his chest the leather-wrapped stump that had once ended in his right hand. From the sickly cast to his features, Dhani could tell he hadn't sought proper medical attention for his wound. While inwardly, Dhani despised having to be in the man's presence, he had to admit, he was enjoying watching him suffer.

Achilles glanced around in puzzlement. "I know this place. It's where I brought you back into this plane of existence years ago."

"Indeed," Dhani drawled. "In a way, you resurrected me—gave me back my freedom and allowed me to begin the retribution I owe my sister, *Miel Se Luuda*. I thought it only fitting to allow you to witness my second resurrection. After all, it's the very least I can do to repay you for your services."

Guardedness shaded Achilles' gaze as he stared at Dhani. Although there was nothing in Achilles' expression to give away his fear, Dhani could smell it on him like a cloying odor. Achilles cleared his throat and bowed slightly. "You honor me, my lord. I assume your human worshippers are around somewhere? I'd granted them refuge here after we lost you in the battle, but I don't see any of them now."

Spread out across the expansive lawns were nearly a hundred *Vam'kir* and *Ba'Kal* diligently patrolling the area. Each was equipped with weapons Dhani had found stashed in the basement of the ranch house. They were trained warriors all, with an innate sense of duty and compelling loyalty. And every last one of them was completely mindless.

Inside, Dhani cringed again at the knowledge of what *Roh Se Kahn* had done. After leaving Keenan at the ranch, *Roh Se Kahn* had gone in search of his lost followers, though not for the reasons Dhani had expected.

It had never been the God's intention to recover the fealty of those who had left his service to join Vane. Without mercy, he'd executed them. And when they had begged for their lives, he'd simply smiled as the power of his darkness engulfed them in white-hot flames.

For several hours, the God had teleported across Europe and the United States, seeking out the followers and killing them until he was convinced their reduced numbers would prevent Vane from interfering again. Then he'd focused on several small shifter communities and *Vam'kir* clans, stealing their warriors from them before they could form a defense. These warriors he had somehow put into a trance, replacing their will with his own. They were innocents. Men and women who had dedicated their lives to protecting their races, and whom *Roh Se Kahn* would now use to finish his war.

The only followers he'd left alive were the three *Vam'kir* in the ranch house, and only for their familiarity with the land surrounding the ranch and intel on how best to defend it.

Dhani shrugged at Achilles' inquiry of the humans. "There were a dozen or so inhabiting the barn. However, I found their presences inconsequential. Much as I found the rest of my former followers to be of no further use to me. You see, I can't very well continue where I left off now that I know my own son has turned against me, can I? It would be foolish of me to put my trust in those who have betrayed me."

The first trace of Achilles' fear began to line his face. "Of course. I take this to mean you have…"

"Forgiven them their sins? Yes. Although I can't imagine *Miel Se Luuda* or the God those humans worship so blindly offering their souls that same forgiveness after I ended their lives. A pity, isn't it? They held so much promise. Then again, I can't tolerate deceit if I am to rule over this world. I thought it best to play it safe for now and imbue those you see before you with fragments of my essence. It has weakened me to an extent, but at least I can rely on their loyalty, and soon I will be made whole again."

Achilles swallowed repeatedly as the color drained from his face. "My lord, I never meant to betray you. Vane gave me no choice. He would've killed me if I hadn't agreed to help him."

"Shhh. You have no need to fear me," Dhani told him, baring his teeth in a false smile. "I didn't bring you here to end your life as I have the others. In fact, I want to show you how grateful I am for all you've done for me. You've provided me with a *Ba'Kal* that possesses two spirits. The light in him will make me powerful beyond anything I could have achieved with my darkness alone. Call me sentimental, but I wanted you to be here to see your progeny granted the gift of becoming my permanent host. Doesn't that please you?"

Achilles' demeanor changed to one of wary delight. "Nothing would please me more. Are you ready to begin?"

"Follow me," Dhani said, leading the way to the large barn to the left of the ranch house.

Inside, Dhani's thoughts raced as he quickly grasped the intricacies of what was going on. Where once he might've been naïve, the months of torture he'd endured at *Roh Se Kahn's* twisted hands had given him insights into the God's mind that he couldn't ignore. He felt like he was watching a dance between two rattlesnakes vying for territory.

The fear Achilles had displayed so dramatically wasn't real. It had been an act to cover up the truth of his real intentions. Dhani could feel anticipation and victory in the man's energy. *Achilles had wanted to be found by* Roh Se Kahn *all along,* Dhani realized. He'd known the dark God would come for him. This was a set up.

Yet, the confidence exuding from *Roh Se Kahn* told Dhani the God was aware of Achilles' deceit, as well. *Roh Se Kahn* was relying on Achilles to betray him and inform Vane of his location. He wanted his son there at the moment his essence was fully returned so he could eliminate Vane as a threat. It was the easiest way to bring down his son on his own turf.

A part of Dhani wondered how the dark God could be so confident about Vane coming to him. Without Sevrick, Vane had no leverage. Then again, Vane's insidiousness didn't exactly account for intellect. The draw of power made fools of everyone, no matter their nature.

The barn had been renovated to accommodate the now dead humans. The divisions of the pens that had once held livestock had been torn down to create a massive open area and the outer walls were insulated. However, there was no heat to stave off the biting chill of the English Channel nearby.

In the center of the barn lay Keenan with his naked body stretched spread-eagled on the hard-packed dirt. At *Roh Se Kahn's* command, Keenan's wrists and ankles had been manacled with thick chains that cut into his skin, held in place by metal spikes which had been driven into the ground. His exposure to the elements was a measure *Roh Se Kahn* had taken to weaken him. The God couldn't take the chance of being interrupted by Keenan when he began the incantation.

"The time has come," Dhani said loudly to the twenty men and women inside the barn. They gathered in a loose circle around Dhani, Keenan and Achilles with their weapons at the ready.

Keenan stared up at Dhani beseechingly. His blue eyes were glazed and skin so pale from blood loss, it nearly matched the color of his ivory hair. He shivered convulsively and licked his lips. "D-Dhani," he stammered. "I kn-know you're still in there. Please, fight him. You can't give up. You're s-stronger than him."

Dhani knelt and smoothed back the tangled wisps of Keenan's hair. When he spoke, his voice contained as much warmth as the icy breeze blowing in from the open doors of the barn. "That's where you're wrong. It's his light that makes *me* stronger. With him, I will rid this world of my sister's abominations and take her powers to spawn my own race. The humans will bow to me, their true God, and serve my race with their flesh."

Fierceness combatted with the despair in Keenan's eyes. "It'll never work. You m-may have found a way to put a sliver of your essence inside my friend, but he has to be a willing host to t-take in the rest of your essence. Dhani would never—"

"He has no choice!" Dhani bellowed. "I still hold his second spirit. When the portal opens, his soul will have no choice but to accept his spirit and my essence with it. They are tied together. Even if he were to reject me, he can't reject his spirit."

A tear slipped past Keenan's lashes as he shook his head. "Dhani, please. Don't let him do this."

Within, Dhani raged against *Roh Se Kahn's* authority. He fought with every ounce of his strength and, for a brief moment, he felt the strangling grip of the God's power over him falter. Then, his tentative control was ripped away. *Roh Se Kahn* channeled his darkness inwards and sent a blast of searing electricity coruscating along Dhani's nerves. Dhani's mind fractured from the pain, though no sound escaped his mouth.

When the pain receded abruptly, *Roh Se Kahn* forced him to stand and begin the spell to open the portal. Even as Dhani's voice resonated with the power of the words, he continued to rebel within. *This can't be happening*, he thought desperately. At any second, he expected — prayed — for Tailor and the others to burst in as they had before and put an end to this travesty.

But no one came.

Keenan's back arched and his agonized cry echoed throughout the barn. Dhani could feel the energy of Keenan's spirit being torn from him like a sickening rift in the atmosphere. At the same time, a cyclone of dark winds spiraled around Dhani, flinging his hair into his eyes and mouth. The portal had been opened and the entirety of *Roh Se Kahn's* essence bore down on him, demanding entrance.

Despite Dhani's battle to refuse the dark God dominion over him, he could sense his falcon reaching out to him from a distance. His second spirit was still far away, yet it called to him pleadingly, and his body pulsated with the need to draw it in. Beyond his will, Dhani felt his soul expand to accept his falcon, and with it, all of *Roh Se Kahn's* essence.

Roh Se Kahn's elation suffused him, then was suddenly torn away as, once more, blinding pain speared Dhani's body. The God's essence, along with Dhani's falcon spirit, were being pulled from him even as they desperately clung to his soul, trying to rip him apart. Dhani fell to his knees, his muscles frozen in torment and head swimming from the volume of his screams, until *Roh Se Kahn's* darkness and his falcon were finally avulsed.

In the haze of the aftermath, Dhani looked up to find Vane standing a few yards to his right, next to Achilles. The cyclone of dark winds surrounding Dhani had transferred to Vane and Dhani watched as the winds narrowed in on the baby in Vane's arms. To Dhani's horror, *Roh Se Kahn's* essence was gradually forced into Sevrick's tiny, squirming form. As soon as the torrent of the God's power had been fully absorbed by the infant, Vane clamped the collar that had been made for Keenan around Sevrick's neck and locked it with the key.

"No!" Dhani shouted above Sevrick's frightened wails.

"At last," Vane said in triumph. Before the twenty warriors could fire their weapons at him, he grasped the collar that had conformed to Sevrick's neck and called out, "Stop! I can feel the darkness my father has instilled in each of you. He commands you. Kill me and I will burn this host alive. It will harm your master and force him into another willing body. If any of you are prepared to make that sacrifice, step forward. Otherwise, you will *stand down!*"

Reluctantly, the men and women lowered their weapons.

Just as Vane relaxed his stance, the sound of multiple guns being fired broke the silence from outside the barn. Vane growled his irritation and turned on Achilles. "You told me this place was safe."

"It was!" Achilles said emphatically. "Other than your father killing your other followers, everything went exactly as you predicted. My lord, we can still pull this off. Sevrick has your father's powers. Take them."

Vane sneered at Dhani. "Not all of them. Kill him. The rest of you, guard the walls!" he yelled to the *Vam'kir* and *Ba'Kal*. "Let no one in until I have secured your master."

Dhani's mind scrambled to catch up with what was going on as Vane tipped his head back and started uttering words similar to those of the spell *Roh Se Kahn* had used to free the rest of his essence.

'Not all of them', Vane had said. Why would Vane order Achilles to ignore the threat outside and kill Dhani? Unless...

Unless Dhani still retained a part of *Roh Se Kahn's* power.

The realization struck Dhani at the same moment Achilles bore down on him with a knife aimed in a backward slash toward his throat. Dhani saw it coming, but he couldn't react fast enough. Vane was going to win, after all.

Chapter Fifteen

From the entrance to the barn, Dhani heard Laya shriek, "Get the hell away from my son!"

Instead of slicing through Dhani's throat, the tip of the blade merely scraped his cheek as Achilles stiffened. Dhani flinched back when Achilles toppled onto his lap, a hilt protruding from the man's shoulder. Dhani looked over to find his mother racing in with hatred blazing in her eyes. Behind her came Tailor, Quinn, Mara, Cy, Rowan and Cain with half a dozen others. They charged the twenty *Ba'Kal* and *Vam'kir*, the clamor of their shouts competing with the deafening reverberation of gunshots.

Joy leapt within Dhani until a staggered grunt beside him drew his attention. Keenan's chest heaved repeatedly as if trying to draw air into his lungs, though the only breaths that passed his mouth were short and pained. The rest of his body was limp and his eyes... His eyes were twin, silver orbs staring out into nothingness. It was the darkness in him, pure and unfettered by the light of Keenan's spirit, which was now gone.

Panic seized Dhani as he shoved Achilles aside. He rushed to jerk the stakes from the ground then freed the chains binding Keenan's wrists and ankles. Keenan's head lolled as Dhani pulled him onto his lap, murmuring over and over again, "No, no, no, no."

He shook his head, heedless of the tears blurring his vision. This wasn't what should've happened. It should be him taking his last breaths—lying there cold and naked and struggling with death. Not his best friend. Keenan didn't deserve this. He was a good man who had spent his entire life running from the darkness in him. Fate had no right to make him to live his final moments absent of the light that had redeemed his darkness.

When Keenan's eyes closed and his body stilled, Dhani clutched him closer and yelled, "No! I won't let you die. I can't."

He looked around in desperation, his mind racing to find something, anything that would keep his friend alive. Through the throng of combatants, he caught sight of Rowan and Tailor fighting their way toward Vane. For a brief second, he thought about calling out to Rowan, but his voice froze. There was nothing Rowan could do except watch his mate die, knowing it had been Dhani's fault.

Dhani tugged Keenan's head to his chest and let out a sob that stabbed his heart. Then he felt something else. A raw hunger stemming from his gut. It was the darkness *Roh Se Kahn* had left behind in him, or rather a shadow of it. Somehow, Keenan's own darkness was attracting it, as if the residue of power in Dhani was trying to join with that in Keenan.

The same power that had taken Keenan's spirit to open the portal.

Dhani's thoughts reeled as an idea began to take shape in his mind. It seemed impossible, but he had to try. He would give anything to save his friend.

Forgive me, he pleaded inwardly to his spirit. To his surprise, his leopard didn't argue. Instead, it rumbled in sorrowful acceptance. Dhani took a deep breath, then against all the laws of his nature, reached for the darkness in him. It rushed forth in a cold fury, only this time, Dhani had full control. He forced the darkness toward his light, the bond between him and his spirit that made him a child of *Miel Se Luuda.*

Though his spirit was willing, the bond resisted with rising ferocity. It repelled the power trying to tear it apart and thrashed against Dhani's determination. Dhani let out an ear-splitting cry as his body revolted. His heart felt like it was being split in two and the pounding in his head was excruciating. Yet, he didn't give in. This was the only way to keep Keenan alive.

After what seemed an eternity, something snapped. Dhani felt his spirit wrenched away and his body spasm uncontrollably. At the same time, Keenan lurched up with a gasp. What felt like liquid fire scorched Dhani's veins until finally, all sensation left his body and he collapsed backward onto the ground. Inside, there was a gaping hole where his spirit had once been and a bottomless pit of darkness where once there had been light.

Above him, Keenan stared down through eyes that had returned to a brilliant, crystal blue. Dhani wanted to weep in happiness at the proof that his idea had worked, but his body was no longer responding.

"What have you done?" Keenan rasped as tears spilled down his cheeks. "You stupid, insane idiot! How could you do this? Why would you make me take your spirit? Did you think I wanted you to die so that I could live?"

With the last of his strength, Dhani whispered the words, "I'm sorry."

Keenan grabbed the front of his shirt with one hand and rattled him. "You were supposed to live this time! We would've found a way."

No, we wouldn't have, Dhani thought even as he felt himself slipping away. When Keenan growled and looked up, Dhani's sight fell listlessly on the battle still raging around them. He saw Tailor dueling with two of the warriors *Roh Se Kahn* had forced to do his bidding, moving swiftly in a dance that seemed more like art than a promise of death. Despite the knowledge that Tailor would end his life after Dhani died, Dhani felt no guilt over it. He knew they would be joined again in the afterlife, and it would be as Tailor had wanted.

A sharp whistle drew Dhani's gaze to a small, yet imposing figure standing next to Laya near the outer wall of the barn. It was Xenessa, he recognized distantly. What was she doing here?

Xenessa said something to Laya and pointed to Sevrick in Vane's arms, then called out, "Tailor!" Immediately afterward, she looked to Keenan and yelled, "Keenan, say the spell. Now!"

Dhani glanced back at his mate, who instantly took down his opponants as if he'd been merely toying with them before. Tailor then straightened to throw a shuriken that embedded itself in Vane's left shoulder just inches from his neck. The impact caused Vane to jerk back and lose his grip on Sevrick. Dhani watched the infant fall and his mind seized in terror until he saw Laya dive for the baby, catching Sevrick in her arms.

The rest happened so fast, Dhani could barely keep track. Laya ran to Xenessa, where both women huddled over Sevrick and began chanting words Dhani couldn't quite make out. Vane teleported to them to snatch the baby back, only to be distracted again by another shuriken to his right arm. The demigod growled as he pulled the blade from his flesh then teleported again, this time appearing behind Tailor.

To Dhani's shock, Tailor's eyes were closed and his expression calm, yet he didn't hesitate to duck the swing of Vane's fist and stab his thigh with a third shuriken. "Keenan, the spell!" Tailor yelled, repeating Xenessa's command.

Dhani watched in awe as his mate continued to predict from which angle Vane would attack next, all the while his eyes closed. Then, the sight was torn away when Keenan forced him to meet his gaze.

"The spell," Keenan murmured in a voice filled with comprehension. His brows drew down in a look of angry resolve and he said, "I'm gonna save you, then I'm gonna kill you."

As he started to recite the spell that would cast *Roh Se Kahn's* essence from their realm, Dhani felt the emptiness in his soul spreading, crushing in on his body. His lungs shut down, his muscles were like dead weights and his vision began to fade. Time seemed to slow with the decreasing beat of his heart, ticking the inevitable countdown to his death.

Dhani expelled a single, final breath, then tensed as a lurching sensation gripped him. For a second time, a dark cyclone of swirling winds encompassed his body. It centered on *Roh Se Kahn's* power still residing in him, but the power twined its way around his soul, refusing to let go. The winds narrowed in on him, circling violently and tearing a scream from his throat.

"Dhani!" Keenan cried out next to him. "No, this can't be!"

Somewhere far away, he heard Vane cry out, "What are you doing? Stop!"

Dhani tried desperately to will his body to move, to grab onto Keenan's hands, but it was no use. A stab of fear pierced him as his body was hurtled into the alternate realm just as it had been one year ago. A deafening silence fell all around him as his senses were taken away, his body once more imprisoned and beyond his reach.

His mind careened in a storm of despair, unable to accept the reality of what had just happened. Death hadn't yet claimed him before the spell had drawn the sliver he harbored of *Roh Se Kahn's* essence into the alternate realm, and his body along with it. His soul couldn't die in this place. He would be trapped here forever.

And not alone.

Radiating waves of anger bombarded him from all sides. Instinctively, he knew they were coming from not only *Roh Se Kahn* himself, but from Vane, as well. The two must've been pulled into the void with him. A small part of Dhani was grateful for the knowledge that the spell had rid Sevrick of *Roh Se Kahn's* essence instead of damning the infant to the same suspended fate Dhani would endure for eternity. Sevrick was an innocent and didn't deserve this punishment.

Yet, the thought of Tailor having to face the rest of his days alone, forbidden to seek out his own death, made Dhani want to scream at the injustice. With his body and soul forsaken the gift of death, Dhani would never find his mate in the afterlife.

There's no hope, Dhani thought. *Nothing except the—*

Suddenly, a blazing light filled his senses, expelling the darkness that tainted his soul. Heat bathed his skin and enveloped him in a pleasure so intense, it dazed his mind. There was warmth, so much warmth and love he could barely contain it, yet it wasn't coming from him.

It was his second spirit. His falcon.

Dhani cried out in joy and, to his surprise, heard his laughter ring out in his ears. His eyes flew open to reveal his body, tangible and aching with fatigue. He was back! Somehow, his falcon had freed itself from *Roh Se Kahn's* clutches and brought him back!

"Sweet Mother," someone breathed. Dhani looked up to find Keenan staring down at him from the tight embrace of Rowan's arms, eyes widened in shock. Keenan fell to the ground beside him and strangled him in a partial hug with his good arm. "Thank you," Keenan said tightly. "Thank you, Goddess, thank you."

"Choking...me," Dhani wheezed past the suffocating crush of Keenan's arms.

Keenan pulled back abruptly then hugged him again, more tears streaming down his face. "I'm sorry. I just can't believe you're back. I don't know what went wrong. The spell was only supposed to banish my father's essence from you, not take you with it."

"It's okay," Dhani said, putting as much assurance as he could into the words. But inside, he was still shaking from what might have been. How close he'd come to a fate worse than death. When Keenan finally drew back, he wavered from his blood loss and Rowan was there instantly. He tore into his wrist then put it to Keenan's mouth.

When Dhani was sure his friend would pull through, he stood and looked out over the crowd of those he'd come to know as family. While their eyes reflected his own astonishment at being there, he could feel their joy as strong as that of his falcon. When his gaze traveled to his mate, his breath caught in his throat and blood surged with anticipation.

Although Tailor's face gave no emotion, his energy hit Dhani like an overwhelming force. It permeated anger, incredulity and possession so savage, it was all Dhani could do to keep standing as Tailor stalked toward him.

There were no words, no hesitation or gentleness.

Tailor grabbed the nape of Dhani's neck in one hand and fisted the back of his hair with the other, then jerked him forward to crush their mouths together. A throbbing pressure mounted in Dhani's groin and his head swam with the intensity of Tailor's tongue driving into him. The immovable cage of Tailor's hard body encasing him made his nerves sing and his heart pound almost painfully. He wanted to strip down right there and take Tailor's cock into him, uncaring of who was there to witness it.

Then a loud harrumph drew them back to their surroundings. Before letting go, Tailor pressed their foreheads together and inhaled deeply. "You are never going to leave my sight again. You hear me?"

The rough authority in Tailor's voice made Dhani chuckle. He had no doubt his mate was completely serious and would follow through with his command, at least over the next few years.

"How…?" Rowan choked, meeting Dhani's gaze, then cleared the obvious emotion catching in his throat.

"How did you bring my mate back? I felt him dying after his spirit was driven out of him."

"I used the residue of *Roh Se Kahn's* power in me to force my leopard spirit into him. Then my falcon's spirit found me to make me whole again."

Everyone froze in shock at his statement.

"My baby," Laya said, breaking the silence and almost shoving Tailor aside to get to Dhani. "I'm so glad you made it back. Xenessa and I were hoping...but we couldn't be sure."

Tailor narrowed his eyes. "Wait, what? You knew there was a chance Dhani could die and you didn't tell me?"

Rowan picked Keenan up and kissed his temple. "We all knew there was a chance Dhani and Keenan could die."

Xenessa spoke up cautiously, cradling Sevrick to her chest who seemed more dazed than scared now. "Things didn't exactly turn out as we'd expected. We didn't know Dhani would give his spirit to Keenan to save his life, or that he even could."

"Dhani should've been pulled back into that alternate realm with *Roh Se Kahn* and Vane," Tailor said angrily. "What secrets are you hiding from me?"

"Whatever they are, it can wait," Rowan said in a tone that brooked no argument. "Right now, we need to clean up this mess." He glanced at a handful of the surviving warriors *Roh Se Kahn* had manipulated, all staring in confusion at several of Rowan's guards who held them at gunpoint. "These followers seem to have amnesia, but I don't want to wait around for their memory to come back. We need to get them to the dungeon beneath my palace."

Love Eternal

Dhani shook his head. "Those aren't followers. They're loyal *Ba'Kal* and *Vam'kir*. I... *Roh Se Kahn* killed all the followers he could find. He didn't want to risk them betraying him for Vane during the incantation to free the rest of his essence. He kidnapped these warriors and forced them to fight for him. When Keenan said the spell to banish *Roh Se Kahn*, the God's influence over them must've been expelled."

Rowan's face paled. "They're innocents?"

Dhani nodded, feeling nausea cramp his stomach as he looked around at the multitude of bodies littering the barn floor. He was responsible for their deaths.

"This wasn't your fault," Keenan said to him, as if reading his thoughts. "Or yours," he said to Rowan. "The blame is on my father."

"Regardless," Xenessa said, "we need to leave this place and erase all evidence of Vane and *Roh Se Kahn's* presence. There can be nothing left behind to give those followers still out there any hope that they can bring *Roh Se Kahn* back."

"Agreed," Cy said grimly, pulling his mate close to his side. In the next moment, his lips quirked up in a smirk as he looked over at Keenan. "So, how does it feel to have Dhani's spirit inside you?"

Keenan smiled. "A little weird, but good. He's accepted me, and I can feel my best friend through him. It's amazing! I can't wait to see what I look like in leopard form during the upcoming full moon."

Tailor furrowed his brow. "I'm not sure how I feel about you possessing a part of my mate," he said in mock territorialism. "It's kinda like you're seeing him naked."

Rowan snorted. "Would it make you feel better if you saw Keenan naked?"

"Hey!" Keenan smacked Rowan on the arm.

"Well…" Tailor canted his head as though thinking about it.

"Tailor!" Dhani punched his mate in the chest with the back of his fist.

Cy burst out laughing at all of them.

When Tailor tucked Dhani under his arm and began to lead him from the barn, Rowan gently lowered Keenan then reached out to grab Dhani's arm. Rowan opened his mouth and hesitated for a few seconds. "All kidding aside, I owe you a debt of gratitude I will never be able to repay," he said to Dhani. "You've saved my mate twice, with no thought for yourself, and gave one of your spirits to him so he could live." He glanced at Keenan, then met Tailor's gaze, though his next words were for Dhani. "This man is the luckiest bastard on earth to have you."

Dhani swallowed heavily at the sincerity in Rowan's eyes, then looked to Keenan. "Keenan's saved my life more than a few times. I was just returning the favor."

Keenan laughed and pulled him in for a quick embrace. "Love you."

"Love you, too," Dhani said. He left the barn with Tailor at his side, feeling for the first time in his life that his future was finally his own.

* * * *

The next day, everyone gathered in the living room of Rowan's palace. Buffet tables had been loaded with every breakfast food known to man by Rowan's cook, and a separate table had been designated to hold about fifteen different kinds of liquor. Tailor joined Cy and Mara at the liquor table and grabbed a bottle of whiskey, bypassing glass completely. It was only nine o'clock in the morning, but nobody cared.

Well, almost no one.

Xenessa glared at her mate when Cy refilled his glass with several more fingers of vodka, to which he simply growled. "Back off, woman. Let me have my cheap thrills. We should both be celebrating *Roh Se Kahn's* defeat."

Xenessa sniffed indelicately, saying, "One more cheap thrill and that'll be your last for the next week."

Cy's humor died quickly and he set his glass on the table.

Mara laughed and took a swig of her beer. "Three and a half centuries old, covered in bulging muscles, piercings and tattoos, and you're pussy whipped in less than a week." She clucked her tongue. "Sad. Just sad."

"Oh, yeah? How 'bout I call Cassie and see how whipped you are for her pussy?" Cy shot back.

"You wouldn't dare."

"Try me."

"People!" Dhani yelled from where he sat on the couch cradling Sevrick in his arms. His hair had returned to its original red and was pulled back into a ponytail at the nape of his neck. "Virgin ears here. Don't make me go over there."

Tailor chuckled at the expressions of guilt on Cy and Mara's faces. "Dick beats pussy every time."

Quinn groaned from his position on the arm of the recliner where Manning sat. "You all give sex a bad name."

"Maybe," Tailor shrugged with a smirk, "but Manning was telling me earlier how much you called out that bad name last night in his bed."

Quinn's cheeks flamed and he smacked his mate on the head.

Manning grunted, then glared at Tailor. "Remind me to thank you when we get back home."

Before Tailor could respond, Rowan walked into the room and cleared his throat. "The council has been notified of the recent happenings. Xenessa, it's agreed that you'll be accompanied by the remainder of my personal guards to interrogate every warrior in our clans to find out if any hold allegiance to Vane or *Roh Se Kahn*. Cy, I give you permission to go with her." To Manning, he asked, "Have you contacted Cher yet?"

As historian of the *Ba'Kal*, Cher's powers came directly from *Miel Se Luuda* and gave her the same ability to discern the truth as Xenessa had. Manning dipped his head. "I've already appointed a group of warriors to go with her to every *Ba'Kal* community. If there are any traitors left among my kind, she'll find them."

Rowan nodded. "I'll meet with you later to discuss the arrangements for the families of those dead warriors who were used by *Roh Se Kahn* against their will. Meanwhile," he said, meeting Tailor's gaze, "I think it's time we were given an explanation. Xenessa?"

Xenessa stiffened, glancing at her mate. "When I communed with the Mother, she provided me with a variation of the spell used to banish *Roh Se Kahn*, as I told you before. Only it wasn't so much of a variation as an…addition. It expanded the original spell made only for *Roh Se Kahn* to include everyone in the vicinity who contained darkness. It was the only way to make sure Vane was thrown into the alternate realm as well."

Dhani stirred in his seat. "That's not what happened, though. *Roh Se Kahn's* essence was in Sevrick, but

Sevrick wasn't pulled into the alternate realm like I was. Keenan has darkness in him, too, but he wasn't pulled in, either."

"Due to circumstance, no. The spell *Miel Se Luuda* gave me wasn't simply one of expansion. It contained protection, as well. The plan was for Laya and me to channel the dark powers in Sevrick. While she recited the original spell, I would recite the addition to it. I could only extend the protection in the spell to one other person, which was why Sevrick wasn't pulled into the void. The spell drew on his powers, yet kept him safe."

"So you were willing to sacrifice my mate and Dhani?" Rowan asked angrily.

"If I had known Keenan would live at that point, I would've had you take him as far away as you could get him before I said the spell. I had no idea Dhani would give him his spirit, let alone that he'd retained enough of *Roh Se Kahn's* power to do so. The moment I saw Keenan regain consciousness, I told him to say the original spell. Because the spell had been activated by Keenan's darkness, it kept him safe as well."

She took a deep breath. "But yes, if he had remained unconscious or died, I still would've gone through with my first plan. Fortunately, that wasn't the case. As soon as Keenan started the spell, I began mine to keep Sevrick in this realm and to send Vane into the other."

"And what about Dhani?" Tailor said through clenched teeth, not bothering to hide his rage. "He'd spent an entire year in that hell realm and you were willing to send him back without even considering another course of action. If you had told us what you'd planned, we could've come up with another way."

"Tailor—" Dhani said quietly.

251

"No," he ground out with a chopping gesture. "I may sound like a callous bastard right now, but I want to know why she didn't even consider using the variation of the spell to save you instead of Sevrick. And you," he rounded on Laya. "You were ready to condemn your own son to the same torture he barely survived before? Why did you even bother coming back into his life?"

"Tailor!" Dhani said again, loudly.

Tailor forced himself to meet the calm acceptance in his mate's eyes.

Dhani looked from Xenessa to Laya, then down at the sleeping baby in his arms. "They were right to do what they did. If the choice had been mine, I would've saved Sevrick, as well."

"As would I," Keenan agreed solemnly.

"*Roh Se Kahn* set everything into motion before all of you got there. I chose to give Keenan my spirit, knowing I would die. If Xenessa hadn't told him to say the original spell, my sacrifice would've been in vain. And if she hadn't said the second spell, I wouldn't have been reunited with my falcon spirit. I'm here with you, right now, because of her."

Tailor scraped a hand through his hair, biting back every 'what if' that crowded into his thoughts. So many things could've gone wrong, and when they had gone wrong, it had somehow worked out for the best. Yet, he couldn't erase the fear that was still riding him.

In the midst of the battle, he'd felt Dhani's impending death. When Dhani had severed the light of his bond with his leopard to give it to Keenan, it had felt like a knife had been driven into Tailor's chest. Only the warrior in him had kept him from abandoning his promise to distract Vane. In those precious minutes when he'd relied on his decades of training to fight a demigod, he'd never felt more powerful and more helpless at the same time.

As he stared at the love in Dhani's gaze, he realized a part of him would always be helpless. They were such complete opposites. His mate was gorgeous and timid with an open heart. All the qualities that had made him a target for abuse by almost everyone in his life. Despite all that, however, he was still stronger than anyone Tailor had ever met. Dhani was his own man, and Tailor couldn't stop him from fighting his own battles.

Grudgingly, Tailor swallowed his fear and nodded. "You're right. I apologize," he said to Xenessa.

"I hope you can forgive me, too. Both of you," Laya said earnestly, focusing on her son. "Xenessa told me there was a chance you might find your other spirit if you were pulled into the alternate realm, and use it to get back. I never meant to consign you to that hell. I'd prayed—"

"It's okay, Mom," Dhani interrupted. "You did the right thing."

"Mom," Laya repeated with tears in her eyes. "I could get used to that."

Manning cleared his throat to draw everyone's attention. "There's still the matter of what to do with your mate, Achilles."

Laya wiped the moisture briskly from her eyes, then looked to Manning. "Yes. I'm aware the penalty for his betrayal is death under our laws. I've known for years it would eventually come to that and I'm prepared to meet my fate with him."

Tailor glanced at Manning sharply. He'd forgotten Laya and Achilles were bonded. They'd taken Achilles alive from the barn and incarcerated him in Rowan's dungeon, but his death would mean Laya's as well. As mad as he still was at Laya, he didn't want to see her die. Especially not after Dhani had finally accepted her into his life.

Quinn snorted. "Like that's going to happen. We'll make an exception for you."

"Quinn," Manning growled.

"What? Like you weren't going to make the same choice."

"I was, but I'm still the *Jaes'din*. The final decision has to come from me."

Quinn flipped his hand in an exaggerated display of obeisance. "Yes, almighty one. Please, give us your wise and honored decision."

Manning scowled at his mate, then looked to Laya. "I—"

"We're not going to kill Achilles," Quinn cut in. "Manning will find a place to lock him up."

With a disgusted grunt, Manning shook his head. "Why do I even bother? You're safe, Laya, and my community is always open to you."

More tears spilled down Laya's cheeks, and this time, she didn't wipe them away.

When Dhani sent Tailor a meaningful stare, Tailor sighed and reluctantly said, "You're welcome to stay with Dhani and me until you find a place of your own in our community."

Cy moved to slap him on the back. "One big, happy family. Brings a tear to your eye, doesn't it?"

Tailor sneered at him. "Fuck you." He took a swig from the bottle in his hand then looked down at it. "I'm going to need more liquor."

"That'll have to wait," Manning told him. "I wish I could give you and Dhani time to spend together, but we need to meet with all the Alphas and Betas to inform them of what happened. We have to double our efforts in finding the last of *Roh Se Kahn* and Vane's followers. If we're going to have any chance at peace, we'll need to make sure those two can never be brought back again."

Everyone nodded in unison, then began filing out of the room. Tailor went with his mate to their guest bedroom where Keenan joined them. It took all of his willpower to leave Dhani there, but he was given little choice. Dhani pushed him out of the room, threatening to withhold sex if he kept hovering like an overbearing parent.

Finally, Tailor gave in and left to find Manning. They called every Alpha and arranged a meeting to take place in a week. They also went over several addendums to the treaty between their kind and the *Vam'kir* with Rowan. Afterwards, Manning booked a flight back to the United States for everyone in two days, giving him more time to heal and allowing them the freedom to run the wilds during the coming full moons.

Hours later, Tailor went in search of his mate and found him in Adreanna's nursery with Keenan. Both men were leaning over the rail of Adreanna's crib, where the little girl and Sevrick were sleeping soundly. Their hushed words fell silent when he entered the room and they both looked up with eloquent expressions.

Tailor frowned in confusion, knowing he had missed something, until the yearning in Dhani's eyes became all too clear. "Oh, no," he groaned.

"I want to keep him," Dhani said in a rush. "He's an orphan now, just like I was. And he has darkness in him, just like I did. I'll be able to understand him and help him when he's growing up. He's all alone now. We can't just forget about him."

Tailor glanced at Keenan who raised his hands in defense. "Don't look at me. I tried to tell him Rowan and I can take Sevrick in, but he's got his mind made up."

"This is the right thing to do," Dhani persisted. "I can feel it. Sevrick deserves a fresh start, and I can give him that. He deserves everything I was denied."

As Dhani went on to name every reason he could think of to convince Tailor to accept the baby, Tailor stopped listening. All the reason he needed was the look of pure longing on his mate's face to convince him. Nothing else mattered.

He walked to his mate and pulled him into his arms, shutting him up with a searing kiss. "If this is what you want, then it's what I want, too. He'll be *our* son. A beautiful baby boy that will grow with our love and know happiness, tears, diapers, two a.m. feedings, throw up, constant supervision, endless crying..." His voice trailed off with a new kind of fear. "I think I need another drink."

"I'll get the whiskey," Keenan said simultaneously.

After Keenan left, Dhani beamed up at Tailor. "You won't regret this. You're going to make a great dad."

Tailor hugged his mate then looked down at the sleeping form of his new son.

I'm a dad, he thought. *Sweet Mother, kill me now or give me the strength to survive this.*

Chapter Sixteen

One month later

Tailor ran to the front door of his cabin at the sound of the doorbell and opened it to find Manning and Quinn on his porch. Quinn was holding their son, Hael, and Manning stood beside him with a large box in one arm and a second on his other side that almost reached his full height.

"You got them both?" Tailor asked excitedly.

Manning grinned. "We picked them up today from the store. Are you sure Dhani isn't going to mind?"

Quinn rolled his eyes. "*Yes*, he's going to mind! Just like I did when Manning got our son the same things. I hope you're prepared to sleep on the couch for the next week," he said to Tailor.

Tailor shrugged before taking the larger box from Manning and hoisting it over his shoulder. "He'll get over it. It's for the baby."

"Right," Quinn drew out in exaggeration. "That's why you're doing this behind his back."

Dhani walked in from the living room carrying Sevrick on his hip. "Doing what behind my back?"

Manning passed Tailor swiftly, patting him on the back. "All yours, buddy."

Dhani narrowed his gaze on the box Tailor held, then glared at him. "You are *not* putting that in the baby's room."

"Of course not!" Tailor said offensively. "I would never put our son's health in jeopardy by putting an inflatable castle in his bedroom, or a racecar bed. He's too young for them."

Dhani nodded slowly. "Good."

"I'm putting them in his playroom."

"With the collection of weapons you hung on the wall for him?" Dhani exclaimed.

Tailor strode to the guest bedroom he'd converted into a playroom for Sevrick with Dhani marching angrily behind him. "One day, he's going to master those weapons. He's a warrior, just like me. Last night, he rolled over to grab my weapons harness. By this time next year, he'll be ready to start training. I thought I'd give him a little incentive for now."

"With a racecar bed and a bouncing castle?"

Tailor set the box next to Manning in the playroom, then took Sevrick from Dhani. Pride swelled in his chest when his son grabbed a tiny handful of his hair and smiled around a gurgling noise. Since Deirdra had been a *Bassen'kir* at the time she'd given birth to her child, Sevrick had been born with a spirit. And his spirit called to Tailor's own as though their paths had always been meant to intertwine.

Tailor couldn't explain it, and he'd given up on trying some time ago. Sevrick was his as surely as Dhani was, and the knowledge was the most terrifying gift of joy he'd ever experienced.

He faced Sevrick to the wall he'd been designing over the past week and said, "You're going to be a fierce, badass little warrior when you get older. Better than your old man. And I'm going to make sure I'll always be there to protect you. Just like your dad," he said, looking to Dhani.

On the wall, he pointed to the weapons he'd mounted, and underneath each one was a plaque that read, 'Baby's first shuriken', 'Baby's first katana', 'Baby's first nunchaku' and more.

Dhani shook his head with a hopeless smile. "You're pathetic, you know that? Our son's going to have issues."

"Yeah," Tailor said, grinning. "But long after we're dead, he'll still be kickin' ass."

Dhani laughed and stepped into Tailor's open arm, tilting his head back to meet Tailor's kiss.

"You know," Manning said thoughtfully, "This baby weapons room has some merit. We should make one for Hael."

"Ugh!" Quinn groaned.

Want to see more from this author?
Here's a taster for you to enjoy!

Keepers of the Gods: Son of Death
Nikki McCoy

Excerpt

As soon as Jamie heard the spray of water hitting tiles in the bathroom next to their room, he sprang into action. It was a short trip to the kitchen where he filled and started the coffee machine, then prepared two mugs with just the right amount of sugar and cream.

Theirs was a small house, but shabby by no means. The kitchen was almost as large as the living room, and while that wasn't saying much, they managed to keep them both free of clutter. This gave their home a cosy atmosphere instead of inducing the claustrophobia one would expect to feel in such small spaces.

There were two bedrooms — one they shared, and one which had been deemed Jamie's office, although that was more of a title than a fact. A jumbled collection of decorations and household items that Loland had accumulated over his years as an interior decorator reigned supreme.

Every week, Jamie was forced to clear a path to his work station, consisting of a worn pine desk, chair, computer and fax machine, but he didn't mind. He loved to imagine the kinds of homes that would eventually house each piece as he was working.

Jamie returned to their bedroom and began to rifle through the clothes inhabiting Loland's side of the closet. Most of them had either designer tags or were close knock-offs. The significance of the names on the material went right over his head but he knew it was important to his partner.

He'd also been keeping tabs on the outfits Loland wore on his dates with his boyfriend. He knew exactly which shirt to match with which pants to give Loland a fresh look every time he went out.

It had been odd at first, helping his lover prepare to meet another man. No other Dom Loland had met had ever had him this flustered. For that matter, no other man had piqued Loland's interest enough for him to want to engage in more than just casual scenes at the club. Jamie knew this one was special. The energy Loland gave off following each date was sizzling with love and lust, and somehow it only enhanced their own relationship.

Loland had informed him that this was another actual date, not a club rendezvous, so Jamie decided on a pair of dark greyy slacks and a long-sleeved, white button-up shirt that shimmered even in dull light. After laying the clothes neatly on the bed so as not to wrinkle them, he went in search of Loland's watch, cell phone, and wallet, lying in various places throughout the room, and lined them all up on the dresser.

He warily eyed his lover's vast shoe collection and was tempted to pick out a pair to save Loland the hassle of having to choose, but he remembered the one time he'd made that mistake. Instead of the usual ten minutes it took for Loland to decide on his footwear, it had taken the man forty minutes to find the perfect outfit to match the shoes Jamie had chosen for him. That had been for the first date and since then Jamie had taken the liberty of dressing the man himself.

Not willing to go there again, Jamie instead walked to the living room and found a jacket for Loland that would go with his outfit and be appropriate for the weather outside. A peek out of the closed blinds covering the window showed that it was going to be a clear, if chilly, night. The perfect opportunity for Loland to try out the new lightweight leather long-coat he'd unearthed at Sears while shopping for a client.

With nothing left to do, Jamie retreated to the kitchen, poured coffee into both mugs, and sipped at his while waiting for the entertainment to start.

It didn't take long. Two minutes later, he heard the shower turn off and watched with a bemused expression as Loland ran to the kitchen, dripping water everywhere, with only a hastily wrapped towel around his narrow hips.

"So I was thinking of wearing my blue sweater, but I don't have any…"

"Bed." Jamie pointed to their room and watched the taller man scramble in that direction. He heard a muffled, "Thanks," and waited patiently for the rest of the ritual to play out.

Loland came hopping out on one foot, trying to walk and put on his trousers at the same time. "Have you seen my…"

"Dresser."

The man hopped back into the room then reappeared five minutes later, asking, "Is that coffee I smell?"

Jamie handed him the second mug still sitting on the counter and tried to stifle his laugh as he watched his lover accept it with glee. Watching Loland enjoy a good cup of coffee was like watching a man in the throes of the best orgasm of his life. It never got old, and it was always as sexy as hell.

His prick swelled to life at the sound of Loland's little added moans thrown in for extra effect. Jamie had to tighten his grip on his own cup to keep from grabbing Loland and swallowing those sounds in a thorough kiss. The quick peck on the mouth Loland gave him didn't help matters at all. Loland raced back to the bedroom while Jamie took a seat on the couch.

"So he's taking me to that new Benihana restaurant they opened up in Paradise Valley," Loland yelled from down the hallway. "I can't imagine how he got reservations there on such short notice. I heard there was a two-month waiting list to get in and that was weeks before they even opened their doors."

"Well, you have been seeing him for three months."

"Yeah, but that was just casual hook-ups at the club. This is our sixth date. It takes us to a whole new level on the relationship scale. Chukka or Memphis?"

"Memphis." Jamie grimaced at the ease with which he had replied. He tried his best to avoid the fashion world like the plague. The fact that he could now make decisions on which style of shoe would fit an outfit best without even looking at them did not bode well for him. "So, you really like this guy, huh?"

It was a needless question. Loland constantly spoke of the man's looks and actions with adoration. His past was still a bit of a mystery, but at this point, Jamie felt as though he knew him almost as well as did Loland. Truthfully, he sounded like the kind of guy Jamie could fall for as well.

But that would never happen.

"Yes," Loland said as he came out and plopped himself down on the couch next to him. "And I know you'll love him too. He has the cutest little dimple on his left cheek when he smiles and have I mentioned his ass? Oh man, I could go on for…"

"Wait, wait, wait. What do you mean 'when I meet him'? He's your boyfriend, not mine." Jamie could feel the familiar sense of panic begin to rise and take root in his chest. He tried to hide the panic he knew was shining in his eyes, but Loland must have noticed before he could cover his face with his hair.

Loland reached out and placed a finger under his chin, then gently began to kiss him — the corners of his mouth, his nose, his eyebrows, the lines creasing his forehead. "I wouldn't introduce you to anyone that would hurt you, baby. I've been a lot more careful since…well, since last time. You're the most important person in the world to me. You know that right?"

Jamie finally looked up through his lashes and met Loland's sincere gaze. There was not a hint of deception or anger to be seen in those soft brown eyes. There never was. He could feel the waves of bright, pure energy rolling into him from the other man that attested to his honesty. He didn't want to rehash the reasons why it would be a disaster for him to meet any of Loland's friends. There was no need to ruin his lover's excitement for the evening.

"I know. And I know what happened before wasn't your fault." He decided to lighten the mood by kissing Loland's mouth and grasping the bulge between his legs in a firm grip. He rarely let his aggressive side show, but every time he did, it was the perfect distraction. Loland gasped and swivelled his hips, silently begging Jamie to rub along his growing erection.

Jamie pushed forwards until his slighter frame was resting atop Loland's across the couch. He ground his hard-on into the crevice between his lover's cock and hipbone. The fabric of his jeans wasn't kind to his sensitive flesh, but the friction felt amazing. He delved his tongue into Loland's mouth and reached up to tweak his nipple with his other hand. Jamie was rewarded with another gasp and a fresh wave of sexual energy.

He nudged copper curls aside with his nose as he kissed his way down his lover's jaw and found the erotic spot just beneath his ear. He bit into the soft flesh above Loland's collarbone and gave the head of his cock a tight squeeze at the same time, drawing out loud pants and whimpers.

The power of taking control always hit him with a rush. It was what Loland needed, and what Jamie desired most in the world to give to him, but he could only keep up this act for so long. As much as he longed to be everything to his partner, he was no dominant.

With more than a little reluctance, he slowly eased back into his true submissive nature and whispered against Loland's lips, "You're going to be late." The dazed look in Loland's eyes almost made him change his mind about releasing him so he could go on his date. The temptation was there, clawing at him as it always did when Loland went out, but he knew that there were things the man needed that Jamie couldn't give to him.

"I can stay home, baby. If you want to spend some time together, I'm all for that. Or I can take you with me. I know he wouldn't mind. We could skip the fancy restaurant and go somewhere private. It would be just the…"

"No. I love you and I'm telling you to go on this date. I can see that this one makes you happy." Jamie quickly kissed away the protest he could see building on the thinning lips of his lover. Loland would probably let him get away with murder in his bid to make him happy in any way that he could, and Jamie did his best not to take advantage of that through of his own selfishness. Loland needed to be dominated just as much as he did. He could tell by the satisfied haze his lover had been floating around in for the past several months that the man he was seeing met his needs.

"Go. Meet this guy, then come home to me so hot and horny you have to drill me through the mattress just to take the edge off." Jamie knew he'd finally lessened his lover's worries when Loland threw his head back and laughed. The sound reached into his soul and cleansed all of his worries about being left alone again in their small home for the night.

"Okay. Are you working a shift tonight?" Loland asked.

"Yea, but only a half one. I should be done by the time you get back."

Loland stood up and straightened his clothes before donning his leather coat. "Do I look all right? Thank you for helping, by the way. Don't know what I'd do without you."

"You're welcome, and you look great. My sexy top. Now go have fun. I have annoying people to piss off."

Loland chuckled as he leant down to give Jamie a chaste kiss, then headed for the front door. "Lock this. Keep your cell phone on you, and call me if anything happens, or even if you just need me to come home for…whatever. I'll be back soon. Promise me you'll call if anything happens."

Jamie tried his hardest not to roll his eyes as the second part of their ritual played out. Loland had always been protective of him. Ever since the episode with the last man Loland had taken an interest in, his lover had become obsessively fussy.

It had taken him over six months to convince the man that he would be fine on his own. He may still get panic attacks and work extra hours just to keep the paralysing fear at bay, but there was no way Jamie was going to let Loland know about that. The man had already sacrificed enough for him.

"Yes, Sir. I promise."

Loland paused in the doorway and bit his lip. The indecision on his face was somehow endearing and exasperating all at once. Jamie wanted to scream at him that he was wiser now. He could take care of himself. But at the same time, he was afraid of losing that special concern that no one else had for him. Loland was his ray of sunshine in a life soured by the ruthless desires of other people. He was a gift that Jamie would never take for granted.

He stood up from the couch and swung his hips in a sultry sway as he approached Loland. In a soft, seductive voice, he said, "I swear to be a good boy until you get home. After that, I promise nothing." Loland groaned into his mouth as Jamie stole another kiss. Their lips met in a bruising clash and Jamie clamped his fingers around the hard sides of his lover's waist. He borrowed confidence from Loland's solid frame and poured as much assurance into his voice as he could muster.

"I'll be fine. Enjoy yourself."

Loland gave him one last kiss before closing the door behind him. Jamie swiftly locked both deadbolts and secured the chain on top. With the added security they had installed into their new home, he felt some relief from the ever-present fear that continuously threatened to steal the fragile hold he had on his self-control. The succour was tenuous at best, and he mentally repeated his mantra of solitude all the way to his office. *Loland is strong. Loland is smart. Loland will keep me safe.* Of course, when Loland said it, it always came out as, "*You are strong. You are smart. You will stay safe for me,*" but no matter how hard he tried, he couldn't instil the same amount of faith in himself that his partner apparently had in him.

And what the hell was up with his notion that Jamie should meet his new Dom?

Loland and Jamie had always shared an open relationship. Well, open on Loland's end. But the inviolable rules in their partnership clearly stated that Jamie was, under no circumstances, required to meet the men his lover dated.

The factor of jealousy was not an issue. Even Jamie couldn't deny that he desired the kind of domination Loland described in his relationships with men he called "Masters" at the clubs he frequented. However, never once before tonight had his lover alluded to an inclination for Jamie to meet whoever was Loland's Dom at the time.

A wave of anguish swept through him as he imagined the humiliation his lover would endure if he brought over his boyfriend. Jamie was awkward at best, with skin so pale he could pass for a ghost due to his reluctance to go outside. His raven-coloured hair didn't help matters, and he was far from muscular…or tall…or even toned.

Truthfully, he had no idea what Loland saw in him, or why the man bothered to keep a lover action-packed with issues. But he wasn't about to tempt fate by embarrassing him in front of a guy Loland was obviously taken with. Then there was always the compounded concerns of his powers. If the guy was slotted to die soon, Jamie would know. And what if his precognition kicked in, giving him a glimpse into the man's future that Loland might not be happy with?

He wouldn't be able to hide his reaction, and the thought of lying to his lover made him queasy. Honesty was imperative in their relationship. Loland had been the first and only person to believe that his powers were real and not a figment of his imagination. He could never betray that trust.

No. When it came down to it, there was no other option. He could not meet this man. His power of precog had taken mercy on him a few weeks after Loland had started seeing his boyfriend, once given the assurance that this guy would make Loland happy. He'd never told Lo about it, but maybe he should. It would ease his lover's mind. But for now, he had Internet complications to tackle.

About the Author

I have always been a lover of books, particularly those with the dichotomy of the strong alpha male and the weaker love of their life which they must rescue. After reading all I could find in M/F books, I decided to give M/M fiction a try and my addiction skyrocketed.

Hot, sexy men times two? No contest. Unfortunately, I was reading faster than the authors could produce. Eventually, I resorted to imagining my own stories and my mind took off from there.

I have to admit, though, I am a bit of a recluse. If not for the joy and humour my husband and four boys bring to me, I would never have ventured this far.

Nikki loves to hear from readers. You can find her contact information, website details and author profile page at http://www.pride-publishing.com.